Forged Fates

Small city art museums, perfect forgeries, brutal murders, Istanbul sex and a tumbling trail of deception and greed are a formula for tense page turning in Larry L. Preston's debut thriller. His tangle of characters and settings take us on a journey that is so seductively believable that you'll be left wondering if it could happen to the characters in your life, your town.

– Paul Chaffee, former Editor and Publisher of the Saginaw News

Bound to enthrall and entertain art lovers and mystery readers alike, *Forged Fates*, offers an insightful and accurate view into the world of high-end forgery and deception wrapped in intrigue and suspense. Preston's vivid characters jump off the page in this thrill-a-minute debut novel.

– Mike Kolleth, Executive Director, Saginaw Art Museum.

Forged Fates

by
Larry L. Preston

Pinckney, Mi

Forged Fates

Copyright © 2022 Larry L. Preston All rights reserved by author.

Published by Wynwidyn Press, LLC

This book is a work of fiction. Names, characters, places, and incidents either are products of the author's imagination or are used fictitiously. Any resemblance to actual persons, living or dead, events, or locales is entirely coincidental.

No part of this publication may be reproduced in any form by any means electronic, mechanical, photocopying, recording or otherwise without written permission of the publisher.

For information regarding permission, write to Wynwidyn Press, LLC, and Attention: Permissions Department, 425 Rose St, Pinckney, Michigan, 48169

Hard Cover ISBN: 978-1-941737-34-7

Soft Cover ISBN: 978-1-941737-35-4

Cover Painting by James Perkins
Author Photo at the Saginaw Art Museum by Thor Rasmussen Photography.
Author Photo at the DIA by Micheal Kolleth
Cover Design by Cara Baker, www.CMBakerDesign.com
Interior Book Design by Bob Houston eBook Formatting

Dedication

Cat Stevens affectionately and respectfully sings of looking for the love of his life, and he knows the rest of his life will be blessed when she's found. I dedicate this book to my lovely wife, Maija, who has and continues to bring countless blessings to my life. Our greatest blessings are our children, Lija, Garrett, and Alec.

Chapter One

Saginaw, Michigan
July 21, 2019

Lukas Novak

Jack's 1866 Bistro in Old Town Saginaw was nearly empty, its large windows staring at the darkening sky lit by a few scattered streetlights.

Nicky Winters and I were quiet in the corner, finding it impossible to believe that our close friend, Adam Lindmark, had been brutally murdered.

"Lukas," she said, "the first time I saw Adam, he was like a splash of golden color. I was working at the Black Cat Café with three or four customers waiting when he came in. Blonde, long, gorgeous. When he moved to the counter, I was so nervous I spilled milk over me, the counter, the floor. I was so embarrassed, but his light blues eyes were kind and reassuring. He gave me the warmest smile."

I love Nicky Winters, and hearing her adoring story about Adam was complicated for me. I could imagine her behind the counter, the beautiful, entertaining barista with her warm, soft voice, knowing each regular's morning favorite: "skinny latte with no whip cream," "cappuccino," or "café au lait." Flirting with the guys, young and old, and making friends with the women. Everyone wanting a flake of her life.

Nicky was working at the Black Cat when I first saw her, in her early twenties with a slim body; like most days, she was wearing a miniskirt, showing off her legs. After I got to know her, she told me the best thing about her were her legs. Nicky was wrong; it would always be her face: angelic and beautifully proportioned with large green eyes and dark wavy hair.

The waitress asked if we wanted another round. Nicky was drifting in her thoughts, so I ordered us her favorite, Tito's martinis, straight up.

"Who killed him?" Nicky suddenly asked.

"No idea," I answered. "I'm trying to think it through. The way he died is so troubling. Brutally beaten and tortured."

"God, it's horrifying. They crushed his fingers and cut the skin off his face," Nicky said and started crying again.

Sliding next to her, I wrapped my arm around her narrow shoulders. She couldn't stop the tears.

"It's good to cry," I told her.

Both of us were numb, and Nicky's description of Adam, "a splash of golden color," was accurate. His energy and good spirits lifted others, and they sought him out. There were probably a dozen people who considered Adam one of their best friends.

Nicky stopped crying and looked up at me.

She was vulnerable, and the tears made her irresistible. I knew, like everyone else, that Nicky wasn't good for me, but I couldn't stop caring.

"Want to talk about something else?" I asked.

"No," she said.

"I don't know a person who didn't like Adam, so was this a random killing? Or is there something about Adam we didn't know?" I asked.

"You were his best friend, by far. What do you think?" She replied.

"Well, he moved around a lot. I mean, this is a guy who had outstanding credentials as an art conservationist and a gifted painter. Yet, he worked at five or six other museums before coming to Saginaw. Doesn't that seem odd?

"Maybe he was searching for the place to call home, and none of the others seemed right," she answered.

"I thought the right woman might cause him to stay. But then again, I don't know," I said.

"Do you think Natalie was the right one?" Nicky asked.

"Maybe, I thought she might be, and then without much planning, he said he needed a vacation and took that trip to Istanbul. He didn't take Natalie."

"Do you think it was a jealous husband or boyfriend who killed him? She asked.

"I don't think so. Adam saw a woman from the Detroit Institute of Arts; it wasn't anything serious. He did say he met a woman in Turkey, but unless someone traveled from Istanbul, I don't see anyone jealous enough to kill him. However, it's obviously a crime of passion. If someone was trying to get even, they did."

"If he was leaving without Natalie, do you think she could have killed him?" She asked.

"Adam told me she had a violent temper, but I don't see her being a killer," I answered.

The more I thought about Adam's death, more confused I became.

We finished our second martinis. "Another two for you?" The waitress asked. Nicky smiled and shook her head "no." Two was usually the right number, and we knew where it would lead. Looking at her eyes and smile, I knew that things between us would be fine for at least tonight.

"I have a 9:00 morning meeting with Detective Clark," I said.

"I thought you already talked to him?"

"I did. Clark said he has more questions for me."

She smiled. "I'm done. Can I stay at your place tonight?"

"Of course."

We both began thinking to ourselves again.

After a while, she said softly, "Lukas Novak, it's time to go."

I remembered many things about Adam and me and didn't hear Nicky.

"Lukas No-vak, it's time to go," she whispered again.

"Right," I said.

I called the waitress over, paid the bill, and we headed to our cars.

"Can I ride with you?" She asked, "I think my car's safe in the parking lot."

"I'm sure it is, and if you get a parking ticket, I'll pay it."

The streetlamp shined on Nicky, leaving half her face in shadow and the other in soft light. Her sculptured cheekbones, arched eyebrows, and dimpled chin accentuated her natural beauty.

I didn't want to think about Adam Lindmark anymore tonight. I just wanted Nicky to myself.

Chapter Two

Murfreesboro, Tennessee
August 16, 2016

Adam Lindmark

It was a sweltering day. The cicadas were singing, air sticky with no relief even in the shadows, the kind of day Adam Lindmark loved. Today he wouldn't be enjoying the summer heat, the forgery needed to be finished and delivered by October 31.

Studying the subtle beauty of the 1880s landscape by Camille Corot was an enjoyable part of Adam's work. Forging a Corot, a Parisian painter, was relatively easy for him after mastering Corot's layering of paints and glazes to create the desired atmosphere. Besides, it's well known that Corot signed some well-done forgeries because he considered it a compliment that someone would copy his work. Even experts disagreed on whether a painting was an original or forgery. This would be Adam's third Corot forgery, the first was at the Chandler Museum in Arizona, and now at the Murfreesboro Art Museum, he'd already completed and sold the first of two owned by the museum.

The first forgery went according to plan. As an art conservationist and curator, Adam searched out smaller museums needing his help to conserve their most valuable and salable paintings. His selection was a detailed process of analyzing mid-size to smaller museums' collections and determining if their finest and most valuable works needed conservation. He'd also examine their financial condition and the sophistication of their staff. He'd then choose the most vulnerable museum and arrange an interview. His five previous efforts led to his employment, and the museums were delighted when Adam completed his work.

The museums didn't know that Adam sold their most valuable paintings to one of Paul Rothstein's clients. Paul and Adam had been friends since their days at NYU. Today he was a successful broker in New York with wealthy clients willing to pay for classic original paintings. To replace an original, Adam would forge a duplicate and place it in the museum. There would always be an unveiling fundraiser, celebrating the beauty of what was thought to be the conserved painting. No one ever suspected they were looking at a fake because the forgery was excellent, and they trusted Adam. Soon after completing his work, Adam would move to his next chosen museum.

Adam wondered if his luck would hold out. He didn't want to take that chance. After finishing the second Murfreesboro's Corot, he was moving on for his last time. He'd discovered that the Great Lakes Bay Art Museum in Saginaw, Michigan had a valuable Adolphe William Bouguereau painting that was worth as much as $4 million, many times the value of the Corot he was finishing. Bouguereau was also his favorite painter. What a fantastic way to end his forgery career, he thought, conserving and copying the work of this respected master painter. With his last sale and forgery behind him, Adam imagined beginning his new life in Istanbul, not as a forger but as an artist.

Before arriving in Saginaw, Adam and The Great Lakes Bay Art Museum had agreed to his employment contract. They couldn't turn down his proposal; he offered his service at a small fraction of what another conservationist would be paid. Why work for such small payment, the museum's board had asked? He quickly convinced them that he came from wealth, didn't need the money, enjoyed giving back to others and took pleasure conserving great art pieces. Some of this was a lie; he loved working on masterpieces and came from money. At one time, Adam was wealthy; his father's greed ended that. Now Adam's life was all about deception.

Stopping in mid-thought, Adam reminded himself he must not become over-confident. Forging the Corot was easy, but he must focus on the details. A mistake could end his forgery career behind prison bars. He brought his full attention to adding highlights to his copy.

He was so focused that he suddenly looked up at the clock on the cabinet on the far wall. "Damn," he shouted. He had agreed to have an early dinner with Chomsky. He wasn't looking forward to this. Chomsky was a nice enough person but listening to hours of his non-stop talk about antique cars was not easy.

"Let's have a good attitude," he said to himself. Listening was part of his job, and he understood that building trusting relationships was very important to his success.

He cleaned his brushes with his usual attention. After putting his paints and everything else away in its proper place, he rolled the easel of his painting and then the easel of the original Corot into a room that had once been a vast walk-in closet. He checked the air conditioning unit that he had installed explicitly for the room. He had instructed the electrical contractor that he needed a backup generator in the event of an electrical failure. Adam checked the temperature to make sure it remained at 72 degrees with 50 percent humidity and was glad he had insisted on a backup system. There was a greater chance of an electrical grid overload with these sweltering days that could cause a blackout. The blistering heat outside could ruin the paintings.

He dead bolted the reinforced door, leaving his copy and the original painting well protected. In his bedroom bathroom, he carefully washed his hands, making sure to remove all the paint. He wouldn't have time for a shower and studied the clothes in his walk-in closet, selecting a silk pair of light moss green slacks, a darker green pullover shirt, and a black sports jacket tailored to fit his long frame. He looked approving at his image in the full-length mirror.

The acorn didn't fall far from the tree, and he thought—what a dashing dresser his father had been. Adam smiled, just like his dad, dressing and living on the edge.

Adam hurried down to the musty 100-year-old basement. Opening the wine cellar, he found a bottle of a 2000 Bordeaux. Perfect, a showy wine to impress his dinner guest. He then moved to the white wines and selected a New Zealand sauvignon blanc for later that evening.

Although running late, he took a few extra moments to check himself out in the mirror at the front entrance before activating the sophisticated security system and slipping outside.

The heat took Adam's breath away. He got into his black Porsche GT2 and fired it up. He wheeled out his driveway to meet Chomsky.

The Five Senses Eatery located in Georgetown Park was known for "the highest quality food, drink, and services." Adam had made the arrangements and now cursed himself for making a dinner appointment on Saturday. Still, Chomsky was the chairman of the Murfreesboro Art Museum's Board of Trustees and its most influential leader. Building trusting relations at each museum was imperative to Adam; he believed that people almost always saw what they wanted to see. If a museum's leaders trusted him and his work, the chances of a forgery being discovered would be minimized.

Arriving a few minutes before 5:00, Adam looked for Chomsky. He was at a prominent table by the two-story glass windows.

"Good evening Mr. Lindmark," said the hostess.

"Hello Adam," said the eatery's owner. "Mr. Chomsky awaits you. This way, please."

"Is it going to be a good evening? "Adam asked the owner.

"Pretty good. A couple of parties of eight a little later tonight."

"Mr. Chomsky," Adam said, "sorry I'm late."

"Ha, ha, Adam, I've never known you to be late, and tonight's no exception."

Adam greeted Chomsky with a firm handshake and handed him the bottle of Bordeaux.

"What's this for?" Chomsky asked.

"A gift for you. A way to say thank you for supporting me on that fundraiser."

"That wasn't a lot of work, and besides, it wasn't for you but the museum," Chomsky replied.

"Nevertheless, thanks. I hope you like it. 2000 Bordeaux, a pretty good year."

"Adam, you should give this to someone who can appreciate it. I'll save it for the next time you come over. Which reminds me, I haven't seen much of Adam lately. What have you been up to?"

"Busy writing a book," Adam said.

"A book?" questioned Chomsky.

"It's a biography on William Bouguereau, who painted in the late 1800s. He was a very accomplished painter …."

Before Adam could finish his sentence, Chomsky interrupted. "Boog-roo, why you should be writing about Bugatti," he said. "It's one of the greatest cars imaginable. I almost bought one. I was outbid at an auction in Vegas."

This started Chomsky's monologue on classic cars that would go on for over an hour. Adam employed his practiced skill of patiently listening. The most interesting subject for any person was him or herself, Adam believed. Through listening, Adam developed a remarkable number of supporters. They loved his company.

After a glass of Chianti Classico and a simple salad, Adam's attention began to waver. He continued to give Chomsky the impression he was fully engaged, but his thoughts drifted to the remainder of the evening with Camille.

She was beautiful and would be waiting for him at her apartment, he thought. Adam checked himself, "be patient, focus on Chomsky."

At 7:45, Lindmark paid the tab leaving a healthy tip for the waitress and a heartfelt thanks to Chomsky for having dinner with him. After a goodnight to the owner and a thankful goodbye from the waitress, Adam made his way to his Porsche, waived one last time to Chomsky, and slowly drove off. Although excited to begin the rest of his evening with a remarkable woman, he didn't want Chomsky to think he was in a hurry. It was also essential to retain control of one's emotions.

As Chomsky strode down the street to his mint condition Rolls Royce, he thought Adam was indeed a special person: intelligent, thoughtful, and always an excellent conversationalist. The Murfreesboro Art Museum was very fortunate to have a man like that working and caring for the museum's treasures.

Chapter Three

Murfreesboro, Tennessee
August 16, 2016

Camille

Adam was hungry for Camille, but soon she would be gone. Like other museums, with other assistants, Adam would end their employment and relationship. He'd use the same reason, as usual, budget cuts. In some ways, it was unfortunate; he enjoyed Camille; yet with his life of deception, again, it was time to start over.

Camille was annoyed. She didn't appreciate sharing Adam, particularly on a Saturday with Chomsky, no less. She was greedy. She wanted Adam to herself. He had explained how important it was for him to have strong relationships with the museum's leaders. She believed the museum was damn lucky to have him. He didn't need to kiss any ass. He was a dedicated conservationist and always working. She had seen his artwork and argued that he'd make more money selling his portraits than slaving as a conservationist.

He was genuinely gifted, she thought. Yes, very gifted. Her attention turned from Adam the painter to Adam, the lover, and she smiled and became aroused. He was incredibly handsome, and he was hers. When together, he focused on her. When making love, he was the ultimate pleaser. Adam was the only man to bring her to multiple orgasms. Now she expected it. Greedy. So very greedy.

Counting her blessings was something Camille did daily. Her parents complained she'd never find a real job when she graduated from Ohio State University with an Art History degree. They were wrong. After her second interview, she was hired as an Assistant Curator at the Murfreesboro Art Museum. It was a museum she had never heard of, but it was reasonably close to her parents' home in Cleveland. The main reason she took the job was Adam. At her first interview, she was prepared and knew the Murfreesboro Art Museum was a quality mid-sized art museum, accredited, and a member of the Smithsonian Society. The conservationist, Adam Lindmark, had outstanding credentials: double bachelors' degrees in Physics and Art History and masters' degrees in Fine Arts and Art Conservation. He'd worked at the Corcoran Museum in Washington D.C. and several smaller art museums across the country. He was new in Murfreesboro and hiring an assistant.

Good-looking, self-assured, but not arrogant, Adam had a gentleness that was hard to resist. At the end of the second interview, he offered her the position. She immediately accepted. Her work was challenging and interesting. Analyzing issues and developing and implementing solutions was work she enjoyed. Adam respected her and was professional in every way. Too professional for her.

She remembered how hard she tried to make their relationship personal. Short skirt, open blouse tactics usually drew an immediate response from most, if not all, guys. Not Adam. He stayed professional. She began to think he liked boys and not girls. She laughed, then it seemed to make sense. Talking to others, she found that several women were in his life, from the area and out of town. She doubted herself. What was wrong with me? It wasn't like she was starving for affection. She had the same boyfriend for over a year, and he visited her, or she visited him almost every weekend. She cared for him, but he wasn't in Adam's league. Seducing Adam took planning and patience. It had worked, and she was proud of her success.

7:45, she opened the Super Tuscan she'd selected earlier. Its cost was out of her price range, but she hoped it would please him. Like Adam taught her, she opened it to let it breathe. She finished getting all the ingredients ready for an original Caesar salad that she'd tossed to perfection when the time was right.

Chapter Four

Murfreesboro, Tennessee
August 16, 2016

Adam Lindmark

Adam thought of Camille during the 15-minute drive to her apartment and the pleasure waiting for him.

She was like many women he'd had. It amused him that the many beautiful and intelligent women graduating from good schools with Art History degrees were dying to find work. He found pleasure, in many ways, helping them.

The Murfreesboro Art Museum didn't have money for an assistant, so he donated the funds with the understanding the money would be used to fund that position. Few knew about his donation; it was best that way.

His assistants were excellent employees and loyal, passionate lovers. Camille, like the others, was beautiful, she even more so. She had magazine model looks: long legs, angular face with large breasts. She was an inexperienced but eager lover.

Parking along the street, he skipped up the stairs of her apartment and rang the doorbell. Hurrying to the door, she hugged him and gave him a big kiss. Seeing the sauvignon blanc, she frowned.

"Ah, you brought wine?" She said, "I bought a special bottle for tonight."

"Well, we've been known to drink two bottles, you know," Adam said with a knowing smile.

"You look fabulous," he added.

"I do?"

Camille believed she was a pretty woman, may be very pretty; but around Adam, she became insecure, craving his praise.

"You're gorgeous, and you know it," he said.

His compliment made Camille light up.

She'd been trying on different tops, skirts, and shorts for a good part of her afternoon. She decided simple was best, a dark blue skirt and a light blue tight-fitting knit sleeveless top. She added a silver necklace with turquoise stones and a matching bracelet. The blue colors set off her tan and light brown hair.

He grinned as he saw her nipples pushing through her blue top.

"I think we need some wine," he said.

While pulling her body against his, he started kissing her neck, then gently on her lips, then his open mouth to hers, finally pulling her lower lip into his mouth.

"Umm," she sighed but stopped and told him, "I wish you didn't waste time with Chomsky."

"I know, but it's so much easier if you have allies looking out for you," he said.

"You don't need allies."

"Oh, but I do, and Chomsky is a good one to have."

Camille turned the conversation away from Chomsky, "I've opened an Italian," she said. "It's a Super Tuscan."

Studying the bottle, "A Sassicaia," he said, "well done."

"Do you like it? The man at the wine store helped pick it out."

"You make me feel special," he replied.

Pouring the wine into glasses, she was happy and smiling. Putting his hand on hers, helping her place the bottle on the counter, he began kissing her and sliding his hand under her top, slowly rolling her nipple between his finger and thumb.

She sighed. "Desert before the main entre?" She said.

"You are the main entre," he whispered.

Playfully pushing him back, she finished pouring the wine.

"Wine and food first," she said.

"Do you have two other glasses?" He asked.

"Do you want to drink the white first?" She replied.

"Let's save the Tuscan for dinner," he said. "What are we having, by the way?"

"Very simple," she said as she pushed up against him. "A Caesar, lamb chops, asparagus, and a raspberry chocolate dessert."

"You are quite wonderful," he said.

Taking out the next two glasses, she waited while Adam opened the bottle of white.

"This will be perfect with the Caesar and your Tuscan perfect with the lamb and the desert," he said as he poured the wine.

She smiled. "I guess together we're just perfect," she said.

"Perfect," he agreed as they clinked glasses.

"To the most beautiful, intelligent, and sexist woman alive," he said.

"Thank you," she modestly said and started tearing up; she was so happy.

Seeing her love for him, Adam thought, why don't I feel guilty? Too many years of deceiving? Perhaps a callous person is all I've become?

Then it flashed into his mind that his cold-hearted use of people would catch up with him. He tried to push it out of his mind, but it wouldn't leave as he sipped the wine and looked at Camille preparing the Caesar salad.

Chapter Five

Saginaw, Michigan
July 22, 2019

Nicky Winters

"It's too early to get up," Nicky groaned as she turned off the alarm and forced herself out of bed. She turned on a lamp, slipped out of her panties, and walked to the bathroom. After showering, she took her time picking out and wiggling into a black mini skirt and white peasant blouse.

"What are you staring at?" She asked Lukas.

"I'm enjoying watching you, even though it's 5:00 in the morning."

She batted her eyes and gave him a knowing smile.

"Your customers waiting for the café to open will be pleased with your selection, particularly the men," he slyly said.

Nicky couldn't recall when she first met Lukas. He wasn't her type. She preferred handsome men. His square face with broad features, stocky build, and dark, thick, unruly hair gave him the look of a movie mob heavy. Later, at a symphony afterglow party, she began seeing him in a different light. She was drinking sparkling wine when he crossed the room to talk to her. It was the first time she noticed his deep, kind voice and dark searching eyes. As they spoke, she decided there was more to Lukas than she had realized.

Despite his appearances, she had grown to care for Lukas, and they became lovers. She liked his muscular body, the way he carried himself with self-assurance. He was independent, witty, and intelligent. One of his friends told her that he was accepted into many prestigious architectural schools. He chose Wayne State University because it was close to his parents in Royal Oak, and he received a full-ride scholarship. After graduating, he stayed at Wayne State to earn a master's degree in urban planning. After working in Detroit at a prominent architectural firm, he moved to Saginaw and worked at a respected firm. Eventually, he started his own office, and with his reputation, no one was surprised that he was doing well.

Nicky learned that more than anything, Lukas cared for people: his mother, friends, clients, and community. He enjoyed giving to others, which made her crazy because she believed some were using him. She was right, but he wasn't changing.

Lukas was a rebound for Nicky. She'd been in a relationship with Adam until he left her when he began his affair with Natalie Collins.

Only recently did Nicky learn it was Lukas who introduced Adam to Natalie. She guessed this wasn't by chance. Lukas knew Adam and Natalie well enough to know they'd be attracted to each other. Soon after being dumped by Adam, she started seeing Lukas.

Nicky wasn't over Adam and that jolt of excitement she felt when they were together. Even after she began seeing Lukas, it didn't stop her from finding other lovers. These affairs hurt him, and he'd take a break from her, but he always returned.

She knew Lukas realized she still cared for Adam. What she believed he didn't know was that she'd slept with Adam the night before his murder. She wondered if Lukas knew? Was he jealous enough to be the killer?

Lukas turned over and returned to sleep. She studied him and gave him a light kiss on his forehead.

"You very kind man," she whispered.

While studying his face, a fear that maybe Lukas did kill Adam raced through her mind.

Perhaps she'd pushed him too far. Was it too much for this caring man to think his best friend made love to her? Is that why the detective wanted to meet with him again?

"Oh Lord, did I go too far this time?" she thought to herself.

Chapter Six

Saginaw, Michigan
July 22, 2019

Lukas Novak

After Nicky left for work, I couldn't get back to sleep. My mind, once engaged, bounced from Adam to Nicky to Detective Clark. It was going to be a stressful day. First off, I had to meet with Detective Clark to talk more about Adam's murder. I didn't know what more I could tell him. I needed to help him any way I could, but I had no clue how. It didn't help any that I couldn't focus.

I thought about what Nicky had whispered to me and her kiss on my forehead. Then my mind went back to last night, the way Nicky and I had made love. Perhaps it was the sadness of Adam's death or Nicky's vulnerability. I wasn't sure. All I knew was she was always a giving lover, but there was something needy and passionate last night. The Sheryl Crow song kept playing in my head, "You're my favorite mistake."

At 6:30, while showering, I thought about what Nicky had said about Adam, "A splash of golden color."

I knew I wasn't golden, more subtle colors in the background. I'm ok with that; I liked myself even though I knew Nicky would always be looking for someone with that 'splash of color.'

A white button-down shirt, a dark blue suit, and a light blue striped tie were more formal than I usually wore to the office. The serious look seemed appropriate to meet with a homicide detective to discuss the murder of my best friend.

I skipped making coffee, opting to have one at the Black Cat, only a couple of minutes away on Hamilton Street in "Old Town Saginaw."

I needed to sit quietly and organize my thoughts. As I got in line, Nicky smiled at me. I wondered if she was thinking about last night too. She already had a double mocha for me when I reached the counter.

"Busy morning?" I asked.

"Always," she smiled. "What time do you see Detective Clark?"

"9:00. I thought I'd come over early and do some thinking before seeing him."

I paid for my drink and found an empty table in the corner. I had about an hour and a half before the meeting.

I began recalling the many times Adam and I drank coffee in the café. Maybe, I thought, in our conversations, there's a clue about his murder.

I recalled our first-time meeting; we were going to discuss the Art Museum. We never got around to that topic. I learned of Adam's ability to learn about his new surroundings quickly. He talked about the history of the Black Cat Café and Saginaw. "The Black Cat," he told me, "was part of Saginaw's prosperous years, located in a brick building constructed at the end of the Civil War." He laughed, "I know you already know this," he said, "but I find it interesting. Saginaw's rich history that is. Flourishing during the late 1800s, from the sale of lumber, and the automotive era of the 1950s and 60s."

"It began suffering in the late 60s," I said, "but is making a comeback."

"I can see that happening," he agreed. "You're an architect; look around this space; it's unique. Sixteen-foot tin decorated ceilings with 12-inch moldings painted dark bronze."

"You don't see this quality of work unless it's a refurbished building," I added.

"Look," he said, "at the history. The brick is darker near the floor, where decades of dust and grime have left their mark. The floor was probably once beautifully varnished oak, and today it's various shades of gray from years of stains from coffee, food, and who knows what else."

"Some of that grime is probably from the Civil War," I laughed.

"I wouldn't doubt it," he chuckled.

We talked about Black Cat's customers; mornings it's busy with those heading to work: doctors, nurses, plumbers, teachers, laborers, and attorneys. At night, it's the gathering place for young adults with tattoos, piercings, and haircuts with rainbow colors. It's where musicians, artists, writers, actors, and other artsy people show up at all times of the day.

I remember how those artsy people loved it when Adam would join in. I swear he could talk intelligently on any subject; he was so bright.

Sipping my mocha, which was finally cool enough to drink, I recalled Adam insisting that I tell him about how it was that I was an architect in Saginaw.

"After practicing in Detroit, I told him, "I moved to Saginaw and joined Duckett and Pomeroy, an architectural firm of 30 people. After a while, I wasn't having any fun working there. I learned that hard work was mandatory to succeed in life, but I believed work should be fun. It was a good lesson I learned from my dad. During a partners' retreat, I realized it was time to change and decided to start my own office.

Shortly after deciding to start my firm, a former associate, Liz Bowers, joined me. We had fun searching for a new office that exuded warmth and sophistication. We wanted to be part of the renaissance on the East Side of Saginaw, along Washington Avenue, where improvements begin with the Children's Zoo that continues along a three-mile stretch ending at the Grand Theatre."

I remembered Adam listening so intently to my story. He made me feel like I was the most important person in the world.

"Are you ok," Nicky said, interrupting my train of thought. "You've been staring at the wall for the past half hour."

"I'm ok, Nicky. I've been thinking about Adam and looking for clues about his murder."

She smiled before heading off to clear another table.

I returned to remembering my conversation with Adam. I explained how Liz and I selected a building on Washington Avenue. It was a home built in the early 1900s by a wealthy family who had made a fortune selling dry goods and other supplies to loggers. The two-story building was brick and featured 10-inch wood casing around all the windows and doors, nine-foot ceilings with plaster cornice in the main rooms. We redecorated with warm colors of bronze, rose, and dark beige."

I remember Adam saying, "you must have felt like you were part of Saginaw reinventing itself. I've read that it's a more diversified economy today and that It's a regional medical center and has broadened its scope beyond automotive manufacturing into aviation, medical, and other technical products."

I added, "And it's still a thriving farming community that gives it a hard-working culture I find appealing."

I recalled Adam laughing, "Appreciating your father's teachings," he said.

Looking at my watch, I realized an hour had passed since I came in. I had no clues more clues to share with the detective. Then I remembered it was in the café that Adam told me about his trip to Istanbul, which he took without Natalie. That he'd go without her surprised me. Adam said he didn't tell her because she has a terrible temper. He also said he had trouble with a Saudi family and feared for his life while there. Maybe this was it. Maybe a Saudi family traveled from Turkey to kill him. Somehow this didn't make sense to me, but I'd tell Clark about it anyway.

I realized, more than ever, how much I missed Adam. His death hurt, and I wanted to cry when I thought about how he suffered before he died.

Chapter Seven

Saginaw, Michigan
July 22, 2019

Lukas Novak

I wasn't surprised that Clark wanted to meet again. Almost everyone knew I was close to Adam. It seemed reasonable I might have an idea of who killed him.

Before leaving the Black Cat, I Googled him. It was always a good idea to go into a meeting as well prepared as possible. I didn't know who had killed Adam, but it only made sense to learn more about the man I hoped would find out.

According to an article in the Saginaw News, he was born and raised in Saginaw's dangerous East Side. Clark was an excellent athlete but not one of the top three in his middle school. He said that the others were in jail, on drugs, or dead. What had separated him from the others was the City of Saginaw Summer Youth Sports Program. He and a few friends would go to as many activities as possible every day.

Clark gave up the dream of playing in the NFL when he received a full academic scholarship to Central Michigan University. He majored in criminal justice with grades so strong that the school gave him a full scholarship for his master's degree. After graduating, he took a job with the Allen Park police department just south of Detroit. After two years there, the Detroit Police Department offered him a position. He spent the next seven years working his way up the ladder to detective. Clark jumped at the chance to return home when offered a detective position with The City of Saginaw Police Department. Clark was now their Chief Homicide Detective.

As I finished my coffee, I decided that while I liked Clark because he was direct, he also made me uneasy. Perhaps his penetrating questions required me to talk about my private feelings. Things I didn't feel like sharing.

Regardless, it was time to go if I didn't want to be late.

Chapter Eight

Saginaw, Michigan
July 22, 2019

Lukas Novak

Arriving at the City of Saginaw Police Department before our scheduled meeting, I informed the front desk officer that I was to meet Detective Tobias Clark at 9:00. In only a few minutes, a well-dressed African American greeted me. Tobias Clark was six-foot-three inches with an athletic build. His youthful appearance disguised his 50 years.

Clark took a seat across from me.

"It's nice to see you again, Mr. Novak. The last time we met, I didn't have the opportunity to thank you for your work and financial support of our community, especially the City's Summer Youth Program. That program means a lot to me, so, thank you."

I appreciated his compliment and told him so. I liked this man even more.

"Detective Clark, what can you tell me about Adam's death?" I asked.

"Before we get to that, let me ask you some questions. How long have you known Mr. Lindmark?"

"About two years. That's when Adam came to Saginaw. At that time, I was Chair of Great Lakes Bay Art Museum's Board of Directors. I was impressed with his credentials and professional demeanor. We got along from the start and became good friends."

Clark looked closely at me. I assumed he'd done his research on me because of my relationship with Adam. Perhaps he considered me more than a person of interest. Maybe I was a suspect?

Chapter Nine

Saginaw, Michigan
July 22, 2019

Detective Tobias Clark

Clark had seen crimes of passion before, and he believed the person who murdered Lindmark had a passionate reason to kill him. Clark had found that Lindmark and Novak were close, maybe best friends in his talks with others around town. He also heard that Lindmark and Nicky Winters were lovers before Novak became involved with her. Some believed that Novak was infatuated with Winters. Clark knew that a love triangle could lead to murder.

He studied the man across the table. Twenty-nine years old and 5'10". Novak had dark eyes matching his full black, curly hair. He was solid, looking naturally strong as his legs and arms were thick. Novak appeared to be into some workout program because his stomach was flat, and he wasn't carrying extra weight. By his looks, he's not the kind of man you'd want to pick a fight with. Perhaps Novak had already been in too many fights? His nose had clearly been broken, and thick eyebrows accented a rugged and scared face.

Clark saw Novak as a leading suspect for murder. After their first meeting, he'd investigated his background. Novak's parents had emigrated from Prague before World War II. He grew up in Royal Oak, a suburb of Detroit. He attended Wayne State University and excelled while earning both a bachelor's and master's degrees. After school, he worked one year with a highly respected architectural firm in Detroit, then moved to Saginaw and joined the regional firm of Duckett and Pomeroy. He'd earned a solid reputation as a creative and thorough architect. When he left the firm to start his practice, his partners were disappointed but genuinely wished him well. They weren't quite as happy as many of their clients moved over to him over the past two years, along with an associate, Elizabeth Bowers.

Novak was known for giving back to the community. He'd been on many community non-profit boards and earned the reputation of being active with each one. His passions seemed to be children, and he'd done his share of work to benefit them.

So, now it was time to dig, to get through Novak's shiny exterior.

"When's the last time you saw Mr. Lindmark?" Clark asked.

"Six nights ago," he answered.

"Are you sure?"

"Yes, we were having drinks at the Lumbermen Club."

"It couldn't have been five nights ago?" asked Clark skeptically.

"No. Why?" he replied.

"Just want to be sure of all the facts, Mr. Novak."

A flash of irritation crossed Novak's face, which Clark mentally noted.

"What did you talk about?"

"His work. He said he's close to finishing the conservation of two paintings."

"What paintings?"

"Adam was conserving paintings by an artist named William Bouguereau. One owned by the museum and the other by a woman in Saginaw."

"What's her name?" Clark asked.

"Janice Wendell. She's a client and friend of mine."

"Did you talk about anything else?"

"He talked about Natalie Collins."

"Not Nicky Winters?" countered Clark.

"Nicky? Well, yes, we did just a little bit. But mostly about Natalie,"

Novak answered.

"Who is Natalie Collins?" Clark asked, although he already knew.

"A woman Adam had been seeing."

"What did he say about Ms. Collins?"

"That he liked her, but soon he'd leave her."

"Do you know this woman?" Clark asked.

"She's my client. I introduced Adam to her."

"What does she do?"

"She used to be a pharmaceutical rep and started buying up commercial buildings, restoring and renting them out. That's how I got to know her. She was so successful; she gave up being a rep for full-time urban development."

"Why did Mr. Lindmark say he'd leave her?" Clark asked.

"Adam was an art conservator. He found museums that needed art conservation work on their finest treasurers. Once he completed his work, he moved on to another city. He moved to many different art museums. I suppose he was thinking of his next restoration project."

"Have you talked to Ms. Collins?" Clark asked.

"Yes. Only briefly," Novak answered.

"How would you describe her state of mind?"

"Hysterical. Have you met with her?" Novak asked.

"No," the detective replied.

"Why not?"

"Ms. Collins said she needed to cry and scream and grieve alone. She said she'd call me later today. So, you're close with Ms. Collins?"

"Fairly close. Adam and Natalie would go out with Nicky and me, and as I said, Natalie is also my client."

"Was Ms. Winters upset that Mr. Lindmark was with Natalie Collins and not her? I heard the two of them were involved."

"They were, some time ago," Novak answered.

"Do you think she still has feelings for him?"

"Yes."

"Does that bother you?" Clark asked him with a penetrating gaze.

"Bother me?" Novak looked a bit annoyed.

"I've been told you have strong feelings for Ms. Winters. I imagine it would be hard for you to see the woman you care for still interested in Mr. Lindmark," he said.

"Yes, it's hard. I recognize I'm Nicky's second choice. If she had her way, she would be with Adam. I've learned to accept that. It made it easier when Adam became close with Natalie, but I won't pretend that it's not hard for me."

"Hard enough to do something about it?"

"Like what?" Novak asked.

"Kill Ms. Winter's other lover? Kill Adam Lindmark?"

"No. I would have done something about it long ago if it bothered me. Besides, I'm neither a killer nor a sadist."

"A sadist? Why did you say that?" Clark asked.

"I heard Adam was tortured."

"What else did you hear?"

"Nothing more. Detective Clark, I've answered your questions now. What can you tell me about Adam's murder?"

"Mr. Novak, this is an ongoing investigation, and the local news leaked information that was unethical. I can tell you we will find the leak at our headquarters and the person will be punished. Now about Ms. Collins, do you think Mr. Lindmark told her that he was leaving her behind?"

"I'm not sure."

"If he had, how do you think she'd react to his leaving?" Clark asked.

"I'm not sure. I know she cared for Adam very much."

"Do you think she'd be angry enough to hurt him?"

"Adam told me that Natalie had quite a temper, but absolutely not; I can't imagine her reacting that way."

"What else can you tell me about Mr. Lindmark?"

"Smart, very smart. Educated. I think he was financially well off, and everyone seemed to like him."

"Do you know anyone who would want to harm him?"

"Detective, I've gone over that question in my mind time and time again. I thought maybe a jealous lover, but that doesn't seem to add up.

As far as I know, Adam wasn't seeing anyone else around here."

"Around here. How about elsewhere?" Clark asked, thinking about this new angle.

"Thank you for reminding me; earlier this morning, I recalled a conversation Adam and I had. He talked about a trip to Istanbul about three weeks before his death. Adam told me he met a woman from the Middle East, and they spent a night together. Her family was so angry that he immediately left Istanbul and hid in another city in Turkey before flying home."

Clark considered this possibility for a few moments before asking, "Do you think they killed him?"

"I wouldn't think so. But maybe. I have no idea. Adam did talk about it before he died. He thought perhaps someone was following him. Then he decided he was wrong."

"How about Nicky Winters? Do you think she could have killed Lindmark?"

"No. Now look, Detective Clark, I assumed you'd be interested in me because of my relationship with Adam and Nicky Winters. Nicky didn't kill Adam, nor did I. If there is anything I can do to help find his killer, I will. If you need me, I'm always around, and I'm not going anywhere."

"That's good because I know we'll be talking again, Mr. Novak," Clark finished as he stood and opened the door.

After Novak left, Clark sat at the interview table and pondered Novak's answers as he wrote up his notes. Novak said that Collins had a bad temper but wouldn't hurt Lindmark. A family in Istanbul wanted Lindmark for having had an affair with their daughter. Novak was dating Nicky Winters, Lindmark's ex, and she wasn't over Lindmark. There are several possibilities but at the top of the list is Novak. Clark pondered this thought for a while. Yes, then, there's Novak.

Chapter Ten

New York City
October 1, 2003

Adam Lindmark

It was a Friday night, Adam's sophomore year at NYU. He was heading to a nightclub in Manhattan to find a woman with whom to spend the night. Adam enjoyed seducing women, and it was part of a life he found very satisfying. He was excelling in the classroom with dual majors in art history and physics. A strange combination, however, both subjects interested him. He had no plan to use either degree because he didn't need to. His grandfather had left him a trust fund when he was 12 years old that today had grown to $15 million. When applying to colleges, he'd scored an almost perfect score on his SAT, and NYU offered him a scholarship if he'd turn down other prestigious schools. The scholarship wasn't important to him; what was important was living in New York City and enjoying women.

At 10:00 on a cool City evening, Adam entered Bungalow 8 on 27th Street between 10th and 11th Avenue, one of the most popular bars in Manhattan. The bar's owner knew the best way to create excitement and enhance patrons was by attracting beautiful women, and Bungalow 8 was very good at this.

Adam found a place at the bar and ordered a vodka and tonic with a twist. He was different than most undergrad students, he wasn't into drinking unless it was excellent red wine. He wouldn't finish his drink. It was there to have something in his hand. While paying the bartender, a dark curly-haired man came up to the bar. Adam guessed he was about his age. The man introduced himself to Adam.

"Hi. NYU, right?" He said.

Adam thought he recognized him, thinking he looked like a taller version of James Caan, the actor.

"Yes, Adam Lindmark."

"Hello Adam, I'm Paul Rothstein."

"Hey Paul, can I buy you a drink?"

"Great, thanks."

Adam waved down a bartender, and Paul ordered a Whiskey Smash. Paul was happy to accept a free drink. Unlike Adam, Paul was financially struggling, and beverages at the Bungalow 8 were not cheap. In addition to attending NYU, Paul also shared Adam's passion for looking for women on Saturday night.

Paul again thanked Adam for the drink and said, "Many attractive women tonight, don't you think."

"I do," Adam said.

While they talked, two women standing at a high-top table watched them. The brunette was studying the blonde man at the bar. As he glanced in her direction, she gave him an encouraging smile.

When Adam and Paul reached the women's table, Adam introduced himself and Paul.

"Life is short he said to the brunette; want to dance?"

So they danced, and after a few songs, Adam suggested he buy her a drink.

The woman liked the look of this tall, handsome man. He was very confident and likable. Over the next hour or so, he bought her a couple of drinks. She noticed that he ordered himself a drink that he had never touched. He asked her questions in a way that soon she was telling him her life story. He was obviously interested in her and a good listener. She asked him if he wanted to see her apartment.

The next morning she heard him getting up before her. She thought he might be slipping out before she woke up. It surprised her when he came to her and said he was going out for coffee and wanted to bring one back for her. She sat up in bed and said that would be great and told him about a coffee shop just down the block.

She wondered if he would come back. He did. They sat at her small table in a tiny kitchen and talked. Actually, she talked, and he listened. He finally said he needed to go. She made sure she gave him her number and told him she'd very much want to hear from him. Adam thanked her for what she wasn't sure. After he left, she realized she didn't have his number or know very much about him. She hoped he'd call. He never did.

For several subsequent Saturdays, she visited the Bungalow 8 hoping to see him but never did. Years later, she thought about him even though she had only known him one night.

The next day Paul saw Adam and asked, "The woman you left the bar with, will you see her again?"

"No," Adam said.

"Didn't you like her?"

"I liked her, and she was interesting. I just think it best not to see her again. We won't be going back to the Bungalow 8; I don't want to bump into her."

Chapter Eleven

New York City and Cooperstown
New York
April 24, 2005

Adam Lindmark

Their chance meeting on that Saturday evening started a strong friendship between Adam and Paul.

They graduated from NYU with honors. Adam entered the Master of Fine Arts program. Paul, excited to stop living in poverty, started looking for a job. With a degree in finance with honors, a robust background working summer jobs at prestigious brokerage firms, and strong people skills, he was offered several positions. Eventually, he decided to work for a boutique brokerage firm in Manhattan.

Adam entered the Fine Arts program because he wanted to become an accomplished portrait painter in the style of the fine masters. Although he appreciated the Impressionists: Monet, Degas, and Renoir and their post-impressionist successors: Gauguin, Matisse, and Picasso; he was fascinated with the sophisticated artistry of the old masters like Rembrandt, DaVinci, and Velasquez. This wasn't a new passion for Adam. As a youngster, he'd spent hours drawing and painting, particularly people. Over the years, he became an accomplished painter and, as a teenager, won highly competitive art competitions in Grosse Pointe, Michigan, his hometown.

Before graduating, Adam asked Paul if he'd sit for a portrait. He agreed and soon realized that this included being still for hours. After six settings, Paul had told Adam that he couldn't do it anymore.

Six months later, over red wine at Paul's apartment, Adam unveiled the portrait. Paul was stunned. Setting in a large, oversized leather chair was a handsome young man driven by inner energy and ambition. The psychology behind Paul's likeness was a perfect reflection. When Paul moved from a cubical to an office, his portrait was given the most prominent wall. His colleagues, clients, and friends were impressed. Many times Paul heard, "your portrait should be in a museum." Although Adam was happy with Paul's portrait, he knew he needed to improve.

After graduating with a master's degree in Fine Arts, Adam continued his education by entering the Art Conversation program at NYU in Cooperstown, New York, a very different environment than New York City. Isolated in the rolling hills of northern New York, Cooperstown was a sleepy town. There's not much to do unless you're interested in visiting the Baseball Hall of Fame or the James Fenimore Cooper Museum. Although Adam missed living in the City, he was excited to learn about conserving paintings.

He found early on that to properly conserve a painting, he needed to understand the practices used by the original painter, each artist's selection of inner framing, canvases, and the underlying ground or foundation applied to the canvas before the actual painting began. It was required for him to study the pigments used by each artist and how they were mixed to become their paint, and each painter's favorite variation of varnishes and lacquers. Many of the artists also made their finished framing, and Adam needed to understand that too.

His background in art history and as a painter helped him understand the unique qualities of each artist and the reasons behind an artist's formulas for making paint and applying it to canvas to create their individual work.

What separated him from other students was his degree in physics and classes in chemistry. He quickly understood the physical and chemical composition of pigments, varnishes, and lacquers and how different solvents interacted with the painting during conservation. He was required to repair damaged areas of the painting, and his scientific background and skill as a painter made him an exceptional conservator. Adam poured himself into his newfound profession in a way that he couldn't have imagined.

While in Cooperstown, his painting of Paul led to opportunities for painting other portraits for Paul's clients; commissions portraying husbands, wives, girlfriends, and children. He honed his skills on each portrait. By the time he completed the art conservation program, he was a consummate portrait painter.

Meeting new patrons and delivering paintings to New York also allowed him to visit Paul and strengthen their friendship, taking them in a direction they never envisioned.

Chapter Twelve

Saginaw, Michigan
July 23, 2019

Lukas Novak

"Hello Lukas, this is Natalie."

"Oh, Natalie, I'm so glad to hear from you. I'm worried about you," I answered.

"Thanks, Lukas. Can we get together to talk?"

'Of course, where and when?"

"How about the Lumberman Club around 4:00 this afternoon?"

"That works; I'll see you then."

Finding a comfortable chair by the fireplace at The Lumbermen Club, I knew the club's interesting history. A three-story building in the downtown area of Saginaw on Washington Avenue was started in 1889 by prominent business and professional leaders, many of whom became wealthy during the lumbering era. The founders appreciated elegance and built a club that reflected their tastes with high ceilings, intricately carved wooden walls, and trim. They added numerous paintings. I saw that their tastes in art varied, from beautiful landscapes to amateurish portraits.

I thought of how Adam and I laughed at some of the nude paintings around the horseshoe bar, rumored to be the favorite prostitutes of the patrons.

Adam, I miss you, I said to myself. I'm sure Natalie does too.

The Club's motto: "We Leave the Burden of our Toil Outside the

Friendly Door" was something Adam and I took to heart as we drank Manhattans many days after work. Today, I wasn't going to be able to leave my burdens behind. Natalie was suffering, and I hoped I could be the person she could pour out her grief.

I recalled meeting Natalie for the first time a couple of years ago. She was interested in urban renewal and asked for my thoughts on buying undervalued commercial properties in Bay City, a community north of Saginaw. She was a pharmaceutical representative and wanted to go into business for herself. She'd already created a limited liability company to own her first property but was getting cold feet before her first purchase. Over the next few days, we developed her business plan to rehabilitate and rent a property. After finally deciding to go forward, she became successful and soon retired from the pharmaceutical sales world, becoming an urban developer.

Natalie lived in many communities growing up. Her father raised her after her mother abandoned them when she was five. One of her vague memories of her mother was an intense argument between her and her father. Her sudden departure still troubled Natalie. A machinist, her father took jobs across the country depending on industrial trends. In each new community, she suffered the challenges of making new friends at every school. Her father, to make up for these difficulties, spoiled her. Whether it was his overindulgence or her genetics, Natalie developed a temper that could erupt into screaming, throwing things, and striking her father and classmates. School officials arranged counseling for her that only intensified her resentment.

In contrast to her unattractive personality, she was exceptionally beautiful. She used her beauty to manipulate both adults and classmates. Through the years, she became increasingly self-absorbed, insisting on getting her way and resorting to cruelty when she didn't.

As she grew older, she had had many romantic relationships; none of which had lasted. The longest had been with Adam Lindmark. She cared for Adam more than any other man and sought to please him, concealing her unattractive tendencies as much as she was able. Adam's death exposed all her self-doubts and left her hollow and deeply depressed.

I introduced Adam to Natalie, primarily acting in my self-interest. I was convinced Adam wouldn't be able to resist a 5'10" beauty with olive skin, full lips, and shoulder-length light brown hair. I was hoping Adam would leave Nicky for Natalie, and I could be the white knight. For the most part, this worked; until recently, Adam and Natalie were inseparable, and most of the time, I was with Nicky.

Upon hearing of Adam's death, Natalie became inconsolable; she hid away and refused to talk to anyone. Before her phone call, I was deeply concerned she might take her life.

She greeted me wearing a classic white silk blouse with mother-of-pearl buttons, tailored chestnut slacks, a black blazer, and low black heels. As always, she was wearing little makeup and had the look of a woman who didn't need to.

With a hug and a sad smile, she said, "Lukas, I'm so miserable, I'm struggling."

She sat in a stuffed leather chair next to mine. She'd been crying. Shaking her head as if it would keep her from crying, she said, "Get me a drink, I need something wicked. An Old Fashioned."

I ordered two from the horseshoe bar.

We sipped our drinks in silence.

"I want to have a wake for Adam. No funeral. I want a celebration. Does that make sense?" She said.

I agreed.

"He didn't have much family, but his friends and I could have closure," she added.

"He had a lot of friends. I know Paul in New York will want to be there. There are others from the museums where he's worked who will want to know. I can reach out to them," I said.

"I just couldn't bear seeing him in a casket," she said and started to cry.

"Ok. Do you want me to make arrangements?" I asked.

"No, I will, but I'll need your help."

We returned to our cocktails and said nothing. I waited for her to lead our conversation.

"Have you heard any more about Adam's death?" She asked.

Natalie started lightly sobbing. I got up and gave her another hug.

"I hurt so much. I needed him. I swear sometimes I want to kill myself," she said.

"I understand."

More silence.

"What have you heard?" She asked again.

"Nothing. Detective Clark interviewed me but wouldn't reveal anything."

"He's the one working Adam's case?" She asked.

"Yes. Clark was asking all the questions. I wanted to learn more about his death, but he said it's an ongoing investigation. One thing I know is that I'm a suspect."

"What! That's crazy," she blurted.

"He talked about my relationship with Nicky and that my jealousy for Adam was a motive to kill him."

"Nicky and Adam ended long ago," she said.

"It ended the moment he met you," I said.

"I know he loved me."

She stood up.

"Excuse me, Lukas, I need to dry my eyes."

She made her way to the Ladies Room. I ached for her and wondered if she knew that Adam was leaving Saginaw and not taking her.

After what seemed like a very long time, she returned and stood beside my chair.

"I'm sorry, Lukas, I must go. I'll call you soon."

I walked her to her car and returned to the Club. Settling into the stuffed chair, I realized our glasses were almost full. I was finishing mine when I received a call.

"Hello, this is Lukas," I said.

"Mr. Novak, this is Detective Clark. I need to talk to you."

Chapter Thirteen

Midland, Michigan
July 24, 2019

Lukas Novak

"Nicky," I said when she answered my call.

"Hi. What are you doing?" She said.

"I met with Natalie."

"And?"

"She's a mess. She wants to have a wake for Adam."

"I'm surprised; she seemed so completely distraught. I didn't think she'd be up for something like that."

"I'm not sure she is. She left before finishing her drink and was crying. After she left, I received a call from Detective Clark. He wants to meet again," I said.

"Why?"

"He wouldn't say. I still think he considers me a prime suspect."

"That's ridiculous," she said.

"I'm going back to my office. Liz and I are preparing for two meetings for tomorrow. Do you want to have dinner?" I asked.

"Yes, I haven't done anything all day but be depressed. Where do you want to go?"

"I need a change of scenery to lift my spirits. The Great Lakes Bay Country Club," I said.

"Perfect. I can dress up and stop thinking about Adam for a little while. Lukas, I feel guilty. I shouldn't want to go out and think of something else, should I?" She asked.

"We've spent plenty of time mourning, and we'll spend even more in the days to come. You dress up, and I'll pick you up at 7."

I reached Nicky's apartment a little bit early. As usual, I waited in her living room until 7:20.

"Nicky, I made reservations for 7:30," I said.

"Call and see if we can be just a little late," she replied.

I called the Club and moved the reservation to 8.

When Nicky came out of her bedroom, I knew it was worth my waiting. She wore a black dress with a black and gold belt and gold earrings, necklace, and bracelet. Her stiletto shoes accented her long shapely legs.

"I'm ready. Let's go. We don't want to be late," she teased.

I gave her a warm kiss.

"You're going to mess up my lipstick," she said and then put her arms around me and gave me a deep searching kiss.

I immediately thought this was one of the reasons I always come back to her.

"Let's eat in," I joked.

"No, I'm all dressed up, and I want to have dinner at the country club."

The Great Lakes Bay Country Club was good for client development and relationships. It had a solid corporate sponsor that had dropped over $40 million into the clubhouse and golf course. It was perhaps the finest clubhouse in Michigan. All the features of the Club were completely upscale, from the dining rooms and bars to the pool, workout, and spa areas. It was the place to be seen. Tonight I was going to be seen with this alluring woman.

"Hello, Mr. Novak," the hostess said.

"I'm sorry for having to move our reservation," I replied.

"That was no problem at all. Ms. Winters, you're as lovely as ever," the hostess said.

"Thank you. I'm the reason we're late. I'm sorry too," Nicky added.

"You didn't mind waiting, did you, Mr. Novak?" the hostess teased.

"Not when I saw her in that black dress."

We laughed as we were seated.

"Enjoy your dinner."

"Thank you," Nicky said.

As soon as we were seated, our server asked if we'd like to order a cocktail.

Nicky said, " I'm having a Tito's martini straight up."

I ordered a glass of Cabernet and leaned back, enjoying being with her.

"Lukas, I wish you'd quit flirting with the hostess and waitresses, " Nicky said.

"Flirting? Will you stop it, I'm with the most beautiful woman. Why would I be flirting?"

Nicky laughed. "Well, that's a good question, isn't it?" She asked.

We studied the menu as we enjoyed our drinks. After ordering, I asked, "Were you busy this morning?"

"Always busy. How about you?

"As I told you, I met with Natalie. It was emotional."

"You said she wanted a wake for Adam?" She asked.

"She does, and I'm sure that many of his friends would like to say goodbye too."

"I agree. If I can be of any help, please let me know. Many people from the Black Cat will attend," she said.

We continued talking about the details of the wake as we ate our salads and worked on our drinks.

"You said you have several meetings tomorrow?" She asked.

"Liz and I worked all afternoon on two sets of plans. Janet Wendell is coming in. I told you we're going to do some remodeling of her home. We'll probably spend most of our time talking about her painting that Adam conserved. I can't tell you how much she loves it. She said it's so beautiful and reminds her of how special Adam was to her. She wants to do something to remember him."

As we ate our dinner, we talked about some of the people that came into the Black Cat that morning. Many wanted to speculate on Adam's killer.

I didn't particularly want to talk about this but told Nicky, "I also heard from Detective Clark."

"What's that about?"

"I'm sure he's still trying to understand what took place. Last time, he told me that how Adam was murdered was leaked to the media, and now it's their continuing lead story. You know, a gruesome murder of a handsome and well-liked artisan. I'm wondering what leads he has other than me."

"Why you? You were his best friend," she asked.

"He mentioned that maybe we had a love-hate relationship."

"What?"

"He talked about you and Adam and you and me. He said love triangles could lead to acts of passion, like murder," I said.

"My god, did you tell him I haven't been involved with Adam for a long time, and Natalie is the woman in his life?"

"I did. I'm not sure I convinced him. I'll know better after seeing him tomorrow at 1:00. Frankly, I'm surprised he hasn't talked to you," I said.

"Well, I hope he does. I'll tell him that Adam and I had nothing going on."

"I'm guessing he wants more information from me before he talks to you. He'll look for inconsistencies in our stories. I'm sure he'll ask if you still had feelings for Adam."

Nicky looked down and then seriously back at me.

"Lukas, I'm not going to lie to the detective. I still cared for Adam. But I care for you too," she said.

I knew I'd always be her second choice, even after Adam's death. A sadness came over me.

The timing was perfect; the waitress broke the silence asking if everything was alright and wanted another drink. Nicky quickly asked for another martini and then looked down at her meal.

"Not for me. Big day tomorrow," I said.

I no longer felt like drinking and sensed the rest of the evening with

Nicky could be awkward.

"Nicky, you know how I feel about you and Adam. You know I never would hurt him, much less kill him."

"I know," she said.

We were quiet the rest of the evening; later, I dropped Nicky off at her apartment.

On the way home, I kept feeling Nicky's doubt; does she believe I killed Adam? As much as I tried to convince myself otherwise, I knew she thought it possible.

Chapter Fourteen

Saginaw
July 25, 2019

Lukas Novak

The following morning I was in the office by 7:00. Liz was already working.

"Good morning, Sunshine," she said.

"My, aren't we the early one," I replied.

Laughing and smiling, she said, "I'm making sure all things are ready for the day. A good idea, don't you think?"

"I thought we were pretty much ready when we left last night," I answered.

"We were. In bed, I thought of a couple of additional items we could go over."

"You're one special person, Ms. Bowers."

Laughing again, she responded, "I know."

Liz was special. She combined being organized and detailed with a genuine interest in our clients. Many relied on her, including me. Liz was raising her two boys alone. I liked her kids and repeatedly told them they were lucky to have a great mother.

Her one flaw, she readily admitted, was her choice in men. Her husband had been an insecure parasite who did everything he could to undermine her confidence. Since the divorce, Liz had dated several guys. Her latest one seemed like a small-town punk. My opinion didn't count, and if she was happy, and she surely deserved it, then I was delighted.

Reassuringly, Liz was the one person who knew I couldn't kill Adam.

Chapter Fifteen

Saginaw, Michigan
July 25, 2019

Detective Tobias Clark

A little before 10:00, Clark called Novak.
"Mr. Novak, this is Detective Clark. Something has come up at my office, and I need to reschedule our appointment."
"Ok, detective."
"You're going to be around, Mr. Novak?" He asked.
"I told you I'd be around, and thanks for rescheduling. I have a full day of appointments."
"Very good. I'll be back in touch."
Clark left his office and drove to the Black Cat Café. Before today, he'd interviewed several people that knew Novak, Winters, and Lindmark. He wanted to talk to Winters this morning before another interview with Novak.
The café was quiet. As he waited to order a coffee, he studied Winters. She certainly was pretty and seemed to enjoy her job or at least talking with her customers. The woman in front of Clark was discussing a new job, her son's flu - apparently he was better - and her lazy boyfriend. Customers at the table closest to the counter were talking and laughing and asking Winters for her advice from time to time. He wondered what, precisely, made Nicky Winters so appealing.
Clark asked for a regular coffee.

"Would that be for here or to go?" She asked.

"To go, please."

"Would you like anything else?" She asked.

"Yes, as a matter of fact. You're Nicky Winters, aren't you?" He asked.

"Yes," she replied, her tone going immediately on the defensive.

"I'm Detective Clark. I need to talk with you in private. When does your shift end, Ms. Winters?"

"At 1:00."

"I'd like you to come to the police station. Will that be an inconvenience for you?

"No. I'll be there as soon as I can," she said.

"Very good. I'll look forward to seeing you."

After Clark left, Nicky called her mother.

"Mom, Detective Clark just came in to see me. He wants to interview me this afternoon," she said.

"Well, Nicky, you were expecting to be interviewed, weren't you?" Her mother answered.

"Yes, but it's still unnerving."

"What's to be nervous about? Tell him the truth. You know nothing of Adam's murder. Have you called Lukas?"

"No," Nicky answered.

"I think you should, and he'll help you be less uptight for your interview."

Nicky's mother liked Lukas Novak. She thought he was the best thing to come into her daughter's life. He helped center her and encouraged her to take advantage of her potential. Hopefully, he'd convince her to go back to college and get her degree. She was happy when Nicky stopped dating Adam Lindmark. Many people liked Adam and thought very highly of him. She didn't. She was a practicing psychologist and believed Adam was polished at taking advantage of people and didn't like Nicky being used.

After her shift, Nicky sped home, poured herself a double shot of vodka, jumped in the shower, and dressed in her most conservative dress.

After brushing her teeth and gargling, she left, arriving at 1:45, and ushered into an interview room.

Clark knew when she arrived but would let her wait. He thought her being anxious may make it easier for him to find the truth. Clark was beginning to believe that Winters was at the heart of Lindmark's murder. He intended to pressure her for some important information.

At 2:15, he entered the room.

"Sorry to keep you waiting, Ms. Winters. I appreciate you coming in," he said.

It was apparent that Winters was nervous. She continually twisted her dark curly hair.

"Ms. Winters, did you know Adam Lindmark?" Clark asked.

"Yes."

"When did you meet him?"

"About two years ago."

"What kind of relationship did you have with him?

"I was his girlfriend."

"And are you still his girlfriend?"

"No. We broke up about a year ago."

"Did you break up with him, or he with you?"

"Detective Clark, is this really important?" She asked.

Clark stared at Nicky and sternly said, "This is a murder case, Ms. Winters, and you knew Adam Lindmark maybe as well as anyone. So yes, these questions are critical. I expect you to answer each of my questions thoroughly and honestly. Do you understand me, Ms. Winters?

Nicky held back her tears and answered in a trembling voice, "I understand."

"Did you end the relationship, or did he?"

"He did. He started dating another woman."

"Who was that person?"

"Natalie Collins," she answered

"And now you're seeing Lukas Novak, is that correct?"

"Yes."

"You may know that I've already interviewed Mr. Novak, and he told me he was seeing you. It's obvious to me that he cares very much for you. Are you aware of that? He asked.

"I know Lukas cares for me."

"More than just caring for you, he's in love with you, isn't that right?"

"I suppose that's true."

Staring intently at Winters again, using his authoritative voice, he asked, "Suppose that's true? You know that's true, don't you, and he'd do anything for you, wouldn't he?"

"If I asked him, I know he would, yes," she answered

"Now, Ms. Winters, we live in a relatively small community, and there aren't many secrets people can keep. I've been talking to people about you, Mr. Novak, and Mr. Lindmark. I found some interesting things. When was the last time you saw Mr. Lindmark?

"I don't remember," she answered in a quivering voice.

"Oh, I'm sure you do, and I want to know when that was," he demanded.

"I think it was about a week before his murder."

Raising his voice, he said, "I told you, Ms. Winters, I want complete and honest answers from you. You're lying to me. The last time you saw him was just before his death. And, you didn't just see him did you?"

Nicky began crying. "I saw him, but didn't sleep with him."

Clark raised his voice yet again. "You're lying to me. We found a used condom in his room. It will be easy to check the DNA, and I'm sure it's yours. Isn't that true?

Crying harder, she answered, "Yes."

"How do you think this made Mr. Novak feel when he found out?"

"He doesn't know," she sobbed.

"Oh, come on, Ms. Winters. If I easily found out, don't you think he knows? He's a very smart man, Ms. Winters. I will tell you how he felt, and he felt betrayed and hurt. Mostly he felt angry. He was angry towards you and what he thought was his best friend, Mr. Lindmark. You said he would do anything for you. I think he would do anything to keep you, Ms. Winters."

"Lukas would never hurt Adam," she cried.

"I'm sorry, Ms. Winters, passion and love lead to many things that are out of character for a person. Even murder. And I'll add this, Ms. Winters, I'm sure Ms. Collins also knows. How do you think she reacted to the love of her life cheating? Did Mr. Lindmark tell you he was planning to leave Saginaw?"

"Yes."

"Did he ask you to go with him?"

"No."

"Did you ask him if you could go with him?" he questioned.

"Yes."

"What did he say?"

"Nothing, he didn't say anything."

"He didn't say no?" he asked.

"He didn't answer, but I hoped I could go with him," she answered.

As Winters left, Clark doubted that Novak would forgive her and thought she believed the same.

Chapter Sixteen

City of Saginaw
July 25, 2019

Lukas Novak

After Nicky Winters left his office, Clark called Novak before Winters could talk to him. Clark wanted to read Novak's reaction to determine if he knew she'd slept with Lindmark.

"Mr. Novak, would you be able to meet with me. I know you're busy, but would 3:00 work for you? It's important."

I was hoping that Clark had new evidence that would lead to Adam's murderer. I made sure I was at his office before 3:00. I took a seat in an interview room. Clark was waiting.

"Thank you for meeting on short notice," Clark said.

I could tell by Clark's demeanor that this would be a difficult discussion. I looked at him, but I didn't answer.

"I'll get right to the point. You know that Mr. Lindmark died on July 12, a Thursday?"

I nodded that I knew.

"Mr. Novak, I told you that this being a crime of passion, I must consider all persons who may be emotionally involved with Mr. Lindmark. I also mentioned that because Ms. Winters had been involved with Mr. Lindmark and you that it raises questions."

I stared at Clark without saying a word.

"I want to go back and ask you further questions about your

relationship with Ms. Winters. Specifically, I want to know if you knew she slept with Mr. Lindmark on the evening of July 11, a Wednesday?"

"What makes you believe she did?" I asked.

"She told me she did earlier today," he responded.

"I don't believe she said that, nor do I believe she slept with Adam before his death," I said.

"Mr. Novak, she admitted that she did after telling her that we found a used condom in Mr. Lindmark's bedroom. When I explained to Ms. Winters, we would be checking her DNA to confirm that she was Mr. Lindmark's partner, she admitted to sleeping with him."

Clark studied my expression.

"I'm sure this makes you angry, Mr. Novak, that the woman you care for deceived you and slept with your best friend. I know it would make me very angry. Angry indeed," Clark said.

I didn't answer Clark, only stared through him, thinking about what he told me.

Finally, I said, "I didn't know they slept together, but I'm not surprised.

"I've always known I'm a second choice for Nicky that she cared or loved Adam in a way that she doesn't me. Am I angry? No. I'm hurt and disappointed. Very hurt and disappointed, but I'm not angry. I don't suppose that will make any difference to you. You need a prime suspect, and I'm your guy."

"Where were you on July 12?" Clark asked.

"I was working at my office."

"I didn't ask you what time did I, Mr. Novak?"

"No, you didn't, but I never left the office from the time I arrived in the morning until about 10:30 or 11:00 that evening," I said.

"Was there anyone else in the office that can confirm that?" He asked.

"Liz Bowers was in the office until about 7:30."

"How about after 7:30?" He continued.

"No, I was alone. I was working on my computer, and the time log will prove that I was there," I said.

"We'll send someone to your office to verify that. Of course, anyone could have been on your computer," he said.

"Yes, they could, but when you look at the architectural drawings and specifications I was working on, you'll find only an experienced architect with knowledge of the specific building could have been using my computer."

"Of course, Mr. Novak. We'll need to verify what you're saying," Clark said.

"I'll be in the office at 7:30 tomorrow morning and ready to meet with your people."

"That doesn't work for me, Mr. Novak. I want to go to your office right now and take possession of your computer."

"That works too, Detective Clark," I said.

"One last question, Mr. Novak, do you believe Ms. Collins knows of Ms. Winters and Mr. Lindmark's evening affair?"

"I don't know. How could I possibly know whether she does? She never said anything to me, and I believe her grief is genuine," I retorted.

"Thank you, Mr. Novak. I will follow you to your office with some of our forensic people."

I left the interview room with Clark following.

At our office, Liz looked at me, Clark, and two other officers.

"Lukas, what's going on?" She blurted.

"Detective Clark believes I may have murdered Adam. He's taking my computer to verify I was working here the night of Adam's death," I said.

Chapter Seventeen

City of Saginaw
July 24, 2019

Detective Tobias Clark

Clark wondered if Novak had known that Winters and Lindmark were together on the way to Novak's office. If he had, did he kill his friend? Novak was a hard person to read, showing almost no emotion. Maybe he hadn't been angry when finding out, or maybe his anger had come and gone, perhaps ending when he murdered his friend.

But there was another murder suspect. Clark knew that his next interview would be with Natalie Collins. He wondered if she would be as stoic as Novak.

At 9:00 the following morning, Clark met with Natalie Collins. He studied Collins and found that she was a commercial real estate developer. What was interesting was her financial condition. After losing some key tenants, it appeared that she was in arrears on her mortgages, had used up her line of credit, and was maxing out on her credit cards. To look at her, He would never have guessed she was struggling financially; when she entered the interview room, she wore tailored black slacks, a white turtleneck, and a white matching jacket. Her shoes and handbag were matching taupe leather. But he did know that appearances could, and often were, deceiving and that people often came in for questioning as if they were an actor in a part.

"Hello Ms. Collins, I'm Detective Clark. Please sit down."

The woman was every bit as beautiful as I had been told, and she knew it. She had been crying, and her eyes were red and eye makeup smeared.

"I know this will be difficult for you because I'm going to be asking you some difficult questions that you are not going to want to hear. However, it's my job to find the murderer of Adam Lindmark. Do you understand?"

"Not completely, no, I don't," Collins replied.

"Well, let me start with the questions. How long have you known Adam Lindmark, and what was your relationship?" Clark asked.

"I've known Adam over a year."

"And your relationship?"

"He was my boyfriend," she answered.

"Would you say you had a close relationship with him beyond just being boyfriend and girlfriend?"

"I was very much in love with Adam, and he was with me," she replied.

"When was the last time you saw him?"

"Monday before his death."

"Where did you meet, and what did you talk about?"

"We met at his house and didn't talk about anything in particular."

"You didn't talk about your financial struggles?" he asked.

"Detective Clark, that's none of your damn business," she angrily answered.

"That's not true, Ms. Collins. Someone murdered Mr. Lindmark in a gruesome way, and I need to find that person. I know you're smart and must have surmised that I must consider you as a suspect. Now, did you talk to Mr. Lindmark about helping you out financially? Yes or No?"

Clark could feel her anger rising.

"Yes, I asked Adam to help me with a short-term loan until I could find tenants for a couple of my buildings."

"And?"

"He said he wasn't able to help me."

"Did he say why?"

"He said he wasn't in a financial position to loan me money."

"What did you say?"

"I told him he most certainly was, and I expected him to step up if he truly cared for me."

"Did he change his mind?"

"No."

"What did you do then?"

"I got up and left."

"It sounds like you were angry."

"I was angry, yet I loved him and wouldn't kill him, Detective Clark."

"And was that last time you saw or talked to Mr. Lindmark?"

"The last," she said.

"Did you also talk about him leaving town? Leaving permanently?" He asked.

"Adam wasn't leaving town," she stated.

"Oh yes, he was. He'd already submitted his resignation to the art museum, effective July 30. He told them he'd be leaving before that and using the last of his paid personal days."

"I don't believe you. You're lying," Collins said as her anger visibly grew.

"Don't believe me? Perhaps you should talk to Ms. Winters. He told her, and she's under the impression that she might have gone with him." Clark said.

"She's a damn liar. Adam didn't even like that bitch."

"He liked her enough to invite her to his house on Tuesday before his death. They drank wine together. He told her he was leaving, and then they had sex."

Natalie's face turned a deep shade of red-purple, and her anger was on the verge of exploding.

"She's a fucking liar. None of that happened. Adam loved me, and he would never do anything to hurt me."

"But, indeed, he did, Ms. Collins. We have a used condom that confirms he had sex with her on Tuesday. Here's what I think, this is a small town; I easily found out from others that Ms. Winters was with

Adam on Tuesday. I think you found out too. I think your anger overtook you, and you confronted him. You demanded to know why he wouldn't give you a loan, why he didn't tell you that he was leaving town, why he had slept with Nicky Winters. His answers didn't satisfy you, and things quickly got out of control. You told him that you would teach him a lesson, and you did. You carved up his face with a knife so that no woman would ever want him again. Then you realized you didn't want him either and killed him."

Now sobbing, she said, "I never saw Adam after Monday night. I never even talked to him. Yes, I was mad at him, but I loved him. I would have forgiven him about the money. I would have. I just needed time to get over it."

"Ms. Collins, where were you on the evening of Thursday, July 12?"

"My God, do you really believe I killed Adam?"

"Where were you?' He repeated.

"I had a drink with a girlfriend after work."

"What time did you finish?"

"Around 7."

"And after, when you left, where did you go?"

"Home, I went home," she said.

"Did you see or talk to anyone after 7:00?"

"No. Wait, I talked to a friend about getting a job," she replied.

"What time was that?"

"About 8:30 or maybe 8:45."

"I'm going to need his name and number to verify that you talked."

"Of course," she said.

"Ms. Collins, if you can think of anything else that places you at home after 8:45 on Thursday night, you need to share that information with me. That's all the questions I have for you today. I don't need to tell you that you're not to leave the area as I continue this investigation."

After she left, Clark weighed the situation. Adam Lindmark was tortured by having his face flayed before being murdered. Everyone seemed to like him. No enemies. Clark had contacted each of the art museums where he had formerly worked, and everyone told him he was the best employee they ever had and were very disappointed when he left. They were shocked to hear about his murder and clearly grieved.

I had several possible prospects: Novak, his closest friend who showed almost no emotion when discussing his lover's affair with Lindmark. Collins, his girlfriend, was the other extreme, emotional and angry when talking about Lindmark sleeping with Winters. It wasn't clear whether either of them knew Lindmark had been with Winters before he told them. Then there was Winters. She, too, loved Lindmark. Maybe he said to her that she wouldn't be going with him. Would she kill him? I needed to dig more to find evidence pointing to one or more of these suspects. Lastly, Novak mentioned that Lindmark feared for his life while visiting Istanbul after sleeping with a Saudi woman.

Whoever murdered Lindmark left no traces behind. No fingerprints, no evidence whatsoever. Even the rope that they had tied him up with had disappeared. There was some rope fiber, but that wasn't any help unless Clark could find the rope in someone's possession. Were Novak, Collins, or Winters careful enough to leave no evidence? They were smart, so maybe. It seemed, however, to be the work of a professional. Did he have enough to get a search warrant for the houses and offices of these three? Maybe he didn't need to if they consented to searches. If they didn't, he'd ask for warrants.

Chapter Eighteen

May 27, 2010
Washington D.C.

Adam Lindmark

Adam started his new job as an Associate Conservationist at the Corcoran Galleries of Art in Washington D.C. after graduating with his Master's in Art Conservation. As his first job, he didn't know what to expect. If Adam didn't like it, he'd quit; he didn't need the money.

What was appealing was Corcoran's collection. Delacroix, Degas, Gainsborough, Monet, and Picasso were all included, although his favorite was a full-length painting of Mrs. Henry White by John Singer Sargent. Adam compared it to Sargent's more famous painting of Virginie Amelie Gautreau, better known as "Madame X," found at the Metropolitan Art Museum. Sargent's genius was illuminating each subject's personality and thoughts. Elegantly dressed in a gown of shades of off-white and pinks accented by satins of rose and cream, Mrs. White stares directly ahead with self-assurance. Madame X, dressed in a sexy tight black evening dress, is looking away from the artist, leaving the viewer with the impression that she believes she's the most beautiful of all Parisian women.

Taken with the portrait of Mrs. White, he sought permission to produce a copy. While energetically working, he imagined his Mrs. White hanging in his regal home one day.

Adam continued to meet with Paul Rothstein, although their time together was different from what it had been in their past. Paul had married and had his first child. He was no longer interested in the bar scene or discussing their sexual exploits. Still, they enjoyed each other's company, and Paul told Adam that his clients continued talking about his portrait and have asked whether Adam would be willing to do more portraits. Adam declined, saying he had little time for anything else between his new job and copying Mrs. White's picture.

On Aug. 27, 2010, Adam learned of his father's death. He wasn't close to his father even after his mother died when he was a teenager. His father had had little time beyond satisfying his desires. *You're So Vain*, a Carly Simon song, summed up what Adam thought of his father:

"You walked into the party

Like you were walking on a yacht.

Your hat strategically dipped below one eye,

Your scarf was apricot.

You had one eye on the mirror, and you watched yourself, gavotte.

And all the girls dreamed that they'd be your partner."

The following day Adam flew to New York and met with his father's attorney and trustee. A life-changing meeting. After moving from Grosse Pointe, Michigan, to the city, his father had lived far beyond his means. He had exhausted the trust fund left to him by his father and had been living off Adam's trust.

Adam's grandfather had bequeathed Adam $12 million, and with growth, his trust should now have a value well over $15 million. He was shocked to learn there was only $550,000 remaining. Having unfettered access to the trust fund as trustee, his father had embezzled more than $15,000,000. Adam questioned the attorney whether he had any recourse against his father's estate or from a fiduciary bond? No, he could only expect about $100,000 from his father's trust and nothing more. He wondered how he'd survive.

Chapter Nineteen

Washington D.C.
New York City
September 2, 2010

Adam Lindmark

The Corcoran Art Galleries granted Adam a leave after his father's death. His passing was surprising; he was only 52. His theft was shocking. Adam was no longer a millionaire. Taking stock of his finances, he had his father's trust, his own trust, a $20,000 bank account, and a new Porsche. His earnings included a small salary from the Corcoran. Adam needed more money to continue his lifestyle.

The copy of the Mrs. White portrait was almost finished; maybe Rothstein could find a buyer. He called him, and they agreed to meet the following day at the Blue Bar in the venerable Algonquin Hotel near the Theater District.

In 1919, a group of journalists and writers began meeting there for lunch. They included Dorothy Parker, Robert Benchley, and Alexander Woolcott and became known as the "Algonquin Round Table." Paul and Adam enjoyed the history of the Algonquin as they had discussed it many times. The Blue Bar, renowned for its blue lighting, was suggested by John Barrymore because he believed blue makes people, most importantly himself, look younger.

While Paul was waiting inside, Adam was in the hotel lobby, as was his habit, petting Hamlet. Hamlet was a tradition too. In the 1920s, a stray cat wandered into the hotel, and the hotel owner adopted it. Given the name by Barrymore, a Hamlet has been roaming the hotel ever since.

Adam made his way to the bar and greeted Paul with a hug.

"I've been giving Hamlet some love," Adam said.

"I think Hamlet's been giving you love because you need it more," Paul said while at the same time ordering Knob Creek Manhattans.

"Adam, I'm sorry to hear about your father. Apparently, you didn't have a funeral for him."

"Thanks. We didn't because it was my father's instructions. He wanted to be cremated and placed in the family mausoleum back in Grosse Pointe. We had a simple memorial service."

"Were you close to your father? I don't remember you talking much about him?"

"No, not at all. I was close to my mother. After her death, he moved to New York City and took on a new life. He became a free-spending playboy. Having an older son did not fit his new image."

"Well, I'm still sorry for your loss. No matter what, it's hard to lose your father," Paul said.

"There's something more than my father that I lost. I learned from my father's attorney and his trust that my father has been stealing from my trust; over $15 million that my grandfather left me."

"What the hell. $15 million. You didn't have any idea?"

"None. My dad was my trustee. Anytime I needed money, he'd transfer the funds without question. When I asked him how much was in my trust fund, he'd tell me I wasn't to worry about money at my stage in life. "Concentrate on school and enjoy life," he'd say. I knew my dad was a free spender, but I never thought he'd steal from me."

"Is there anything left for you?'

"Yes, some in his trust and mine. Not enough to live the life I want. I need to generate more money. I'm about to complete a copy of a John Singer Sargent full-length portrait. Do you think any of your clients would buy it?" Adam asked.

"Probably. Two or three ask me about you. One person, in particular, wants to know if you have connections to sell high-end original art. At a discount, of course," Paul said.

"That's odd. What does he have in mind?"

"No idea, I never asked. I'll tell you what; I'll call the client who's asked about you. His name is Deacon Carter. Frankly, he's a badass and scares me. But he's loaded, and he loves art, particularly portraits. I'll ask him about your Singer and explore what else he has in mind."

"Thanks, I appreciate your help. And I'm not poverty-stricken, at least not yet, so I'll buy the next round," Adam said.

"Oh no. You've been buying my drinks forever. Today's my turn. Another Manhattan?"

Paul called Deacon Carter and told him about Adam on his way home. They agreed to meet at Paul's office next week and discuss Adam.

Deacon Carter was one of Paul's better clients. He was managing $30 Million for him, and he had other brokers too. Carter had been a professional boxer. He looked like a tough guy—about 6 foot and solidly built with graying close-cropped black hair. Carter loved the fight game and had framed pictures of boxers on his office walls, including some of the fighters he managed. Watching fights in Vegas, particularly with his boys, was his passion.

Carter owned a demolition company. A picture of a crumbling building at the entrance of his office was one of the first implosion demolitions in the country; Carter proudly told Paul. He made most of his fortune demolishing buildings in Latvia and Russia. The black market was expected, and Paul was confident Carter excelled in that environment.

Carter also owned nightclubs, and Paul wondered if it was a way to launder money. He never asked; he knew that everything he was doing for Carter was completely legal.

After arranging to meet Carter, he called Adam and asked him to send him pictures of his Sargent copy.

"Did you talk to Carter about original artwork? Adam asked.

"Just briefly, he sounded interested. I'll get back to you after we meet."

Carter, dressed in black slacks and shirt, a dark gray jacket, and cowboy boots, showed up on time. His hardcore look made Paul nervous, and there was no one he worked harder to please.

"Mr. Rothstein, I had my accountant go through my statements, and I see your returns aren't as good as some of my other money managers."

"Mr. Carter, thanks for stopping by. Well, you said you wanted me to be more conservative with your funds compared to your other brokers. I know they've invested in emerging markets, and China is doing well right now, yet they're taking more risk. Keep in mind that my funds have less risk and complement your other managers. When the markets go down, my investments will outperform theirs. That's why you have all of us working for you in harmony."

"I agree. The markets at some time will go down. We'll see how your strategies do then."

"I'm confident you'll be pleased," Paul said nervously.

"Ok, on to other business. You say you have a friend that wants to sell a copy of a Sargent he's finished painting. Do you have any pictures?"

"I do. Take a look at my computer screen."

"Sargent did beautiful work, didn't he?" Paul said.

"He did. And, apparently, so does your friend. This portrait isn't Madame X, but it's certainly beautiful. How large is it?" Carter asked.

"Over 6 feet by 4 feet."

"I'm afraid that's too large for me. However, I have a friend that may have an interest. Her collection is superior to mine, and she may not be interested in a copy. I'll check with her and get back to you."

"That would be good. I'm sure my friend will appreciate your help," Paul said.

"Paul, I have another topic I want to discuss. What do you say we go find a place to have a cocktail and talk?" Carter said.

"Ok. Where shall we go?" Paul asked.

I'll meet you at the White Horse Tavern on Bridge Street in 30 minutes."

The White Horse Tavern is an upscale pub located in the Financial District since the late 20th century and owned by the same family since 1976. Carter was a regular.

The bartender called out to him, "The usual Mr. Carter?"

"Yes, Jack. Make it a double. I have an important meeting with my friend," Carter responded.

Jack, the waiter, came over to Paul and asked him what he'd like.

"Whatever, Mr. Carter's drinking. I'll have the same."

"You know Paul, you've done well for me. You're more conservative than others. Then again, I live in a highly risky world. It's comforting to know that some of my assets are more safely managed. But that's not why we're here. I have a friend, or maybe I should say a business associate, who collects art. Art, in a serious way. She has contacts in Europe helping her buy art. She's always looking to add to her collection. I bring her up because she is a patron of the artists from the Realist period: Sargent, Waterhouse, Bouguereau. I'm not sure about your friend's history, but I'm sure he knows about these types of artists."

"He has an art history degree, and he's copying a Sargent," Paul said.

"Here's what I want you to tell your friend: my associate will buy his copy. She wants to start a relationship with him. However, she wants him to use his contacts to help her find paintings from the 1880s. She has already collected several Impressionists. She is looking for more of the Realist genre for her collection. Tell your friend she will pay his price for his copy. She, in turn, wants him to go to work and find her originals. Also, tell your friend this is not a person to play games. She is reasonable, but she can be unforgiving if she senses that someone isn't straightforward. Will you give him that message?"

Paul left the White Horse and called Adam and relayed Carter's message.

Adam asked Paul, "Who is this new person? Can I trust her? What does she want me to do?"

"I'm not sure who she is or if you can trust her. Carter says you can. She wants original paintings from the Realist period. Carter didn't say how you were to find them. I think she's looking for something in the black market. She could go to an art dealer if she wanted to buy in the open market. I don't know if you can help her, but these wealthy people made their fortunes playing hardball. Give serious thought before you begin a relationship with them."

Chapter Twenty

Washington D.C.
Chandler, Arizona
September 30, 2010

Adam Lindmark

Original artwork? Adam couldn't guess what Deacon Carter was talking about. Paintings purchased at a discount? Black market? Adam wasn't going to steal a painting from a museum. Surely he'd be a prime suspect and convicted or at the very least destroy his reputation. That's totally irrational. No, he needed a sustainable plan. Perhaps doing high-end copies like the Sargent? But copies didn't have nearly the value of original work; besides, it took him over a year to copy the Sargent. The math didn't work.

As Adam drove through the night back to D.C., rolling in his head were thoughts of selling originals. Suddenly he had a crazy idea.

What about selling a fake as an original? No, wait, how about conserving an original painting and forging a copy of the original? Then, put the fake back in the museum and sell the original.

"Adam, what are you thinking? That's nuts?" He said out loud.

Certainly, people at the museum would notice they were getting a fake. But what if the artwork badly needed conservation, then when the fake was installed, it would look different from the original because of the restoration? That could explain the difference. They wouldn't recognize it as a forgery.

Driving and talking to himself, "What if he worked for smaller museums whose staff didn't have the expertise to know a forgery from an original? That might work. He'd research to find smaller museums with quality originals that Mr. Carter and his friend wanted. Adam had read that the hardest part of making money from stealing a painting was finding a buyer. Perhaps he'd have a buyer before he stole the original."

Continuing to think and talking to himself, "He'd go to small museums forging a painting or two and then move on. If he did it right, his chances of being discovered could be reduced. If caught, he'd go to prison. That was the risk." A pretty boy in prison gave him the chills.

There must be more to his plan. He'd need to generate enough dollars to get out of the game at some point. He could then move to Europe; he always wanted to live in Istanbul. He'd be a different person starting a new life. Besides, he didn't have family, and Paul was his only real friend. How many dollars would he need to get out? What paintings would be less likely to be discovered as a forgery and still generate enough dollars to live a new life? So many questions to answer.

"Damn, this could work," he suddenly shouted.

When he got back late that night, he began researching smaller museums and identifying their finest works. When he finished his investigation, he'd ask Carter what he'd pay for particular originals.

Would Paul go along with this crazy scheme? Maybe, if he had a financial incentive.

The next few weeks, Adam narrowed down his list to seven smaller museums. His top choice was the Chandler Art Museum in Arizona. Two days later, he flew to Arizona, visited the museum, and inspected their collection. He was particularly interested in two paintings: a landscape by Camille Corot, a French artist, and a portrait by William Adolphe Bouguereau, also French, who worked in the late 1800s and early 1900s. Secretly photographing both paintings, he planned to share the photos with Paul and Carter.

Adam found that the Chandler Art Museum was understaffed and lacked an experienced curator. Like most small museums, it didn't have a conservationist though they needed one badly. Adam needed to conserve the originals and forge the copies offsite in the strictest privacy to make his plan work. The Chandler Museum didn't have the necessary space, and he'd need to convince them to allow him to work at another location approved by the board. He was confident he could assure them it would be in the museum's best interests.

After two days of searching, Adam found a home he could lease, having space for his conservation lab. Satisfied, he headed back to D.C., and if Carter had an interest in either of these paintings, he'd start.

After sharing the photographs with Paul, Adam said he estimated that each painting had a value of over $1 million, and he'd sell each to Carter based on an agreed appraised value with a 40% discount. To encourage Paul to help, he'd share 10% of his payments with him. Adam estimated the Corot at $1,250,00 and the Bouguereau $2 million.

Paul was doubtful that Carter would be interested, but three days later, Carter told Paul his research found the Corot's value to be $1,000,000 and the Bouguereau at $1.2 million. Carter made it clear he needed the Corot in four months, or there was no deal. He also said he wasn't interested in the portrait.

"This might work," Paul said to Adam in a call later that day.

"Do you trust Carter?" Adam asked.

"No, but what do you have to lose?"

"If we don't have a ready buyer, then selling the painting on the black market will be hopeless," Adam said.

"Let's assume he doesn't want the Corot. You can put the original back in the museum and keep the copy for yourself. You're only out the time and trouble of moving to Arizona. On the other hand, if we can sell even the Corot, it'd be worth it, especially considering the payments would be tax-free," Paul reasoned.

"I'll think about it," Adam told Paul.

"Well, don't take too long; you only have four months to complete the Corot forgery."

"Why the time constraints?"

"I think he wants the painting as collateral for a black-market transaction. Artwork is black-market currency," Paul said.

"Ok, I'll let you know tomorrow," Adam promised.

Adam ultimately agreed with Paul's logic, and the terms were agreed to with Carter within days. Adam then called the Chandler Art Museum and spoke with the chairman of its board. He explained his desire to live in the West and described his credentials. After emailing his resume to the chairman, Adam interviewed with the Chandler Art Museum Executive Committee within days. He indicated that his salary demands were below market because he was financially independent.

"What's important to me is where I work, what I'm working on, and whom I'm working with," he told the committee. After meeting with the Museum's staff the following afternoon and having dinner with two executive committee members, he accepted their offer.

In a whirlwind of activity, he gave the Corcoran his notice of resignation; flew back to Chandler; rented a home; returned to D.C., packed his belongings; and hired a moving company to deliver everything to his new home. He started work one day after his two-week notice of resignation ended. Within days, he was conserving the Corot when he received a call from Paul.

"Carter didn't want the Bouguereau; however, his business associate does and accepted the terms we discussed with Carter."

"Art forgery could be rewarding and very risky," Adam told Paul, "Anyway, it's now my life."

"And mine too, Paul said. "So you better be good at what you're doing. These people can be dangerous. You understand me, Adam? Dangerous," Paul stressed.

Chapter Twenty-One

Paris, France
The 1880s
Chandler, Arizona
October 30, 2010

Adam Lindmark

It was the ancient Greeks who began putting their names to individual pieces of art. Earlier masterpieces created by Egyptians, Babylonians, and Chinese were anonymous. The artists of those ancient times were content to follow the preceding artist-craftsman and accept the standard method of creating art that reflected their cultures and not the individual's interpretation. Once the Greeks began signing pieces of art, forgery began. Even the great Michelangelo, many believe, was a forger early in his career.

The craft of forgery is one of science and art. It involves research, preparation, and painting skills. Like few other forgers, Adam was skilled in all phases and also had the charm to deceive others effectively.

There are different types of forgeries and fakes. One uses photography combined with printing techniques making it virtually impossible to determine the fraud from the original. The production of fake Dali', Chagall, Matisse, and Miro prints has become a billion-dollar business. The modern reproduction techniques make convincing reproductions of smooth, two-dimensional images. The three-dimensional quality of forgery demands a higher level of understanding and skill. It, too, has echelons of sophistication. Some forgers use modern painting techniques to create the fake. In other words, they are looking only at the surface of the painting and fail to understand the process the Old Masters employed to create an exceptional work of art. By looking only at the surface and not understanding the entire process, a forger may accurately paint the outlines and coloring but fail to capture the three-dimensional essence that defines the finest works.

The great forgers profess a deep respect for the discipline of drawing and the craft of traditional picture-making, particularly true of forgers of the great Realists.

Adam appreciated the Old Masters' craft and would faithfully follow it as he settled into his new house in Chandler. It provided him with all he needed, a living area and studio space with plenty of windows.

He quickly made friends with board members, staff, and supporters of the museum. His love of conservation and painting took over his life. He was also financially incentivized to be successful, and the quality of his work would be the difference between his freedom and jail.

A significant factor in Adam's selection of a museum was the quality of the art. He admired Camille Corot and recalled an art history professor pointing out that Claude Monet once wrote, "There is only one master here-Corot. We are nothing compared to him."

Corot used his drawings, leading to painted studies and then the final piece of work. A noted historian explained, "He began outdoors, blocking in the subject fairly completely, usually in pencil but sometimes in oil; then in the studio, using oils, he repainted from memory, making the drawing and the effect of light and shadows more precise; next he returned to the site to analyze in detail various elements of the landscape; finally he retouched the painting in the studio, sometimes over a period of years, until he considered it perfect." Corot stated that "Nothing should be left imprecise."

Corot was known for his landscapes, but he very much liked figures to animate his paintings. He wanted to have company in the woods, in the valleys, along rivers, to see animals and people rambling around. His most valuable works include these figures, and Adam was careful to select those because they were more interesting to paint, and more importantly, they brought a much higher price.

Adam completed the Corot painting, meeting Deacon Carter's deadline. He flew to New York, delivering the original to Paul and Carter. Adam harbored doubts whether the scheme would happen, but it did. Paul created an offshore account for Adam in the Cook Islands. Some enterprising attorneys worked with the Cook Island government designing laws providing account holders complete confidentiality and prohibiting creditors from attaching any funds. It was more secure than other offshore arrangements and a massive windfall for the Cook Islands. $540,000 in Adam's new account, his forger's life was underway.

While Adam admired Corot, the William Adolphe Bouguereau painting was what excited him. Bouguereau was his favorite artist. Adam honored the painter's craftmanship of bringing his subjects to life. Consequently, a portrait by Bouguereau was considerably more challenging than a Corot landscape. Adam had mastered forging a Corot now; he would need to apply all his talents to convince others that his forgery of a Bouguereau was an original.

In the late 1800s, Bouguereau was more famous, respected, and financially successful than his Impressionist contemporaries: Degas, Monet, and Renoir. He was a man of tradition, studying art history and valuing the works of antiquity and the Italian Renaissance, particularly DaVinci, Michelangelo, and Raphael. Bouguereau loved drawing and was an expert at his craft, bringing human figures, animals, trees, and inanimate objects to life. He grew up in Bordeaux, but the center of the art world was Paris. His uncle paid his expenses so the young artist could live and study in the art capital. Soon many called him a genius, gaining success early in his career. By the time he was in his late 20s, he had earned prestigious commissions for portraiture and decorative arts. He moved from painting traditional scenes of saints, centaurs, martyrs, and nymphs to peasant women and their children and pets. It was these later paintings that Adam, like so many others, found appealing.

Starting with Impressionism and followed by Post-Impressionism,

Expressionism, and Abstraction, the art world dramatically changed. Art critics were excited about writing about something new. Art dealers enhanced the number of painters whose works could fill their galleries and generate sales. Art historians soon forgot and ignored Bouguereau and other traditional painters and rarely mentioned them in their exhaustive histories. Not surprisingly, the value of Bouguereau's paintings fell sharply. By the 1950s, a collector could purchase a quality Bouguereau oil painting for a few thousand dollars. Slowly art patrons began again to appreciate the sophisticated techniques and artistry of the Realists, and the value of their paintings grew. The 1990s saw a Bouguereau painting selling for over $1 million. Adam recently read that one of his paintings sold for over $10 million.

Adam's selection of Bouguereau fit all his needs. He loved his work, and the value of these paintings would significantly enhance his offshore account. Nevertheless, to forge a Bouguereau, Adam would need to understand the man's inspiration and techniques.

He read that Bouguereau would bring Italian model-women to his studio with their young children. Once in the studio, he'd roll around on the floor to play, laugh or quarrel with them. He recorded their movements as they tumbled on the floor. One woman said that Bouguereau spoiled her children so that she could do nothing with them at home or elsewhere. Bouguereau's paintings of mothers, their children at play created poetry and a celebration of innocence and the human spirit.

Bouguereau has been classified as a Realist painter due to the photographic qualities of his work, though he rarely worked from photographs. Those seriously studying his work argue he created a new school of painting unique to himself, combining Neo-classicism, Romanticism, and Impressionism, and best described as a Romantic Realist. He combined the unique gift of painting as an artist and scientist. His masterpieces followed the same process: A croquis or a quick sketchy drawing of a live model followed by a grisaille study or an oil sketch. He then prepared highly finished drawings for all the figures in the composition and drapery and foliage. He would complete detailed studies in oil of heads, hands, and animals, followed by a full-scale preparatory drawing the size of the final painting, called a cartoon. Once completed, he'd begin the finished painting incorporating his deep knowledge of anatomy, pose, foreshortening, perspective, and modeling.

Adam wouldn't need to follow many of Bouguereau's pre-painting processes because he'd be working directly from the original, eliminating many steps Bouguereau would take. Having the original available to study was an enormous advantage for Adam compared to other forgers. Most needed to work from studying a painting in a museum and photographs. It was often up to the forger's memory to depict the fake as closely as possible. On the other hand, Adam could spend countless hours studying the original to replicate it as close to perfect as possible.

Although Adam circumvented many preparatory sketches, he followed the other steps in creating the finished work. Bouguereau painted on a semi-absorbent canvas, primed with the first coat of insulating glue, a preliminary layer of white often tinted with grey or red-grey. He would then apply two or three more layers of the same grey.

Like each Old Master, Bouguereau used his paints, oils, and varnishes. Adam's research revealed Bouguereau's preferences, including the type of brushes he used. He found it particularly fascinating when examining his powered colors, called pigments, and mediums, the liquids he used to hold the pigments together. The chemical structure of the paints used by the Old Masters were the same used by painters from the earliest days. Adam's training as a conservationist taught him to use the same materials to withstand scientific examination. He understood the many sophisticated techniques used to detect forgeries: digital imaging of a painting using ultraviolet-induced visible fluorescence; infrared reflectography; and digital x-radiography. These practices disclose much about the artist's workings, including materials and processes, and reveal what the human eye can't see. Ultraviolet light records low-energy radiation that materials re-emit in the visible range, called fluorescence. Different painting materials exhibit characteristics identifying the pigments, mediums, drying agents, lacquers, and varnishes used by the painter during exposure to UV radiation. Adam's goal was to create a forgery that no one would suspect as a fake by looking at it. If ever suspected and a higher level of scrutiny was employed, he sought to avoid detection by using Bouguereau's processes and materials to replicate his work.

Adam knew selecting the correct pigments was an essential step for a forger. Hundreds of pigments were used by Old Masters partly because of the many substances capable of coloring a painting. Some artists used pigments from insect juice or urine. Most used a few common pigments. Frans Hals and Rembrandt used only four pigments, flake white, yellow ochre, red ochre, and charcoal black. Bouguereau's palette was slightly wider. Adam's list of pigments for forging his work would also include raw sienna, red ochre, burnt sienna, vermilion, raw umber, burnt umber, terra verre, lapis lazuli, and ivory black. Each pigment has an interesting background. Flake white is made by exposing lead plates to vinegar fumes, causing a white scum that becomes the pigment. This lead pigment is toxic and has been replaced by other whites, such as titanium and zinc. Terre verre is also known as green earth, a transparent color created from cow dung. Using any modern replacement could reveal the painting to be a forgery and would be avoided by Adam.

Understanding the canvases used by the artist is also essential. A cotton canvas was most common. To avoid detection, forgers often buy a painting from the same time period as the original and then remove the paint, retaining just the ground and creating their forgery on the old canvas. Adam wouldn't need to do this as he would tell the museum that he was relining the painting. Relining is the process of removing the original canvas and replacing it with a new canvas.

Following Bouguereau's painting process was also important. Adam knew that Bouguereau used thick paint for lay-ins of broad strokes to begin his work. He never left them in this state. He'd use his palette knife with incredible skill going over it in all directions, eventually evening out and stripping until the surface acquired the desired finish and transparency.

As Bouguereau moved forward, observations, notes, and incredible talent enhanced his execution. As he painted, he used different types of siccative, a drying agent that works on topcoats and the depths of the paint. It's an accelerated drying additive causing thick coats to harden evenly. It's colorless and will not alter light colors. The first siccative he used was the kind employed by house painters and known as siccative soleil. A second was composed of a mixture that included flour and oil and was Bouguereau's personal receipt.

In the ensuing days, Adam was fully absorbed in using the right materials and following the techniques and methods used by this Old Master.

After starting the Bouguereau, he realized he had little time or interest in his curator duties. He needed help. Agreeing with the board of directors, he hired an associate curator with his funds. Adam posted a want ad in trade magazines and was surprised by the number of applicants. He interviewed his top three choices and selected a young woman with a degree in Fine Arts from the University of Arizona. This began Adam's pattern of hiring assistants at each museum he worked, relieving him of his curator duties to focus on conservation and forgery. Each assistant was attractive, intelligent, and capable. Each would become his lover until he moved to the next museum.

After 14 months, the Bouguereau forgery was complete. Again Adam personally delivered the masterpiece to New York. The funds transferred to Adam's offshore account came from an anonymous source known only to Deacon Carter.

After a year and a half in Chandler, Adam began his new job at the Boise City Art Museum. Adam's offshore account had grown to over $1 million as he headed to Idaho. It was only a start; he'd need to find more museums and forgeries to live the life he imagined. In the meantime, he was pleased that the Chandler Art Museum's board members, patrons, and visitors were delighted with the conserved Corot and Bouguereau paintings. Only they weren't conserved paintings; they were fakes.

Chapter Twenty-Two

Boise City, Idaho
Cedar Rapids, Iowa
Topeka, Kansas
Murfreesboro, Tennessee
April 20, 2010 – September 22, 2016

Adam Lindmark

Adam's research revealed that the Boise City Art Museum had two valuable paintings that needed restoration, a Winslow Homer and a Jean-Leon Gerome. Adam sent pictures of the paintings to Paul, and he confirmed, after discussing with Carter, that both paintings would be purchased under the same arrangement.

Winslow Homer is considered by many to be the finest American painter of the 19th century. The quintessential Yankee New Englander was self-reliant, strong-willed, practical, and terse. Although he lived in New York City for nearly twenty years, he never painted an urban scene. He'd spend his time in New England and the upstate New York traveling to the seashore, the mountains, and farmlands, painting the simple life he admired. He was a realist whose gift was his directness, a strong sense of design, and the ability to get to the essence of things. These talents were well represented in the museum's painting of a young woman reading a book under a lush maple tree. It was Boise's most valuable work, a painting that Adam fully appreciated.

"Ottoman Merchants" was one of Jean-Leon Gerome's Academic style works painted in Paris during the same period that Homer was painting in the United States. He was a prodigious painter, and some argue he was the world's most famous living artist by 1880. His work at the Boise City Museum badly needed conservation, but Adam believed he could restore its beauty and present it to Carter.

Boise City in the winter of 2010 was unusually arctic. A significant change from Arizona and Adam questioned his choice, but the financial reward of forging works by Homer and Gerome overweighed the winter's cold. The staff and board of directors were also factored into his decision. The staff had limited experience, and board members were welcoming and provided little interference. Working with people he liked and with great paintings made it hard for him to leave Boise City, but in May 2012, he finally decided it was time. Adam thought back to the great paintings he'd copied and now before him was Iowa City and the opportunity to forge a portrait by Thomas Gainsborough. This opportunity was simply too hard for him to resist, so he moved to Iowa.

The selling of Homer and Genome paintings added more than $1.2 million to Adam's Cook Island account. Before leaving, the Boise Museum threw a party for Adam and happily provided glowing references that helped him secure his next museum.

Thomas Gainsborough, an English painter, was one of the masters of 18th-century art. His range of subjects, quality, and originality includes naturalistic landscapes, inspirational images of children, and glamorous society portraits. His paintings are admired throughout the world, making them valuable. His portraits were particularly appealing to Adam, and the Cedar Rapids Museum owned his "Mrs. Harold Grimsley" masterpiece. Gainsborough depicted the stunning Mrs. Grimsley seated in a gown of beige, greens, and shades of pink with one hand on her hip and the other gently touching her cheek. In the background are drapes of burgundy and carmine, setting off her pale skin and large brown eyes. Adam would indeed find pleasure in spending time with this woman. He thought to himself as he started work that he'd want to own the original for himself. He knew that was impossible because he needed to sell the painting, and he'd never take the chance of betraying Carter.

Adam's efforts included conserving a painting by Elisabeth-Louise Vigee Le Brun, a prominent French painter from the same period as Gainsborough. He estimated that together the paintings to be worth $3 million. Carter and his associate negotiated with Adam and Paul, and it was decided that $2.4 million would be the base price. When finished in Iowa in October 2012, Adam moved to Topeka, Kansas applying his trade on a painting by another world-famous artist, John Constable.

Constable's Suffolk landscape painted in 1827 of a cornfield bordered by a flock of sheep would be worth $2 million, Adam estimated. The museum also owned a portrait by Giovanni Boldini, a late 19th century Italian, of two young women that needed considerable help from Adam. Adam guessed the most the Boldini would appraise for would be $700,000. Beginning in 2013, he finished both paintings by 2015.

Adam questioned how much longer he'd continue living from museum to museum. It seemed that eventually, one of his forgeries would be discovered. He was suffering nightmares of being in prison and forced to do unthinkable things. His overseas account had grown to close to $6 million. Maybe just one more city would be enough?

The trouble was It was hard to quit, as he enjoyed the people, the work, and the tax-free money. Perhaps Murfreesboro, Tennessee, would be his last museum. In their collection were two high-quality works by Camille Corot, who seemed like an old friend to Adam after studying his work over the years.

Was it time to start his new life? He'd been considering where he would move? He thought Europe would be best. When he was young, he'd traveled extensively throughout the continent with his parents and then later by himself while in undergrad. Istanbul always stood out to him. A mysterious city, well suited for him to hide in the shadows and start anew. To make sure that this was the place of his future dreams, Adam decided at some point to take a break and explore the ancient Turkish cultural center. Somehow he believed it was his fate to journey there. For the time being, Istanbul would have to wait as the chance to paint two more Corot paintings waited him.

Chapter Twenty-Three

Murfreesboro, Tennessee
October 31, 2016

Adam Lindmark

Having moved to so many museums over time, Adam quickly adjusted to living in Tennessee. He had two challenging paintings to work on, both by the French painter Camille Corot. Within a year, Adam finished the conservation and copying of both works and sold them to Paul's client, Tobias Carter. It was becoming hard for Adam to play the role of a trusted colleague, knowing that he was a total fraud. He desperately needed a change and was ready to start his new life immediately and decided to visit Istanbul and measure his compatibility with his possible new home.

Chapter Twenty-Four

Istanbul, Turkey
November 10, 2016

Adam Lindmark

For 8,000 years, people have gathered along the waters of the Bosphorus, a trading center connecting the Black Sea, the Sea of Marmara, and the Mediterranean Sea. Istanbul's importance from an economic, political, artistic, and religious perspective is highlighted by the fabled names who coveted the great city: Constantine I, Attila the Hun, Genghis Khan, Tamerlane, Ivan the Terrible, Catherine the Great, and the British Empire. Once known as Constantinople, Istanbul has been described as where "East meets West." It was the center of the Christian religion for more than a thousand years, eventually conquered by the Ottomans and becoming a centerpiece of the Muslim faith.

Beginning as a teenager, he studied its past and present-day life and believed it the most incredible metropolis in the world. Warnings that it was too dangerous a city, particularly for a blonde-haired Christian, were unfounded. The richness of its culture and people were exciting, begging to be explored and offering him the opportunity to redefine himself.

After leaving Murfreesboro, Adam met with Paul in New York. They discussed their success, and Paul pressed Adam to name his next museum and was disappointed to hear that Adam would take a break from forgery and do some traveling. Maybe his days of faking paintings were over, and he'd decide that over the next few months. Paul argued that their customers would be very disappointed and he feared disappointing them. Nevertheless, Adam held firm and said traveling to Istanbul would provide him the chance to assess his life.

The following day, Adam purchased a one-way ticket to Paris. He spent a week taking in the great museums, restaurants, and musical events of the "City of Light." While enjoying the city, he wanted to make sure he covered his tracks if someone would ever try to find him once he started his new life. He paid for everything with cash, including his one-way ticket on the Orient Express train to Istanbul.

Adam always wanted to ride the legendary train, absorbing the glamour of traveling made famous by Agatha Christie's 1934 novel, *Murder on the Orient Express*. Adam pictured the fictional Belgian detective, Hercule Poirot, having breakfast in the luxury art deco carriage and later in the day sipping cocktails with fascinating travelers as the Express raced across Europe. It was a 10-day trip from Paris to Istanbul, stopping in Budapest, Romania, and Bulgaria before arriving in Istanbul. On the trip, he practiced reading and speaking Turkish. He'd been studying for months, and although his language skills weren't the strongest, he'd hope to communicate in some essential way. He'd soon find out.

It was a short walk from Istanbul's eastern train station to his hotel. Adam selected the Eminonu District to live in for the next month or two. The district bordered the Bosphorus and was a short walk to the waterfront, where excellent seafood restaurants were under the Galata Bridge. It wasn't very far from the Golden Horn Bridge that would take him across to the modern side of the city and its adventurous nightlife he'd heard so much. He'd selected the Legacy Ottoman Hotel, an architectural work of the Ottoman Empire. It was a magnificent 5-Star hotel. Adam's well-appointed suite provided a panoramic view of the Bosphorus, the Golden Horn, and the Galata Tower overlooking the city, as well as the ferries transporting people across the open water.

Soon after checking into the hotel, he set off on his new adventure. Wandering the ancient narrow streets was the experience he'd longed to discover. The sidewalks were crowded with people, the electric trains running dangerously close to anyone who might slip off the narrow sidewalks. Adam was fascinated by the people and the many ways they dressed. Most of the women were wearing clothes they'd wear in the U.S. However, there were differences. Western-style fashion, including uncovered heads, forearms, and calves, was prohibited until recently. Many older and some younger Turkish women continued this conservative style in public, including headscarves and long jackets that completely cover their arms and legs. He wondered how uncomfortable they must be on hot summer days. Adam saw a few women in a burka, the black full-body coverings, including the veil. Most of the women with burkas were visitors from other countries with a stricter interpretation of Islamic dress traditions, or so Adam had heard. The local men were typically dressed in black pants and button-down short-sleeved white or light blue shirts. There were also businessmen and women dressed in modern suits, skirts, and jackets.

He walked from the Legacy Ottoman Hotel to the Hagia Sophia and Blue Mosque. He passed by the walled gardens of the Gulhane Park, where the Topkapi Place and Archaeological Museum could be found within the many acres of sidewalks bordered by beautiful trees, blossoming bushes, and rich colored flowers. He loved gardens, but they would wait because he was on a mission to experience the two great mosques of the city.

The Hagia Sophia was once known as the Church of the Holy Wisdom, built in 537 by Emperor Justinian; the church was converted into a mosque in 1453 and remained an incredible display of architectural genius and aesthetic magnificence. It's controlled by a non-profit organization and is open to all visitors.

Crossing the busy streets and train tracks, Adam settled down on a park bench to study Hagia Sophia's deeply colored red walls topped by a central dome and flanked by two semidomes. How could this incredible building have been constructed in the 6th century and survived to this day? As he admired its impressive beauty, he turned to face the opposite direction. Across the park stood the Blue Mosque. After the Turks conquered the city, Sultan Ahmet I's ambition was to create a structure more remarkable than the Hagia Sophia. The Blue Mosque, completed in

1616, sits on a rise that once was the palace of Christian Emperors. Looking back and forth, Adam pondered whether the Sultan had achieved his goal. The Blue Mosque central dome, surrounded by semidomes, is supported by four giant columns. Undeniably stunning, it rivals the Hagia Sophia, and together they create one of the world's most incredible displays of architecture.

Adam often visited these mosques, wandering around inside. He would lie down on his back mid-floor, as would others, to study the wonderful marble columns, colonnades, and rich colored walls and ceilings.

He also became a regular at a few places along the narrow streets. One of his favorites was a hookah café that sat above the street that bordered the walls of Galhane Park. It was a perfect place to watch people moving along the busy streets and his fellow café patrons. He played the game of guessing who they were and what they'd be doing once they finished with their hookah smoke. He wasn't the only one studying the patrons; along the walls were cats enjoying themselves. Istanbul loves cats, and they are pretty much everywhere. Adam had read that one of the ancient empresses loved cats, and so too the entire city. This legend may have saved the city from the plague. The story goes that the cats would eat the rats whose fleas carried the plague. Fewer rats and fleas meant less threat of the pandemic. Adam didn't know if any of this was true but enjoyed thinking about the city's past.

Another favorite of his was sipping Turkish coffee in the Grand Bazaar. The Bazaar covers a network of sixty-one streets. Every day as many as 30,000 traders in 4,500 slips haggle with untold numbers of shoppers. Twenty-two gates lead into the Bazaar. The roof, in many places, is an arcade of brick domes and arches ornately decorated with brilliant-colored paints. Adam enjoyed searching the streets for antiques, paintings, books, carpets, decorative pottery, hangings, spices, and jewelry.

One day, he considered buying an enamel bulb covered with red, purple, and green painted tulips. Questioning how to get it home, he decided not to buy it. A couple of days later he changed his mind and tried to find the shop. He hunted for hours down one street and another, not having any luck. Finally giving up, he sat down at a café to take in a coffee. While studying the passers-by, he realized he was sitting next to the shop he'd been hopelessly looking to find. He laughed at his bumbling but was sure thousands of others had been lost in the Bazaar's maze. Finishing his coffee, he finally made his purchase.

The Bazaar and Istanbul's nightlife exposed Adam to the city's hidden and extreme dangers.

Chapter Twenty-Five

Istanbul, Turkey
November 20, 2016

Adam Lindmark

After living in smaller communities for years, Adam came alive walking at night along the waterfront, watching the lights shimmer across the water, listening to the many voices from the crowded streets, taking in the smells of the street vendors and restaurants. Adam's anticipation grew while crossing the Golden Horn Bridge and walking down the cobblestone street, entering the Nevizade District, Istanbul's most colorful and active area for nightlife. While many clubs courted the tourist crowd, Adam instead sought out clubs the locals frequented. He enjoyed meeting new and exciting people, and he found these clubs were full of patrons eager to talk to the tall blonde. Trying his best to speak Turkish seemed to help him find new friends.

The Ergenekon Night Club was his favorite. Combining mystery, energy, and pounding music, Adam sought out the club on many nights. The entrance was like walking through a cave that opened into a narrow room with a long-lit bar. There was a stage for bands and a large dance floor at the far end. Most nights, he found himself on the rooftop enjoying a drink, talking to interesting people, watching beautiful women, and looking at the sparkling lights along the Bosphorus shoreline. Many women approached him, but he was careful not to be too friendly with any women who seemed to be with a boyfriend, husband, or other suiter.

Some nights he walked home alone, but others he'd spend with an alluring woman. It reminded him of fun times with Paul in New York City.

His frightening departure from Istanbul started not in this club instead at his favorite café in the Bazaar.

Chapter Twenty-Six

Istanbul, Turkey
November 25, 2016

Adam Lindmark

To Adam, sipping Turkish coffee in the Grand Bazaar was an exciting adventure, peering into a different world; so many exotic people searching for treasures in the hundreds of stalls filled with unusual and alluring goods. Ironically, as Adam was thinking of alluring, a mother and daughter wearing burkas walked by. The daughter was slender, and even with her veil covering most of her face, he could tell this was a beautiful young woman. She stared at him and, after passing, turned back and gazed at Adam before her mother noticed. He couldn't know for sure, yet he thought she was smiling at him. Whether she was or wasn't didn't matter because he'd never see her again.

That evening at the Ergenekon Night Club's rooftop, Adam drank and listened to the music throb up from the floor below. Like other nights he was mesmerized by the lights on the Galleta Tower when he realized a stunning woman was staring at him. Dressed in a tight black mini skirt that showed off her long slender legs, she stood studying him. Her hair was equally as black and set off her olive complexion. Her eyes, large and dark, complimented a stunning diamond neckless that glittered in the club lights.

"Hello," she said with an inviting smile.

Smiling, Adam was sure he knew her but couldn't remember where.

"You don't remember me? That's very disappointing. I thought we made a special connection, if only briefly," she said.

Adam loved the mystery.

"Would you care to join me?" he asked.

"Only if you can remember who I am."

She pouted at him as he studied her face.

"Do I need to give you a little hint?" She asked.

"No. Would you please sit down and let me study your face? I do know you, I'm sure. You say we only met briefly?"

The woman sat down next to him.

"Yes, briefly and only just today," she said.

Adam grinned.

"I didn't recognize you without your mother."

She laughed. "My mother and my burka."

"Your eyes are very memorable," he said.

"You are very memorable—a handsome man like you sitting alone in a café. You looked lonely. It would be a shame for you to be lonely in this lively nightclub. I was guessing you're Dutch or maybe Swedish."

"You're a good guesser. My mother was Swedish and my father German, but I'm an American. And your English is excellent," Adam said, complimenting her.

"For many years, I was taught by English-speaking teachers and professors."

"Can I guess where you're from?" He asked

"Yes. I'm interested in your guess."

"Saudi Arabia," he said.

She smiled. "Someone told you."

"Who could possibly tell me?" he answered.

"Then how did you know?"

"I was told that some Saudis, being from a stricter religious culture, sometimes find pleasure in the Istanbul nightclubs after changing to western clothes," he said.

"And what do you think of these men and women?"

"After we smiled at each other today, I thought to myself that it's a pity that I'd never see you again. And now, like a miracle, you are sitting with me, talking to me and looking more beautiful than any woman I've ever met."

"My, you're charming. Are you also a good dancer?" she asked.

Halfway through the second song, a large dark-haired man approached the woman and quietly said something. She turned away from him, smiled at Adam, and continued dancing. The next song, she pushed against him, holding herself tight. Rotating her body to the music, she whispered in his ear.

"Do you know where the back entrance is by the bathrooms?" She asked.

He nodded.

"Ok, I'll meet you there in half an hour. Go back upstairs but be at the back door in 30 minutes," she said.

Abruptly she turned and walked to the man that had approached her.

Promptly on time, Adam was at the backdoor. Together they walked outside into the dark.

"I hope to hell you have a car," she said.

"No. I walked from my place."

"How far a walk is it?" She asked.

"15 minutes."

"God, 15 minutes in these shoes," she complained.

She bent over and took off her black stilettos.

"Ok, I can walk barefoot. Let's go. Which way are we heading?"

"Towards the Galleta Bridge. My hotels in the E District."

After 5 or 10 minutes, she stopped. "I need to text my friend," she said.

"Is that man your boyfriend or husband?"

"No. My bodyguard."

"Your bodyguard? You need protection?"

"My brothers think so. They're worried about me and this necklace," she said.

They moved across the bridge to Adam's hotel. Before going in, she put her shoes back on. They took the back stairs to his suite. She immediately kissed him hard and put her tongue down his throat so far he thought he'd choke, unzipping his pants while kissing and biting his lower lip until it hurt. Adam knew this was a hungry woman. After his pants were down, she began giving him a blow job. She then slipped out of her black skirt, pulled down the coversheets, and dragged him on top of her. He wanted to remember this evening and asked, "What's your name?"

"Elena."

She didn't ask his name and began biting his nipples hard.

Their sex was more an act of violence and ended with her multiple organisms. Finished, she pushed him aside. "Thank you. Whoever you are," she said.

She got up and, after a few minutes in the bathroom, put on her clothes.

"I'm leaving now. I'll get a taxi downstairs," she said.

Adam jumped up, put his clothes on, and followed her into the hallway and down the stairs.

"I don't need you to come along," she sternly said.

"I want to make sure you're safe."

She gave him a condescending smile and called a number on her phone. She told the person who answered where to pick her up.

"My family won't be pleased that we were together. I don't know your name. It's better that way. I won't tell them your hotel, but they have ways of finding things out. My brothers can be very difficult when angry, and they'll be furious. You'll want to stay out of sight for a while. Perhaps hiding would be best for you."

The taxi pulled up, and she opened the door but, before getting in, said, "My brothers are very dangerous, so please take my warning seriously. Hide."

As she left, Adam asked himself, "What the hell was I am into?"

Chapter Twenty-Seven

Istanbul, Turkey
November 19, 2016

Adam Lindmark

Adam took her warning seriously. Having already paid for his hotel suite for another two weeks, he nevertheless packed early the following morning and went downstairs to get a coffee before leaving for the train station. To cover his blonde hair, Adam put on a baseball cap, just to be safe. After pouring a coffee, he noticed three large men go to the hotel clerk. After a brief conversation, the clerk handed a man a key; it was the man Adam had seen in the nightclub. After the men entered the elevator, Adam slipped outside and found a place across the street where he could watch the hotel entrance and not be seen. Fifteen minutes later, the men left in a car parked in front of the hotel. Nervously, Adam went back to his room, finding all his clothes and other things strewn across the room. Fortunately, his identification, including his passport and all his cash and credit cards, was with him.

He quickly repacked and found the back entrance to the hotel. He hurried to the train station and bought a ticket to Ankara. He regretted leaving Istanbul, but he knew his life was endangered. On the train, he tried to recall all the things he had told Elena He mentioned he worked at a small museum in Michigan. "God, why did I tell her that?" he scolded himself. It wouldn't be difficult to track him down. He'd worry about that later; for now, he was going to hide.

After booking into a second-rate hotel in Ankara, Adam hid for three days before hiring a driver to take him to the airport. He bought a ticket to New York City with the remainder of his Turkish Lira and was relieved when his plane left the ground. On the flight, Adam knew that his lack of discretion endangered his life, and the threat could follow him to the U.S. and maybe when he returned to Istanbul. He knew he would be returning to be his permanent home. He loved everything about the city, but for now, he decided to put some time between his recent encounter and his eventual move. When he got back to the U.S., he'd hoped there might be a new museum waiting for him.

Chapter Twenty-Eight

New York City
Saginaw, Michigan
November 30, 2016

Adam Lindmark

Paul was surprised. Adam was back in New York after a short time in Istanbul. Since leaving, Adam hadn't talked to Paul or anyone else; he completely stopped using his phone and computer. He bought a burner phone in Istanbul for local calls but made no calls to the U.S., ensuring no one could trace him when he made his permanent move to Istanbul.

Over dinner, Adam and Paul chatted about Paul's wife and two children and about the money they made over the sale of the two Corot paintings. Unsure if Adam would begin forging again, Paul reminded him of their profits. Adam was proud of his work and his recent delivery of the original Corot paintings. They were some of Corot's best works, and the buyers got a good deal. Paul reviewed the transaction with Adam.

"You made $765,000 minus my 10% of $76,500. I hope you're happy with the arrangement," he said.

"Without your contacts and buyers, this would never work," Adam replied.

"Actually, Adam, it's enhanced my relationships with the buyers, and I'm managing additional millions for them. Once deposited in my account, I'll transfer your share of the money to your Cook Island funds. So Adam, where's your next museum? Paul said hopefully.

Expecting the worst, Paul was delighted when he heard Adam say, "Saginaw."

"That's great. Why Saginaw?"

"Two reasons, they have a William Bouguereau, a favorite of mine, and I need time before returning to Istanbul. But this will be my last museum. Frankly, I'm tired of my life. I was in Murfreesboro for 18 months. I meet people and build relationships. I spent time with a woman I enjoyed being with, and I cared for her. One of the last times I was with Camille, she cried. Paul, these were tears of happiness, being so happy to be with me. But then it's over. I had to move on. Flying home, I thought about this and how Murfreesboro Museum's people were delighted with my work. You know, they had a champagne celebration at the unveiling of the Corots. They had no notion that I'd deceived them and were looking at forgeries. Then it's goodbye. Time to tell Camille it's over. I didn't want to leave her. I wanted to stay; she's been wonderful. I hurt her, and she didn't understand. She didn't understand I was a total fraud. Then I start looking for another museum and begin deceiving all over again. I need to get off this merry-go-round."

Paul and Adam stared quietly at their drinks. Then Adam continued, "I spent time in Europe and seriously considered not coming back. But fate entered the picture. I met one of the most beautiful women I've ever known. She seduced me. As it turns out, she's from a wealthy Saudi family. When our short romance ended, she told me that her family would be furious and might kill me. She advised me to hide. So I'm back, for now."

Paul was hesitant to say anything. Maybe Adam would change his mind and not go to Saginaw if he did.

After a long pause and a couple of sips of his Manhattan, Adam continued, "I wasn't looking forward to finding a new museum. It isn't easy finding a suitable one. That's where fate again intervened. Before leaving for Istanbul, I had an interesting email. It was from Sheila Reading, the Great Lakes Bay Art Museum Director. She said she'd been at a national conference for the American Museum Association. In a breakout session on conservation for smaller museums, she talked to people from the Chandler and Topeka museums. They both spoke highly of me. When she heard I worked on a Bouguereau painting, she reached out. She wrote me that her museum has a Bouguereau painting that needs work. Judging by the picture she sent me, the painting is so dark you can barely see the bright colors Bouguereau used. It also needs repairs. It's a lovely painting of a teenage peasant girl sitting on a stone fence. It's not his best work, but still worth over a million. In a week, I'll be flying to Saginaw and meeting with their director and a couple of board members. I'll be back in touch after we meet."

Trying to encourage him, Paul said, "Adam, I know it won't be your biggest payday, but still, you'll make around $600,000 doing one forgery in Saginaw. Don't forget by living in smaller communities; you're not spending much of your savings, so your Cook Island account must be quite healthy?"

"Not as much as I'd like. You're right; another Bouguereau will help."

For years Adam had been moving from community to community, always with the same purpose. Looking for smaller museums that needed a conservator and curator, he'd find ones that, most importantly, had at least one piece of art he could conserve, fake, and sell. For a while, Chandler, Arizona, Boise City, Cedar Rapids, Topeka, and Murfreesboro, Tennessee were all his homes.

Each location worked as planned, with Adam forging one and sometimes two valuable artworks. After settling into each new city, he immediately searched for his next museum. Adam was meticulous in his study and selection. Many weekends he would fly to some smaller town and visit their art museum. Only those cities that absolutely met his criteria would he select and begin seeking a position. Now fate had turned his way, the Great Lakes Bay Art Museum found him.

Ten days later, Adam flew from JFK to Detroit and then to the MBS airport. MBS is an anachronym for Midland, Bay City, and Saginaw. An area the community calls the Great Lakes Bay Region. The three smaller communities are no more than thirty minutes apart, and each has its own identity. Adam thought that his start in Saginaw was going well. The airport was small and very modern. Sheila, the museum's director, insisted on picking him up at the airport, but Adam explained that he would rent a car to explore Saginaw and the surrounding area and meet her at the museum that afternoon.

Adam was pleased that the Great Lakes Bay Art Museum was in a home designed by architect Charles Adams Platt, who had designed a wing of the Corcoran Gallery of Art in Washington, DC. in 1928. While working at the Corcoran, Adam had admired not only their fine paintings but also its architecture. It seemed to him that fate was truly stepping in, and Saginaw was the right fit for him, for his last stop.

Sheila Reading met him at the entrance to the museum. She was a tall, pretty woman of early thirties with auburn hair. She was well dressed in a tailored blue suit with a matching dark blouse. Adam encouraged her to talk about her background, and she explained that she was hired six years ago to raise funds to build wings on both sides of the Platt home. She worked with community leaders to complete the project including, modern glass and steel wings on each side of the original building contrasting sharply with the historic red brick home.

Admitting that she planned to use Saginaw as a stepping-stone to go to a more prominent museum, "I just never left. I liked the area and purchased a home north of Bay City along the shore of Lake Huron, and now I'm focusing on conserving the Museum's artworks, particularly paintings."

Adam smiled. "Maybe you'll find Saginaw to be your last stop," she prophesized.

"If everyone is as friendly as you, maybe I will," Adam said.

Sheila toured Adam through the museum. Adam thought he was off to a good start; he was building a relationship with the director; and found its collection included many fine paintings and sculptures donated by the lumber-era descendants. One of the finest was the painting "Peasant Girl in Early Evening" by William Adolphe Bouguereau. Studying it, Adam appreciated its beauty and potential monetary value to himself.

Meeting with the executive committee, Adam was introduced to Lukas Novak, the museum chair. He was another important person to build a relationship with, he thought. The interview was brief as the committee previously discussed Adam's credentials and work experience. They wanted him. Adam explained to the committee that one of his requirements was finding a home where he could live and use it as his studio. He said that in every other museum, they allowed him to conserve the paintings in his home away from the distractions of the museum life. The committee was concerned with this arrangement, but Adam reassured them that he'd pay for insurance and any improvements to the home to ensure the painting's preservation and safety, like all other museums. When they heard his low salary requirements, they offered him a position that Adam accepted. Afterward, Lukas Novak treated everyone to dinner at his favorite restaurant, Jack's 1866 Restaurant. The owner had restored a former bank dating back to the end of the Civil War into a beautiful restaurant.

Over dinner, Adam found out that Lukas was in his late twenties and an architect who'd lived in Saginaw for about seven years. Adam urged Novak to give him a short Saginaw history. This information was essential to Adam; he knew the more he learned about a community and its culture, the easier it was to build relationships and, most importantly, to be trusted.

Lukas explained, "In 1831, Alex de Tocqueville, the French philosopher and traveler, made his way to Saginaw, the farthest American outpost of civilization. He found the wilderness just as it appeared six thousand years ago. He also said many found Saginaw to be uninhabitable due to swamps and hordes of mosquitos. Lukas laughed, and everyone joined in.

Adam showed so much interest in the story that Sheila added, "For many years, these challenges prevented Saginaw from growing. That all changed after the Civil War. Beginning in the late 1860s through the 1890s, Saginaw was the pine capital of the world. Using its rivers to bring white pine from Northern Michigan to Lake Huron and on to Chicago, it made many families wealthy, and some of their wealth stayed in Saginaw, remaining as parks, beautiful homes, art collections, and trust funds."

After dinner, the committee planned to take Adam to a performance by Kenny G at the Grand Theatre. Although Adam was tired from his day of travel, he was happy to join them as they were excited to show them the renaissance in downtown Saginaw, highlighted by the restoration of their historic theatre.

Giving his full attention, Adam listened as Lukas and Sheila explained that It was constructed in 1927 for early talking movies and hosted everyone from Charlie Chaplin to James Dean to Jewel over its lifetime. A Saginaw family generously used millions of their funds to restore the building beyond its original splendor. They then donated it to a public charity.

Adam was impressed with the theatre's beauty and its acoustic quality. More, he liked the advantages of living in this new community, including trusting people and, more importantly, a painting by Bouguereau.

After the performance, Adam was ready to call a night, but Sheila insisted they have cocktails. The theatre's very chic Leopard Lounge provided the chance to discuss Adam's start date. He said he needed to find a place to live and told them he could spend days, sometimes weeks, looking for a home that met his living and painting requirements. Sheila excitedly told him of a restored house that became available on Washington Avenue that dated back to the early 20th century. The owner recently moved to Naples, Florida, and Sheila was sure she could convince the owner to rent his home to Adam. Everyone agreed to meet tomorrow for lunch, and in the meantime, they would check with the owner, and Adam could inspect the house.

The Washington Avenue house turned out to be Adam's favorite among the previously places he'd lived. Looking out the front and back windows, Adam smiled, appreciating the views of the large backyard leading to the Saginaw River and, in the other direction, Washington Avenue and the Children's Zoo.

Fate, too, was smiling, welcoming Adam to Saginaw.

Chapter Twenty-Nine

Saginaw, Michigan
December 15, 2016

Adam Lindmark

Soon after he started, the Great Lakes Bay Art Museum's Board held a welcoming party for Adam, providing him with the opportunity to develop relationships with crucial museum contributors. Adam enjoyed these parties because he genuinely looked forward to getting to know people and establishing friendships. That evening he renewed acquiesces with Lukas Novak. Lukas introduced him to one of his clients, Janice Wendell, while offering them glasses of Pinot Noir. Janice was a lifelong resident of Saginaw and a descendent of an 1800s lumber baron.

"Hello, Mr. Lindmark; I'm Janice Wendell."

"Yes, hello, I've heard about your love of art and the museum. Please call me Adam."

"Thank you, Adam, and please call me Janice."

Janice was in her late sixties with short wavy white hair and horn-rimmed glasses. She had a glowing smile and wore a light pink lipstick that set off her white dress with patterned pastel flowers. A pearl necklace and matching earrings set off her looks. Although slightly overweight, she carried herself like a younger woman.

"Tell me, Janice, when did your appreciation of art begin?" Adam asked.

"I was so fortunate that my parents loved art and took me on their travels to New York and Europe. They dragged me to all of the finest art museums. In the beginning, I hated going to see more boring art. When I was 12 or 13, I started to enjoy it, and I've been an enthusiast ever since," she said.

"Like you, I was fortunate. My parents loved the arts. Well, actually, my mother loved the arts, and my dad loved going to art parties."

Janice laughed, "Well, the parties are fun don't you agree?"

"I do indeed. Thanks for being here tonight," Adam said.

"I've been told that you're going to clean the museum's Bouguereau painting."

"Janice, that painting is a primary reason I've come to Saginaw. Bouguereau is one of my favorite artists, and to have the opportunity to conserve one of his fine works is exciting."

"Oh, I didn't know you appreciated Bouguereau so much. You know I have a Bouguereau."

"What? Did you say you own a William Bouguereau painting?" he said.

"Yes. I must tell you, and I know I'm biased, but I believe mine is much nicer than the museum's. It's a peasant mother with two beautiful daughters playing with a ball."

"Well, Janice, as they say on the American Roadshow, 'You truly have an American treasure,' even though it's by a French artist. How did you come to own his work?" Adam asked.

"On our honeymoon, my husband and I were searching to buy a painting to remember our time in Paris. We looked and looked but didn't see anything that both of us were excited about. Before leaving for home, we went into a small gallery in Montparnasse and saw the painting. We asked the price, and it was affordable, so we asked to see its provenance. The dealer had a detailed history of ownership dating back to 1882. There were no gaps, and the current owner and his family had owned the painting since 1922."

"That's a great love story about you, your husband, and William Bouguereau. I hope your husband wasn't jealous," he said.

"No, no, he loved him too. You know when we bought the painting

Bouguereau wasn't in fashion, and the cost was low. I'm delighted that the art world is beginning to appreciate his work once again. My goodness, the price of my painting has increased dramatically. I had it appraised, and the cost of insuring it and adding more security to my home is costing me a fortune. It's worth it, though; I love that painting. When I had it appraised, they told me it could use a good cleaning. Is that something you might be interested in?"

"Very much," Adam answered.

"I'd like to show you my Bouguereau? Would you come to dinner?"

"With your husband?" Adam asked.

"No, he passed away years ago. And you, are you married or seeing anyone?"

"No one," he answered.

"Well, I think we should invite Sheila and Lukas too, that will make it more fun, don't you think?"

"That would be perfect," he smiled.

"I can't wait to show you my Bouguereau!" she said.

"And I can't wait to see it!"

Adam was euphoric about a second Bouguereau. He started planning what he wanted to accomplish when having dinner with Janice Wendell, even before leaving the museum's party.

Days after the party, Adam leased his new home and arranged his furniture, art supplies, and other personal belongings to be shipped to his Washington Avenue address. He then flew to Tennessee, and on the flight, he thought about visiting Camille. Since Istanbul, Adam hadn't been with a woman but decided it was best to leave Murfreesboro behind. Arriving, he took his Porsche out of storage and began driving to Saginaw. The weather in Tennessee and to the Ohio border was excellent, considering it was still March. That all changed when he reached southern Michigan. It began to rain and freeze; not good weather to be driving a Porsche on I-75. He checked into a hotel in Dundee and waited out the storm, regretting he hadn't reached out to Camille.

Once Adam began working at his new museum, he focused on his curator duties while waiting for his belongings to arrive from Tennessee.

He was pleased that the Great Lakes Bay Art Museum was doing a good job cataloging and booking exhibitions through Sheila's leadership. The first would take place a few weeks after his arrival; a Marilyn Monroe exhibit was shown in several cities across the U.S. had arrived from Austin, Texas. Adam's new place of work was busy, and he enjoyed everyone's enthusiasm.

He also visited the Black Cat Café and met Nicky Winters, the cute barista that caught his eye. Adam asked her out for drinks, and she gladly accepted. Two martinis later, Adam drove to her apartment. It was always fun for Adam to find a young woman eager to go to bed and found Nicky less violent and dangerous than his last lover in Istanbul. For that, he was grateful because he didn't feel like making a sudden exit from Saginaw.

For the next few weeks, Adam and Nicky met frequently. He heard, however, that Lukas Novak was interested in Nicky. Adam's rule was never to be with any woman involved with a museum director or supporter. Maybe he wasn't violating his rule because Nicky said she wasn't dating Lukas. Although she knew him, he'd never asked her for a date. That seemed odd to Adam, but maybe he had his reasons.

It may have been a coincidence; sometime soon after, Adam was invited to have cocktails with Lukas and his friend, Natalie Collins, at the Great Lakes Bay Country Club. When he arrived, they were sipping drinks in the bar lounge. She was stunning. Wearing a tight cinnamon skirt with a complimentary color sweater, Adam was immediately taken by her. The conversation over drinks was almost exclusively between her and Adam. Lukas rarely said a word and seemed to be concealing a slight smile. At the end of the drinks, Adam and Natalie agreed to have dinner the following evening. On the way home, it occurred to Adam that Lukas was indeed a clever man. He was glad he was and knew he would not see Nicky in the future without Lukas with her.

Dating Natalie, and not Nicky, was excellent timing because, within days, Janice Wendell invited Adam to dinner with her other guests, Sheila Reading and Lukas Novak. Adam arrived a bit early for dinner with an outstanding Napa Cabernet and a bouquet as a gift for the hostess. Adam saw her Bouguereau for the first time. It was magnificent; two young girls, one sitting between her mother's legs the other sister slightly off to the side, rolling a deep red-purple ball. Sitting on a stone wall, the mother was looking adoringly at her innocent daughters. The children's skin was so natural. Adam thought if he touched their hands, he would feel their delicate softness. His appreciation of the painting was apparent without saying anything.

"It's quite tremendous, don't you think?" Janice asked.

"This is one of Bouguereau's finest works. I've seen many, and yours rivals those in any museum. I'm not sure many people know it exists," Adam said.

"Yes, and I want to keep it that way. I don't want people to know I have a multi-million-dollar painting hanging in my home. You must promise me that you will keep my secret. Sheila and Lukas already know, and they've been very good at keeping my confidence."

Her cooking skills matched Janice's taste in paintings. She served mushroom brie baguettes, coq au vin, asparagus, and chocolate mousse. The conversation was interesting, talking about portrait painters, American literature, Broadway plays, and Saginaw history, including Janice's stories about her family in the 19th century. Over a fine port, Lukas had the opportunity to ask Adam if he was seeing Natalie. Adam smiled and thanked Lukas for introducing them, "yes, we're were getting along very well."

The evening ended with Adam agreeing to conserve Janice's painting for only his cost of materials. He said he wouldn't be able to start it until the museum's Bouguereau was completed. This made Sheila happy, and Janice, too, was pleased with the arrangement.

During the evening, when everyone was busy, Adam went back to Janice's Bouguereau and, taking out a small measuring tape, took down its dimension to the closest eighth of an inch. He estimated this painting would sell for between $5 and $10 million. It would provide him with enough money to live his life comfortably. On the other hand, he coveted this painting for his own. He was conflicted; sell it or keep it? As he thought about its beauty, he again entertained the thought that perhaps he'd forge a second painting for Paul's client and keep the original. He knew this would be his last forgery, and then he'd hide away with his new identity in Istanbul. It would be risky, but he could plan a quick exit from Saginaw. He needed to think about it, yet loved both the idea of owning one of Bouguereau's finest works and increasing his offshore account by $4 million, perhaps $5 million. Anyway, he knew tomorrow he'd begin looking for a painting from Bouguereau's period that had the exact dimensions. He'd remove the paint from that canvas and use it to paint his second forgery.

Working on the museum's Bouguereau was a complete joy for Adam. Relying on the exhaustive research from forging the Chandler Museum's Bouguereau, he restudied all Bouguereau's materials and techniques, making sure there were no inconsistencies in the grounds and layers of paint. He made a trip to New York to purchase some pigments he didn't own and couldn't acquire in Michigan or on the internet. He was always driven by details in all his prior work but knowing that when he was working on Janice's painting, he needed to be perfect because he may sell the forgery to an unknown buyer and keep the original. Previously, Adam never planned to play games with Paul or any of his buyer-clients; now, if he did, he was unsure of the scrutiny his work would put through. It needed to be his finest forgery. First, he needed to complete work on the museum's Bouguereau.

Adam worked on it for eight months, repairing and cleaning, knowing he'd sell it to Paul's client. His forgery he'd rehang at the museum. Adam had already explained to Sheila and Lukas that he would reline the museum's painting to strengthen and add to its longevity. Relining would avoid possible questions about the painting having a new canvas. When nearly finished, he studied the original and the forgery a hundred times, making subtle changes. When finished, he placed it next to the original in bright sunlight. He was pleased that with his closest scrutiny, he could barely see the differences. He was confident that no one would identify it as a fake. He then placed the forgery in the original frame and rehung the painting in the Museum. He draped it and wouldn't allow anyone to see it until the formal unveiling.

While working on the museum's painting, planning was taking place for Janice's Bouguereau. After much going back in forth in his mind, he finally decided that he'd paint one forgery that he'd return to Janice. He'd paint a second forgery that he'd sell to Paul's client. He'd keep the original. With Janice's forgery, he'd tell her that he'd relined it so that he wouldn't need a proper time-period canvas for this fake. The second forgery would require a canvas from Bouguereau's time with similar dimensions as Janice's painting. One day when he was close to finishing the first Bouguereau, the time-period frame and canvas that he'd purchased arrived from a gallery in Boston he'd found online. He was satisfied when he unwrapped it, finding it in excellent condition. The landscape painting itself was amateurish, but that wasn't important. It only mattered that the artist was French and painted in the late 1880s, just like Bouguereau, and the canvas was in good shape. He would remove the paint and the underlying ground to the bare canvas and then paint his forgery.

Meanwhile, Sheila arranged an elaborate cocktail party to unveil the museum's Bouguereau, and when the day arrived, everyone agreed it was a great success. Sheila, Lukas, other board members, and patrons closely studied Adam's work and found his conservation outstanding, not realizing they were looking at the fake.

Sheila was particularly excited as she used the event to raise funds beyond her expectations. One person at the party was paying particular attention to the museum's painting: Janice Wendell. From the time she'd initially agreed to have Adam conserve her painting, she began having doubts. Adam, sensing that she might be reluctant to turn the painting over to him, let his work on the museum's piece speak for him. It worked. Janice gushed about the forgery's extraordinary depths of colors. She cornered Adam later in the evening and told him she imagined how magnificent the colors in her painting would be once he had completed his work. She excitedly asked him when he would start. He told her that he was visiting a friend in New York and would be back in a week. They could arrange to deliver the painting to his studio when he returned. Before he left, he invited Janice to his studio and discussed how her painting would be conserved. Janice was thrilled. "Please hurry back as quickly as you can to start your work," she pleaded.

Putting his arm around her, he said, "There's nothing more important to me than working on your Bouguereau."

Chapter Thirty

New York City
September 18, 2017

Adam Lindmark

Setting in Paul's office in Manhattan, Adam beamed as he delivered the museum's original Bouguereau painting.

"I know your client's going to be happy with this painting. It's an excellent example of Bouguereau's work. You've confirmed the price, and we're all set?" Adam asked.

"We're set, and the person buying the painting is very excited to take possession. Aren't you glad you're back to work? A very nice payday for six months work."

"It is a good payday. Let's celebrate and find a place to drink. I also need to go over some things with you," Adam said.

"Ok, but please not the Blue Bar at the Algonquin Hotel again, " Paul pleaded.

"Come on. I love that place—all its history. I hear John Barrymore, in 1927, told the owner: 'change the lights to blue because it hides his wrinkles,' by the way, I can use some of that too," Adam said.

"Yeah, right, you look like you're 25. Adam, come on, it's a long ride over there," Paul again begged.

"Really, how many times do I come to the City, and I'll buy our drinks," Adam said.

After an Uber ride to the hotel bar, Adam ordered Manhattans for them, and Paul watched him studying the etching of famous Broadway plays framed along the walls.

"Ok, Adam, what are we talking about?" Paul asked.

"I told you that there's another Bouguereau in Saginaw. Well, I've seen it, and it's magnificent. It would be a prize in any major art museum. I took a trip to the Detroit Institute of Arts and saw their well-known Bouguereau, "The Nut Gatherers." The painting in Saginaw is better. More figures and interesting subject matter: little girls playing with a red ball with their mother fondly watching. I've done some research, and with Bouguereau prices going up, it's worth $5 to $10 million. A widow owns it, and she's agreed to let me conserve it. I'll forward some pictures to you, and after you see them, talk to your client and see what the starting price could be. I'm thinking no less than $5 million, but maybe as much as $10 million. Now, aren't you glad you came with me to the Blue Bar?" Adam asked.

Laughing, "Yes, Adam, I'm happy. Time for a second round. I'll show Carter the pictures when I deliver the first Bouguereau. This would be our biggest payday. Damn, you could net over $4 to $5 million on this one," Paul exclaimed.

"I know, and I've already started work on it. I purchased a painting from the same period, and I've already prepared the canvas and began the foundational painting. I'll be done by mid-July. Leading me to the second thing I want to discuss, could you find someone to make me a new identity? Passport, credit cards, everything. Can you do that?" Adam asked.

"How in the hell do I know? I've never done it before. I'll look into it. Does this mean you're going off the grid?" Paul asked.

"When I'm finished with this next forgery, I'm done. The timing is right. We've made a lot of money, and if I disappear now and the forgeries are discovered, they will never find me or trace anything back to you. You know the old saying 'pigs get fat and hogs get slaughtered,' I don't want to be a hog. If you find me these new credentials, it protects you too. It's also a good time for me to get away from Natalie."

The cocktail waitress brought them their second Manhattans.

"Are you still seeing that crazy?" Paul asked.

"I am, and she's getting crazier. Paul, she's becoming more and more erratic and violent. When she losses her temper, she's out of control. She's now throwing things, and I'm not talking about pillows. First, it was glasses and then books, and now it's a wine bottle at my head. I believe she has a chemical imbalance or something. She wanted me to go on a vacation with her to Monaco; when I told her no way, she went nuts. Screaming, punching, then throwing the bottle. I tell you, I'm staying with her for these last months because I'm terrified of what she may do if I tell her it's over. I will keep her as happy as I can until I disappear, and the sooner, the better. Someone once told me for every beautiful woman; there's a guy sick of fucking her. It's true. I'm tired of fucking Natalie Collins."

Chapter Thirty-One

Saginaw, Michigan
December 23, 2017

Adam Lindmark

Before Christmas, Adam arrived back from New York and arranged to have the museum pick up Janice's painting and deliver it to his studio. He invited Janice to see his conservation tools and supplies. They shared glasses of Champagne while walking through his process for cleaning and repairing her painting. He explained how tedious his work was, like cleaning the entire painting with a Q-Tip and using the proper solvents to avoid damaging the paint while removing the aged varnish and lacquers. He showed her the damaged areas of the painting and how he would delicately restore them to their original state. He explained why he would reline the painting and how the process worked. After the second glass of wine, she politely asked if she could visit her painting from time to time. "In the past," he said, "I don't allow visitors, but for you, Janice, I'll make an exception. My work will take months, and I know you'll be lonely without your girls."

Chapter Thirty-Two

Bay City and Saginaw, Michigan
June 28, 2019

Natalie Collins

Natalie Collins knew she was beautiful; no one needed to tell her. As a little girl, whenever she was with her father, shopping, walking, or going for ice cream, people would compliment her father on his beautiful daughter. By the time she was in 3rd grade, Natalie also thought she was the smartest of anyone in her class, and she was.

Natalie moved to Bay City, Michigan, when she was 15. Her father, a machinist, raised Natalie by himself after her mother left them when she was five. Natalie understood that her mother was a painter, but she had only one memory of her, a violent argument with her father. Pictures revealed an attractive woman, slender with olive skin and long brown-blonde hair. Natalie took after her mother but had an exceptional natural beauty beyond her mother's.

In high school, she was the prom queen, class president, and academically one of the tops in her class. She decided to go to the University of Michigan and graduated with honors in Business Administration. She had numerous job opportunities from companies offering different roles. Ultimately, she became a pharmaceutical representative with a major company because she believed she could use her looks and intelligence to make a lot of money. The company hired her because they too thought she would be exceptionally successful in convincing doctors, particularly men, to buy their products. They coveted her so much that they gave her a region, so she could continue to live in Bay City. Natalie understood that between Saginaw, Bay City, and Midland, there were five hospitals and plenty of doctors she could approach. One of her professors had told her that being attractive could open doors for her, but it was up to her abilities to become successful. Natalie took that advice to heart and learned all she could about the drugs she was selling.

As predicted, Natalie was successful and immediately one of the leading national salespersons. She was making more money than she had imagined. She used some of the money to travel to New York City to look at art galleries, take in Broadway plays and buy clothes from expensive stores. Throughout these days, Natalie developed her own look by wearing very little makeup and dressing like the beautiful women strolling down the Champs de Elise in Paris. She enjoyed selecting expensive, elegant clothes to fit her Parisian look.

While selling pharmaceutical drugs, she dated many men. After five years, she was tired of selling drugs and dating disappointing men. She loved the music of Leonard Cohen and often thought about his song lyrics, "I'm just waiting for the miracle to come." That's how she felt about men; she was always waiting for the perfect man to be her partner, enhancing and not diminishing everything she loved about life.

At 26, her ambition led to buying her first commercial real estate property. It was undervalued because of a lack of tenants. She knew if she brought in tenants, she'd be successful. After providing the needed improvements, she convinced new tenants to move in, and that's how her success worked, and immediately she began making money. She had help from an architect, Lukas Novak, who advised her to develop a business plan that would describe her competition, marketing strategy, financial projections, and staffing. In the beginning, she followed her plan. She was so successful that she wanted to expand faster. She quickly found banks willing to loan her the money she needed to purchase more properties. At some point, she failed to heed Lukas' advice to retain enough capital to survive the bad times. He warned in troubled times, if she had capital, she could survive and purchase properties with even greater depressed prices.

Natalie ignored his advice because she had complete confidence in herself and her abilities to achieve any goal. Her life was filled with getting her way, from her spoiling father, charming doctors to buy her drugs, and convincing tenants to lease her properties. Anyone that challenged her soon discovered that behind her beauty and charm was an anger storm that could rage out of control.

She liked Lukas Novak and appreciated his business and urban planning wisdom. She also thought he was attractive. He loved art, music, and giving back to the community. These were things she prized. He was single, and she found this particularly interesting because he never gave her the feeling that her good looks impressed him. She'd never needed to flirt with a man to get a date. With Lukas, it was different. She opened the door for them to go out, but he never took the opportunity. Later she found out that Lukas was interested in another woman, Nicky Winters.

One day Natalie received a phone call from Lukas asking to have drinks. He wanted to introduce her to his friend, Adam Lindmark. She had heard of Lindmark. He was the new conservationist at the Great Lakes Bay Art Museum. She would like to meet him sometime but wasn't interested in being set up. Lukas urged her to meet for a simple drink. Eventually, she agreed.

They met at the Great Lakes Bay Country Club. She told Lukas they needed to meet before Adam arrived to talk some business. So they were halfway through their first glass of Cabernet Franc when Adam joined them. By the time she finished her second glass, she knew her "miracle" she'd waited for had arrived.

Natalie and Adam had dinner the following night and were inseparable for the next months. He enhanced her life: intellectually, sexually, completely. They'd had fun going to New York and Miami or simply watching television on a Saturday night. They made a beautiful pair. Both were tall, slender, and beautiful; Natalie had an olive complexion and dark eyes, and Adam, blond and blue.

One day Natalie was at Barnes and Noble looking for a book and saw Adam having coffee with another woman. Both were leaning towards each other, obviously sharing something special and laughing and smiling.

They were enjoying each other's company, and she felt her jealousy and anger rage. She was accustomed to having her way and had a violent temper when she didn't get what she wanted. Her father recognized this since she was young and warned her about her acts of anger that could erupt at any time. As much as he loved his daughter, he was genuinely concerned about her personality disorder.

Natalie left the bookstore without confronting Adam. They'd planned to meet that evening, and while she waited, her jealousy grew. When he came into her condominium, Natalie flew into a rage, accusing him of going behind her back and cheating on her. She saw them telling secrets and laughing. He tried to explain that woman he was talking to was an adviser from the Detroit Institute of Arts, and everything was utterly professional. She wouldn't have it and began screaming and demanding the truth.

"You have the truth," he said, "there's nothing more to talk about."

This didn't satisfy her, and her jealousy completely took over. Finally, Adam said, "I'm not talking about this anymore. When you calm down and regain your senses, we can talk."

He left. For one entire week, they didn't speak. Finally, Natalie called him and apologized for her behavior. He accepted her apology but told her that they needed to take some time off from one and another. She was shocked. She thought he'd beg her to come back; now, she was doing the pleading. No matter what she said, he told her he wanted to think about things and would call her when he had thought things through. Natalie had never felt such strong emotions: anger, jealousy, and loneliness. She needed Adam in her life and would do whatever it took to make that happen.

Natalie's angry explosion confirmed to Adam that she had become too possessive. He had felt this way before and had considered ending their relationship but hadn't. Hannah Spencer, the woman that Natalie saw having coffee with Adam, was the Director of the European Art Division at the Detroit Institute of Arts. Natalie's observation that the two enjoyed their conversation was correct, as they had much in common. She grew up in Manhattan and was educated in Europe. One of her previous positions was with the Corcoran Gallery in Washington, which was Adam's first place of employment. He had told her that the original house of Great Lakes Bay Art Museum had been designed by the same architect who designed a major wing at the Corcoran. They also agreed that Bouguereau was a great artist. His painting was the reason she was visiting. He wanted to tell her about the second Bouguereau owned by Janice Wendell but didn't because he promised confidentiality and his intention to forge two copies. Twice Hannah invited Adam to visit The Detroit Institute of Arts to see Bouguereau's "The Nut Gatherers," one of his finest works. He hadn't planned to go, but he decided he would go after the incident with Natalie.

He arranged to meet Hannah at the DIA and then have dinner. Adam had already made reservations at the Detroit Athletic Club.

At the Detroit Institute of Arts, Adam was again utterly taken by Bouguereau's "The Nut Gatherers" and thought to himself that Janice's painting was its equal, most likely better. More than ever, he wanted to own her painting. Afterward, Hannah and Adam had dinner at the Parc restaurant on Woodward Avenue overlooking Campus Martius Park. They then walked to the Detroit Athletic Club to look at its art collection. Hannah told Adam that she had heard it had a value nearing $50 million. After looking through the various rooms that displayed its paintings, they had a glass of Port on the rooftop restaurant, and both thought it best that she spend the night with him. Hannah left early the following day, and as he lay in bed, he felt tired of Natalie. Yes, she was beautiful, but she wasn't that interesting, and she wasn't all that good in bed. Frankly, she was always focused on Natalie, which had become quite tiresome. He was concerned about how she'd react. He knew it wouldn't be a happy ending; to avoid this, he'd stay with her until he escaped to Istanbul.

Chapter Thirty-Three

Saginaw, Michigan
New York City, New York
July 10, 2019

Adam Lindmark

Having worked on Janice's Bouguereau for over a year, Adam was finishing both forgeries of her painting and began focusing on final preparation to start his new life. Years ago, he had an attorney in New York prepare a will and trust; now, he wanted to update those documents and prepare a new power of attorney. He thought it best to do it in Michigan since he currently considered himself a Michigan resident, and Michigan law would govern the things he wanted to be done.

Lucas gave him a name of an attorney, and Adam met with him and signed the updates and a power of attorney naming Lucas as his agent. He planned to have Lucas sell all his belongings in Michigan and pay himself $100,000 for wrapping up matters. The balance of the sales proceeds were to be donated to the Great Lakes Bay Art Museum. His attorney prepared a letter of instruction to carry out Adam's wishes. He also prepared a trust amendment naming Lucas as his trustee if he was unable or unwilling to act for himself. The trust provided that upon his death, after paying for all his debts and expenses, his estate would be divided equally between Lukas and New York University to provide scholarships for art conservation students.

Adam rented two mini-storage units from Carl Williams, a friend of Liz Bowers, planning to place his Porsche in one unit and the remainder of his belonging in the other. His goal was to make it easy for Lukas to liquidate his possessions. Slowly he cleared out his property, placing them in the storage unit, with Lukas helping him move his property. When alone, he put the neatly packed original Bouguereau painting in a properly sized wooden box. Adam planned to retrieve the painting on the way to the airport when he left town.

Williams was curious about what Adam placed in his units and where he planned on going. Adam sidestepped all his questions and was polite only because of his friendship with Liz. Adam thought Williams a complete loser and wondered how she could find him attractive.

He listed his assets on a spreadsheet, except his Cook Island account and $100,000 of cash in further preparation for leaving. This list he'd give to Lukas to help him wrap up his affairs. He also calculated that after the Bouguereau sales, he would have nearly $15 million safely protected in his Cook Island account and would leave $150,000 in his bank account would be enough to pay Lukas and leave funds for the art museum.

Meeting with Lukas, he explained that he was leaving Saginaw. Lukas was disappointed.

"Adam, are you sure you want to leave? You have a home here. People care for you and respect you. If you're looking for a home, Saginaw can be that place. You've been a vagabond for years. Don't you want to have a permanent place?"

"Lukas, it's not that easy, and I can't explain why. Please believe me, you've been a very good friend, and I appreciate our time together; now it's time for me to move. I'll be in New York for a few days and then back to make final arrangements. I've stored all my property that I'm leaving behind in two rented storage units, including my Porsche. I've prepared a letter of instruction requesting you to sell everything and how I want you to distribute the proceeds.

"Adam, have you told anyone that you're leaving?"

"No, not now. I'll eventually tell Natalie. I'm holding off to the very end because it will make it that much easier. I'd like to tell Nicky too, if that's ok?"

"Of course it's ok. She's going to be very sad. She's fond of you, as you know."

"I don't plan on telling anyone else," Adam said.

The following day, Adam flew to New York and met with Paul. He carried with him the forged Wendall's Bouguereau. They met at Adam's favorite, the Blue Bar. He had the painting safely tucked away in a black carrying bag, and as he waited for Paul, he thought, this is the last time I'll ever be here. He walked over to the hotel side of the building and studied all the etchings of great theater performers and performances. He slipped over to the hotel desk; they asked if they could help him. Sadly, he said no and just wanted to give Hamlet some attention.

Adam walked back to the Blue Bar, and Paul was waiting. They ordered Manhattans and reminisced about their days at NYU and all the fun they had at the bars. Paul said he would very much miss Adam, for he was his oldest and best friend. Like the Algonquin Hotel and NYU, Adam knew he would never see him again. Paul handed him a briefcase and in it was a new passport, credit cards, and all other papers necessary for Adam to start his new life.

"Whatever it cost, Paul, take it out of the proceeds from this next painting. It's the very best of all the paintings that we've sold. I'd like to own it myself if I could. When the $5 million has been transferred into my Cook Island account, let me know. In the meantime, I'm going to complete arrangements in Saginaw," Adam said.

They had a second Manhattan and talked about Adam's plan for his life. He said he wasn't entirely sure.

"I'm going to live in a place that no one will ever recognize Adam Landmark. I'll probably paint again. I love painting, especially portraits of women," Adam said.

After wishing Paul the very best, Adam got an Uber and headed to JFK Airport.

Chapter Thirty-Four

Saginaw, Michigan
July 16, 2019

Adam Lindmark

Back in Saginaw, Adam packed up the last of his personal items he wanted to keep. His furniture he'd leave behind; it was all new and well-kept, and a future tenant would be happy he did. He gave some of his better artwork to Lukas, Natalie, and the art museum. He was leaving the following night and was prepared for his new life.

As he sat down with a glass of cabernet sauvignon, he received a call from Paul. The money had been transferred into his account. Adam told him this was the last time he was using this phone and thanked him again, and said goodbye for the last time. He then wrote a long letter to Natalie explaining, as much as he could, that he was leaving. It was very heartfelt; however, he didn't plan on seeing her again. It would be too emotional. Adam was concerned that Natalie's temper would take over, and the last thing he needed was to be injured just when he was leaving. He thought about telling Nicky that he was departing and thought better of it. Nicky was Lukas' girl, and he didn't want to cause trouble.

Sometimes coincidences or fate happens; while finishing the second glass of wine, there was a knock on his door. It was Nicky Winters.

"Hello Nicky, I was just thinking about you," he said.

She smiled.

"I wormed it out of Lukas that you're leaving," she said

"I hope you didn't tell anyone else."

"I didn't. Can I come in?" She asked.

"I'm happy to say goodbye to you in person rather than leaving a note or message. I'm drinking a Cab; want some?" He asked.

"I've already been drinking martinis. Ok, I'll mix my drinks and have wine," she said.

After pouring her a glass, he told her how much he'd enjoyed his time in Saginaw. All the friends he made and none more so than Lukas.

"You're fortunate to have him in your life. You know he's exceptional?" He said.

Nicky didn't answer; she drank her wine and smiled at Adam.

"I remember the first day you came into the Black Cat. I spilled milk making your drink. Do you remember?" She asked.

"I do. You seemed a bit confused," he replied.

"I was. It was seeing you. Can I have another glass of wine?" She asked.

"Really, do you think you need another?"

"No, but this is the last time I'll ever see you, and I don't want this to end. What about Natalie? Have you talked to her?" She asked.

"No, and please don't tell her I'm leaving. I've written a long letter to her, and I'm going to have Lukas give it to her."

Nicky laughed. "You coward."

"I'm truly a coward. I admit it. I just don't see any upside in seeing her again; there'd be over-the-top emotion that I don't want to deal with. Changing subjects, I've got a few bottles of wine left in my cooler. I was going to give them to Lukas, but maybe you want them?"

"Maybe I do."

The two martinis and two glasses of wine were affecting Nicky. As Adam walked into the kitchen, she got up from the couch and weaved behind him. He pulled out four bottles and sat them on the counter.

"Yes, they all look good to me. Open this one. I want a glass of this. What is it?

"Chateauneuf du Pape. You really want another glass?" he asked.

She slurred, "Yes, I absolutely do."

Adam knew this was a mistake but opened the bottle and poured her and himself another glass taking them back into the living room. As she plopped onto the couch, he handed her the glass.

"Like I was saying, I remember the first time I saw you. Right then, I thought you were gorgeous and wanted to have sex with you on the countertop. If I had asked, would you have done it?" She asked.

"No, Nicky, not on the countertop. That was a long time ago, and now you're with Lukas. That's ancient history."

"Adam, look at me right now. I mean, really look at me, in my eyes. Tell me the truth, do you want to fuck me on this very couch?

"Nicky, I wouldn't do that; it would hurt Lukas if he found out, and I don't want to hurt Lukas, do you?"

"No, I care for Lukas, but nobody has to know. It will be our secret, and you're going away forever, so it won't hurt him or Natalie."

Before Adam could answer, she slumped to the side of the couch, spilling the last of her wine. Adam looked at her and thought she was incredibly sexy. He went into his bedroom and returned with a pillow and a blanket. Cleaning up the wine that had spilled, Adam put her head on the pillow. He took off her shoes and placed the blanket over her.

"Good night Nicky, you little nymph."

Adam finished his glass of wine and looked at Nicky sleeping. Then he went to his bathroom and brushed his teeth, and got in bed. He wasn't sure what time it was when he woke up, but it felt great. Nicky was sucking on his cock, and as he looked down, he could see she was naked. She stopped and looked up at him.

"Had you forgotten how good I am at this?" She asked.

"No, I didn't forget."

She pulled herself over him and started kissing him on his mouth, neck, stomach, and was going lower when he pulled her up to him and put his hand between her legs. At this point, Adam was no longer thinking and just enjoying.

Early the next morning, Nicky was out of bed, showered, returned, and kissed Adam.

"I'm glad you still enjoy my company. Take care, my love," she said as a last goodbye.

She left without taking her three bottles of wine and headed to the Black Cat with a slight hangover but feeling better than any time she could remember, a bit euphoric.

Adam got out of bed and felt the wave of guilt smother him, "Damn it, Adam, what were you thinking? Obviously, you weren't."

Chapter Thirty-Five

Saginaw, Michigan
July 25, 2019

Lukas Novak

I'm hollow. I ache. Nothing is as it was. My best friend's been murdered. Now I find out from Detective Clark that he wasn't my best friend, really. He slept with my woman the night before he died. I loved her, and she cheated and betrayed me with him.

And now I am accused of his murder.

Later that afternoon, I made myself go into the office, not that I would accomplish anything.

"What's wrong? Did they find Adam's murderer? Are you ok?" Liz said as I blankly walked into the office.

Slumping into my chair, staring vacantly at the wall, I heard Liz sit down.

"Ok, what happened?" She asked.

There's no one else I could talk to but Liz.

"Detective Clark told me that Nicky was sleeping with Adam the night before his murder."

"He's playing you. That's not true," she responded.

"No, he says Nicky admitted it after he told her that they had their used condom and it would have her DNA on it. What's wrong with me? I'm in love with a woman that treats me this way?"

Liz got up and grabbed my hands, and started pulling me up.

"Liz, what are you doing?"

"You're getting up, and we're going to get a drink," she said.

"I don't want a drink."

"I know. Too bad. I feel like a drink, and you're joining me. C'mon get up."

"You're insufferable," I said.

Whether I needed a drink or not, I didn't know. I was numb. We drove over to Tommy's Pub, picked a table, and ordered two vodkas and tonics.

"I'm Clark's lead suspect."

"He said that?" asked Liz.

"No, but it's clear what he's thinking."

"But you didn't do it, and Clark has no evidence you did. So screw him. And Nicky, dump her. She's toxic."

She was right on all accounts.

I started feeling better as the vodka kicked in. "I'm sure Clark will be talking to Natalie. If she doesn't know about Nicky, this will kill her. She thought she and Adam were forever," I said.

"Oh shit," I thought as Carl Williams, Liz's boyfriend, walked in and joined us. He's nothing but a lazy small-time thug, and I wasn't sure what Carl did. Liz said he owned some mini-storage units and did odd jobs for friends. She wasn't sure if he did anything useful and didn't know his friends nor want to know them.

"Hello, Carl. What's new?" I said.

"Liz didn't tell you about our trip to Las Vegas? We had a great time."

Carl considered himself a big-time gambler. He frequently visited Vegas, each time bragging about his winning. Carl was too dumb to count cards, so he wasn't winning every time, just sounding like an idiot.

Baiting him, I asked, "How did you do?"

"Made some money. That's why I like to go," Carl said with a wide grin.

I was getting up to leave when Liz changed the subject, and Carl ordered us a round.

Liz jumped in, "We saw Celine Dion. We had great center seats in the fifteenth row. She was incredible. I insisted we have dinner at a restaurant at the Bellagio called *Le Circe*. It was fine French dining. It made me think of you."

Carl added, "Lukas, I had Australian venison with an apricot-cherry sauce. It was an inch and a half thick."

"A chocolate souffle that was incredible," added Liz.

Strangely, Liz was right; listening to them talk about their lives and having fun made me feel better.

"Lukas, I'm sorry about your friend. He seemed like a good guy." Carl said.

"Thanks, Carl."

"Do they know who killed him?" he asked.

"They're working on it," I said.

Carl's question triggered in my mind something I told Clark during our first interview. It didn't seem important; now, the more I thought about Adam's tortured murder, it seemed to make sense. Adam told me that he'd taken a trip to Istanbul and had an affair with a wealthy Saudi girl. Her family was very religious, and she warned him to hide because they could be violent. So he did. He moved to Saginaw. However, he was paranoid and thought he saw some of the people he'd seen in Turkey. I assumed he was wrong because nothing ever happened. Maybe it finally did. I needed to revisit this with Clark.

"Something wrong, Lukas?" asked Liz.

"I just thought of something," and told them about the Saudis.

"Tomorrow, I'll remind Clark, but he'll probably believe I'm just trying to mislead him."

I knew the evidence was confusing, a well-liked man brutally killed. Who was his murdered? I knew that Detective Clark thought it was me. It made sense because Adam slept with Nicky Winters, my girlfriend, the day before his death. My thinking was clouded and incoherent about Adam's death and the realization that Nicky's continued lack of discretion would never change.

Then there's Natalie Collins, Adam's girlfriend, known for having a fiery temper. If she knew about Adam and Nicky before Clark told her, would her violent nature lead to murder?

How about Nicky? She loved Adam and said she wanted to leave Saginaw with him. What if he said no? Would she kill him?

Maybe it was the Saudis that killed Adam for revenge?

One thing I knew, my life couldn't get much worse.

Chapter Thirty-Six

Saginaw, Michigan
July 26, 2019

Detective Tobias Clark

Continuing to look for clues, although he couldn't find Lindmark's cell phone, Clark obtained his phone records. There were calls to Winters and Collins. None to Novak. More interesting were numerous calls to a New York number. He traced it to Paul Rothstein.

Clark needed to talk to Novak and Collins about Lindmark's phone records and was surprised he received a call from Novak just before calling him. They would meet at 10:00 at Clark's office.

Novak arrived promptly.

"What did you want to see me about Mr. Novak?" Clark asked.

"There was something I remembered last night."

I told Clark again about Adam's paranoia about a Saudi retaliation.

"I don't know if this means anything, but I wanted to share it with you," I said.

"You mentioned this before; why talk to me about now?"

Clark looked suspiciously at me.

"Please, Mr. Novak, I'm sorry; I think you're making up a story to point me away from you."

"Believe what you will, detective. More recently, his fear was triggered by something. I'm not sure what was causing it." I said.

"Did he tell this to you more than once?"

"Three or four times. He was most frightened at the Detroit Institute of Art. We were sitting in their courtyard drinking when he saw a man he thought he recognized from Istanbul. He was so upset he insisted we leave without finishing our drinks. Over the next couple of days, he brought it up again. He thought someone was watching him at the Black Cat Café. He took a couple of days off work and stayed home. When he came back, he said he must have been mistaken. He brought it up again about two weeks before his death. He thought someone was following him," I said.

"Think hard, Mr. Novak. Can you think of anything else that could help our investigation? Did he say what the man looked like?"

"He said he was a big man with black hair and dark complexion. He asked me to be on the lookout if I saw someone like that. I'm sorry, Detective Clark, that's the only thing I can think of."

"Did you see anyone that fits that description?" he asked.

"Never."

After Novak left, Clark called Rothstein's number.

"Hello, is this Paul Rothstein?"

"This is Homicide Detective Tobias Clark in Saginaw, Michigan. Do you have a moment to talk, Mr. Rothstein?"

"Yes. Please wait a moment and let me close my door."

"Mr. Rothstein, did you know Adam Lindmark?"

"Yes. What's this all about, detective?"

"You didn't know he was murdered on July 17?"

"Oh my god, no. Adam?"

"Yes, and I have some questions for you. Mr. Lindmark's phone records indicate you had numerous conversations with him before his death."

"I talked to Adam many times around that time. He said he'd finished his work in Saginaw and was taking a break," Rothstein answered.

"Taking a break?"

"He said he wanted to do some traveling in Europe."

"Didn't you think it odd he didn't reach out since July 17?"

"No. Not if he was in Europe. I'd be surprised if he called me."

"What else did you talk about?" Clark asked.

"Nothing specific. Adam said he was tired of moving from museum to museum. He thought it might be time to find one place to call home. We talked about him moving to New York. That it would be a great city for him."

"What else?"

"We talked about a woman he was dating, Natalie, and my wife and children. Again, just how is everyone doing type of thing."

"Did he ever talk to you about an experience he had with a woman from Saudi Arabia?"

"He did. He went to Europe just before he moved to Saginaw. He said a beautiful woman came on to him in a nightclub. They went back to his hotel. When they finished, she told him her family was powerful and that they would hurt him if they found out she'd slept with him. She warned him to hide out for a time. So he came back to the U.S. and moved to Saginaw."

"Did he ever talk about it again?"

"He did. From time to time, he still worried that maybe her brothers would track him down and kill him."

"When was the last time Mr. Lindmark talked about being found?"

"Not that long ago. Maybe weeks before his death."

"Did he give you any details?"

"He said he thought he'd covered his tracks well, but maybe it wasn't enough."

"What else can you tell me, Mr. Rothstein?"

"Adam was a great friend. We've known each other since our days at NYU. His death leaves a big hole in my life. If there is anything else you need from me, don't hesitate to call."

"Thank you, Mr. Rothstein, for your cooperation."

Clark then called Natalie Collins.

"Ms. Collins, this is Detective Clark."

"Yes, detective, tell me you've found Adam's murderer and can stop suspecting me."

"Ms. Collins, did Mr. Lindmark ever talk about some trouble he had with a Saudi Arabian family when he was in Europe?"

"No. He'd never talked about anything like that," she said.

"Are you sure?"

"Yes, Detective, I'm sure. What's this all about?" she asked.

"Just following up on a lead. Sorry to bother you."

Natalie said goodbye, but Clark had already hung up. She then called Lukas and asked to meet later at the Black Cat to talk about Adam's wake and other things.

After getting their coffees, they found an open table.

"I had an interesting call from Detective Clark this morning," she said.

"Really?"

"He wanted to know if Adam ever talked to me about a problem he had with a Saudi Arabian family. Do you know anything about this?" she asked.

"He had told me that he might be in trouble with the brothers of a Saudi girl that he met in Istanbul. He cut his vacation short because the woman warned him her brothers could be violent. So he came back and moved to Saginaw," I said.

"Nothing more? He never said anything more about this threat?"

"It worried him from time to time?"

"Do you think they murdered him?" she asked.

"Natalie, I didn't kill him, and I don't think you did either. So who did? I think it's possible that the Saudi family found him," I said.

"Lukas, I also wanted to talk to you about a wake for Adam. Even though I was terribly hurt he slept with Nicky, I still loved him. I want proper closure. Do you want to help me?"

"I will, even though it's hard to think of Adam as a friend after what he did."

"Have you talked to Nicky?"

"No, and I don't plan to," I said.

"I understand completely."

Natalie was understandably empathic.

"What kind of wake did you have in mind?" I asked.

"A celebration; I'm hoping we could share the cost," she said.

"Natalie, Clark told me you have some financial challenges. I don't know if you are, but I can take care of all the costs. If you want, in the future, you could pay me back," I said.

"Thanks, Lukas. I've been trying to keep it quiet, but I lost a couple of important tenants, and it's hurting my cash flow. So I appreciate your offer. It would make it easier for me. I'm curious about Adam's estate. I assumed he was loaded, but we never talked about money," she said.

"He told me he went to an attorney and had a will and power of attorney made out. He named me his agent and personal representative. I don't know if he did. I haven't seen any documents."

"Did he tell you who prepared them?"

"No. He said his friend in New York had an attorney friend that helped him. He asked for, and I gave him a name of an attorney in Saginaw. I don't know if they ever met."

"Have you talked to Adam's friend? What was his name?" She asked.

"Paul Rothstein. No, I haven't. We'll need to let him know about the wake. I'll give him a call tonight."

"Thanks for meeting. Life is strange, isn't it? I mean Adam's death, him sleeping with Nicky, we're suspects, and it's up to us to arrange his wake," she said.

I shook my head. "And don't forget I'm supposed to be his personal representative and have no idea what he owned or where it's located."

Chapter Thirty-Seven

Saginaw, Michigan
August 4, 2019

Lukas Novak

Later that evening, I called Paul Rothstein. He wasn't happy to hear about Adam's death from a homicide detective.

"Adam told me he signed a power of attorney naming you as his agent," Paul said.

I didn't know that, but it wasn't important because, like all powers of attorney, it ends on the death of the person creating it.

"Adam said he wanted you to wrap up his affairs in Saginaw after he left. He said that if you agreed, you would sell all his property, including his Porsche. After you paid expenses," Rothstein said, "he wanted the balance of his money to go to the Great Lakes Bay Art Museum."

Then Rothstein told me something else I didn't know.

"Adam's grandfather and father had trusts naming him beneficiary. He said those agreements called for all Adam's debts to be paid upon his death and the remainder to be distributed as Adam directed. He had named the New York University Art Conservation Department."

Finding out that Adam had trusts created for him made sense to me. I was guessing this is what made him financially secure.

"Paul, Natalie, and I are planning a wake for Adam, and we're hoping you can be there."

"I'll be there. Just give me the date, time, and location. I want to say goodbye to my old friend."

Over the next few days, Natalie and I planned Adam's wake, and a week later, I stood in the back of a bar we chose to celebrate his life. It was a full house. Not only did his friends from Saginaw attend, but people from all over the country. When we notified the museums where he'd previously worked, they were shaken, and many promised to attend.

Quietly watching, I considered the twelve passionate testimonials. Some said Adam always listened and didn't judge. One friend said he didn't know any more caring person than Adam Lindmark. Others wanted to say something on Adam's behalf, two from Murfreesboro, including a man who talked about cars. Other speakers were from Chandler, Boise City, Cedar Rapids, and Topeka. Many were crying.

Paul Rothstein was there with his wife. He, too, was crying, and I sensed more profound grief in his eyes than anyone else.

One person in attendance was Clark. He watched people sign the guest book. He probably was thinking he'd have a lot of people to investigate. Neither Natalie nor I spoke. Clark probably noticed. Maybe he also saw that we were crying. Nicky spoke and made it clear she loved Adam and would forever. Natalie's face flushed with anger.

The wake continued, and Adam's friend played guitar and sang Adam's favorite songs. Some people tried to dance, but so many people crowded into the bar that it was difficult. The drinks were poured and put down freely. Nicky came up to me and muttered something that I didn't understand. She was crying, but I wasn't sure if it was for Adam or her betrayal. Natalie stared at us and stormed out.

Chapter Thirty-Eight

Saginaw, Michigan
July 24, 2019

Detective Tobias Clark

After more interviews, Clark believed that Novak and Collins probably knew that Winters slept with Lindmark before he told them. After sleeping with Lindmark, Winters visited the Black Cat Cafe, hinting, perhaps bragging, about being with him. I assumed the news traveled fast.

My investigation of Novak and Collins revealed the difference in character between each suspect; I was beginning to know them much better.

Novak grew up in Royal Oak and was very close to his mother and father. He was an excellent student and could have attended many top schools across the country. Instead, he chose Wayne State University to stay close to his parents in Detroit. It didn't hurt that he received a full scholarship. His father passed away two years ago, and he did everything to convince his mother to move to Saginaw. She decided to stay in her house where Novak grew up. Son and mother met regularly either in Royal Oak or Saginaw. They enjoyed taking walks along the rail trails, the Dow Gardens in Midland, or the riverfront in Bay City.

Interesting to Clark was Novak's boxing background. His father had been a professional boxer in the Czech Republic and taught his young son. With natural strength and agility, Novak became a Golden Glove winner.

Novak's career ended when he punched an opponent so hard that the boy ended up in the hospital even with protective headgear. Novak couldn't bear the guilt of having injured the other boxer. He never boxed again. However, he continued to train as if it was his profession. His basement was complete with an entire workout facility, including a speed bag and a hanging heavy punching bag. Clark saw that Novak looked in good shape, particularly for an architect. He now knew he was physically fit like few others.

Clark saw the influence of Novak's parents. He was warm and caring person like his mother, and physically and mentally as tough as his father.

Novak was a natural leader, and although he was involved in many community activities, he was passionate about the arts and was Chairperson of the Board of Directors of the Great Lakes Bay Art Museum. Clark's investigation revealed that Novak was understated and highly respected. Perhaps his only flaw was loving Nicky Winters. Anyone who knew the two couldn't understand why he was faithful, even when she wasn't.

Natalie Collins was a different story. Behind her incredible looks and polished charm, she was a very hard woman. Some called her a bully with a temper. One person said her company was having financial difficulties caused by her disrespect of tenants. One story had Natalie blowing up and threatening a tenant's life if he didn't sign a new lease.

If Novak or Collins knew that Winters and Lindmark had been together, I questioned whether Novak's character would allow him to murder his friend. On the other hand, Collins' reputation for rages and retaliatory threats made her a compelling suspect. Could she kill the man she claimed to need badly? Claimed to love? Perhaps, Clark thought.

Chapter Thirty-Nine

Saginaw and Midland, Michigan
July 25, 2019

Lukas Novak

The day after Adam's wake, I told myself to remember all its details. I was sure I'd never again experience such emotion: disbelief, sadness, and joy. And hatred too. I thought about Nicky's tearful words about Adam. There was no doubt she loved him. Yes, she loved him in a way she'd never care for me. What was wrong with me? I couldn't move on with this woman. I weighed the tender moments we had together, the joy I felt when I was with her, and the deep hurt when she was with other men. Unexplainably, the balance always tipped in favor of wanting to be with her.

I pondered the expression on Natalie's face as she listened to Nicky. I'm not sure I'd ever witnessed hatred in anyone's eyes like hers.

While contemplating people's emotions, I received a call from Nicky. "Hello, Lukas. We're doing the LPGA event together, right?"

Well, this was a total surprise. Nicky and I volunteered to work on the LPGA event at the Great Lakes Bay Country Club for the past couple of years. We always worked the hospitality suites and had a good time welcoming and helping guests enjoy themselves.

"I haven't given the event any thought, Nicky. I'm not sure about us."

"Look, I know you must be hurt that I slept with Adam, but I've always been upfront with you about my feelings. I loved him. I'm guessing you weren't surprised when you found out I was with him. Lukas, please remember I care for you in a way not possible with Adam. I've never told you this, but I love you too. I do. So let's move forward. I know I want to."

Nicky had never told me she loved me. I weighed her words and what they meant. Finally, I knew that I wanted to move forward too.

"Are you still there?" She asked.

"Ok, let's do the tournament again," I said.

"I'm guessing Natalie won't be joining us this year," Nicky said.

"The look she gave you at the wake, I don't think she ever wants to see you again, and I think it's a good idea if she doesn't," I replied.

"Her look was pretty scary, wasn't it?'

"No, it wasn't pretty scary. It was as if Natalie's hate for you unhinged her," I said.

Changing the subject, "So we're doing the tournament?" Nicky asked.

"Yes, I'll contact the people at the club to work it out. I don't think I'll talk to Natalie. It's best to give her time and space."

"I absolutely agree," Nicky said.

Chapter Forty

Saginaw, Michigan
July 25, 2019

Lukas Novak

The day before the tournament, I received a surprising call from Natalie. She said she was looking forward to doing the tournament again.

"Are you sure?" I questioned.

"I'm sure. I need to keep busy, and working the tournament keeps my mind from going to places it shouldn't go."

"OK," I said, "that makes sense."

So, I gave her the days, times, and suite locations on the course.

"You know Nicky will be there too," I said.

"I know it's fine. I've moved on. I'll see you at the club."

Well, I thought, this is a side of Natalie I'd never seen. She's more mature than I thought possible.

Chapter Forty-One

Midland, Michigan
July 27, 2019

Lukas Novak

I enjoy working the LPGA event with Nicky, and we have fun helping people enjoy watching the world's greatest women golfers. Some years Natalie volunteered too. She worked in several roles wherever they needed her, checking golfers in, looking for balls that went into the rough, and controlling crowds around the tees or greens. Nicky and I always worked the hospitality suites. There were seven or eight constructed along key parts of the course for sponsors who were served drinks and food while watching their favorites.

The rules prohibited volunteers from drinking, which never stopped Nicky. She brought her rum and added it to a glass of coke that she refilled during the day. She even wrote her name on the cup in black marker so others wouldn't use it or throw it away.

Everyone got along splendidly during the two days that Natalie worked with Nicky and me. I was surprised.

After the last day, Natalie offered to meet Nicky and me at Natalie's favorite bar in Bay City for a drink. We declined, saying it had been a long day and we were heading home.

"I understand," Natalie said.

"Let's get together another time, soon," Nicky said.

"Of course," Natalie said.

Frankly, I was relieved the tournament ended with no conflict between Nicky and Natalie and having drinks was pressing our luck.

Chapter Forty-Two

Saginaw, Michigan
July 27, 2019

Lukas Novak

I asked Nicky if she wanted to stop for dinner on our way home. She told me she wanted to head to her apartment. After dropping her off, I drove home.

Around 9:30 that evening, she called and said she was terribly sick and vomiting.

"Come over right now," she pleaded.

Immediately I drove to her apartment and let myself in. She was lying on her bathroom floor crying.

"Lukas," she sobbed, "I'm in so much pain. I can't stand it." She seemed confused and was having trouble breathing. I called 911 and watched helplessly as she writhed on the floor in complete agony. After what seemed like hours, the ambulance arrived and raced her to Hope Medical Center.

The next morning at 6:00, I called Natalie to tell her that Nicky was in critical condition at the hospital. The doctors weren't sure of the cause but suspected she had an allergic reaction to something she ate or drank but were also considering the possibility that she ingested poison.

I had called Clark earlier and told him about Nicky. He said it sounded like poisoning and would send officers over to search the golf course and clubhouse for evidence of poison.

Natalie drove immediately to Saginaw and joined me as I frantically waited for the doctors' update. At 11:00 that morning, they gave me the news. Nicky was dead. I fell apart. I seem to remember Natalie consoling me. She must have driven me home at some point. It was an agonized blur.

I stayed in bed for days. I didn't answer the phone, except to tell Liz I was alright. I'll never see Nicky again was a realization I couldn't accept, and finally, when I did, the torment was too much for me, and I'd cry out her name over and over.

Early one morning, there was a knock at my door. Clark and two other police officers greeted me. Clark read me my rights and placed me under arrest for the murder of Nicky Winters.

Chapter Forty-Three

Saginaw, Michigan
July 28, 2019

Detective Tobias Clark

Clark studied Novak. It looked like he hadn't slept, showered, or eaten in days. His grisly beard and matted hair enhanced the dark bags under his eyes. He yelled at Clark, demanding why he was being arrested.

Later at the police station, while he was fingerprinted and processed, Clark considered Winter's and Lindmark's murders. He thought they must be connected, and Novak and Collins were the obvious links. For the moment, he ruled out other suspects. He'd arrested Novak but knew Collins had the motive and the opportunity and maybe the means to kill too. He had no evidence she was the killer. Novak was different. After hearing Winters' symptoms, police searched the course grounds and found Nicky's plastic cup, with her name printed on it in black marker. It tested for 1080 poison, a type of rat poison. When they informed Clark, it affirmed his thinking.

Clark had a judge issue search warrants for Novak and Collins's homes and places of business.

A thorough search of Collins' home and her commercial buildings revealed no evidence pointing to Winter's murder. On the other hand, searching Novak's home revealed a slight trace of poison on the shirt he'd worn at the golf event. Clark surmised that Winters was poisoned on the event's last day. There were hundreds of people around while Winter was volunteering. All were suspects, yet only one had traces of poison on their clothes.

Clark arrested Novak. He had to arrest him but was bothered because he didn't think he profiled as a murderer. He'd been wrong before and would let the court decide his fate.

In the interrogation cell, Novak stared at Clark with dark resentful eyes.

"Why did you arrest me? I would never harm Nicky and wouldn't and couldn't kill her. What makes you think I did?" Novak asked, almost pleading."

"Mr. Novak, I know you're very smart, so I'm going to read you your Miranda rights again before I start asking you questions."

After finishing, Clark asked, "Tell me about yesterday's event at the Great Lakes Bay Country Club?"

"Detective Clark, I didn't have anything to do with her death. I've nothing more to say until I have my attorney present."

"This is your chance to tell me what happened. You don't want to do that?"

"I'm being set up either by you or someone else. Perhaps you're feeling the heat from your captain for getting nowhere in Adam's murder. Now a second murder of my girlfriend, and you plan to pin both on me. I want to call my attorney."

"I'm just trying to get to the truth Mr. Novak. But ok, you can make your call, and then we can talk about Ms. Winters and yesterday."

Lukas called one of his friends who specialized in criminal law, and she quickly followed up and arranged a $150,000 bail for Lukas' release. She then met with Lukas at the jail.

"Lukas, what the hell is going on?" His attorney asked.

"They think I murdered Nicky."

"I read the file. They say she was poisoned yesterday at the women's golf event."

"I know, and I was with her the entire day. I picked her up in the morning, and we drove together to Midland. We worked together all day as volunteers. Sometime early the next morning, they told me she died of cardiac arrhythmias."

Lukas started to cry and then abruptly stopped. His attorney watched the emotions flood through him.

"I remember what my father used to tell me," Lukas said, while staring down at the table, talking more to himself than his attorney, "when the going gets tough, the tough get going. Well, things couldn't get much tougher, so I'm going to get damn tough. Someone killed Adam and Nicky, and I will find out who. I'm looking forward to inflicting some serious getting-even when I do."

There was a knock at the door, and Clark entered.

"Hello counselor, I want to talk to your client," he demanded.

"Detective, my client is distressed over the death of the woman he loved. This is not a good time, and I've already arranged bail for Lukas. I'm going to take him home now. You can talk to him sometime in the future," Lukas' attorney made clear.

"I see you've arranged bail, and I suppose you'll tell Mr. Novak not to answer any of my questions anyway. So, I'll arrange for his release. I'll contact you tomorrow for that interview," Clark said.

Clark looked at Novak and nodded. He sensed that he wasn't the murderer, and measuring the determined look on his face, Clark knew Novak would be looking for Winters' murderer too.

Chapter Forty-Four

Saginaw, Michigan
July 28, 2019

Lukas Novak

Clark left the room, and two officers entered and took me away. Within an hour, I was home, lying on my bed, alone and immersed in darkness. There was one thing that I knew; I would fight back. Fight back hard.

The following day I called Liz Bowers. She knew about the arrest and intuitively understood it would be best to wait to talk to me. She assured me she didn't believe I had anything to do with Nicky's murder and would always be on my side. Knowing Liz was on her way over to see me, and hearing her reassuring words, gave me strength. I told her to let herself in that I'd leave the door open. I couldn't remember the last time I'd slept and decided to take a shower and shave my beard off before Liz arrived.

I wonder what Liz thought when she saw me. I know I looked tired, but hopefully not defeated.

"Someone killed Nicky, Liz. I'm going to find them," I pronounced. She hugged me.

"Lukas, life can be so cruel, but you're strong and caring, and you will survive all of this and come out the other side with the strength you never knew you had inside you." She gave me another hug.

"And there's no way you'll be convicted; there's no real proof."

"Sit down," I said, "help me go through the entire day in detail."

When finished, I said, "There were hundreds of people who could have put poison in her drink. But who'd want to?"

"Lukas, maybe this isn't a good time to talk about this, but maybe Natalie. She had the motive. She was very jealous of Adam, and she knew Nicky slept with him. She was around all day," Liz said.

"I know Natalie was very possessive of Adam, and it hurt her to hear about him and Nicky, just like it hurt me. I just don't see her being a killer any more than me, and I don't think she's Adam's killer either. Consider this, Liz, I can't figure out who. Maybe if I could understand the why behind the murders, it would lead me to the killer."

Later that afternoon, my attorney and I met with Clark. I retold in detail everything that had happened the day at the golf event. Clark tried to guilt me into admitting I killed Nicky because of jealousy. I told him the simple truth; I'd rather die than have Nicky dead. After over two hours of going over the same details, Clark told me I was free to go.

Chapter Forty-Five

Saginaw, Michigan
July 28, 2019

Detective Tobias Clark

After they left, Clark thought that either Novak was the greatest liar he'd ever met, or he didn't kill Winters. "If it wasn't Novak, then damn it, who did? And who killed Lindmark?" he said out loud to himself. It was up to him to figure it out. What about Collins? Or how about some Saudi family that Lindmark had trouble with? Or how about some unknown person from Lindmark's past. He wondered whether the two murders were even connected. It was hard for him to believe they weren't.

From listening to Novak, he was sure of one thing; Novak would be searching for Winters' murderer too, even though he demanded that Novak leave the detective work to him and his people.

Chapter Forty-Six

Bay City, Michigan
July 27, 2019

Natalie Collins

Remorse was a feeling she rarely felt and didn't like it. She tried to block it out every time she started thinking of Lukas. She wanted to simply bask in the glorious feeling of her cunning and a plan perfectly executed. It was the expression on Lukas' face at the hospital she couldn't shake out of her mind; his grief and sadness completely swallowed him. She tried to focus on her satisfying revenge, but now Lukas was arrested for murder. She had considered this; it was part of her plan and thought he'd get off. The reality was pushing hard on her, and now she questioned whether he would. Even if he did, she worried that his grief would be endless. When devising her plan, she never considered that.

"Focus on Nicky with Adam and how much you hated her," she said out loud. "Forget about Lukas," she shouted.

She reminded herself of her deep hate, the unforgivable hate she felt at Adam's wake. Watching Nicky talk about Adam and crying to Lukas, Natalie knew then she would kill her. She just didn't know how she'd do it.

Her planning had begun with asking herself, what would be the most effective way to murder Nicky? She decided poison would be the easiest. What poison would she use? She didn't know. How could she arrange not to be caught? She didn't have a clue. She only knew she'd find answers, making sure that bitch died.

She'd started by researching poisons. Knowing she couldn't use her computer as it could be traced back to her, she remembered that once she studied an architect, Albert Kahn, who had designed many of the finest buildings in Detroit. He'd also designed a building in Bay City she planned to buy. To find out more about Kahn, she visited the Detroit Public Library, making a day of visiting the library. A young man was delighted to assist her and show her the computers open to the public. This time she'd visit the library for a very different purpose.

Her focus had had a clarity that only hate and revenge could foster. At the library, she'd had some resistance from an employee about using the computer; apparently, you needed to reserve a time. This young man didn't know what hit him when Natalie turned on her charm and sex appeal. Soon he was helping her get started and said if she needed any help to ask for him. He'd stop by just in case she needed anything. She assured him that wasn't necessary, but if she needed help, he'd be the only one she'd ask.

She'd started researching Albert Kahn, just in case he showed up, and when he didn't, she turned to research poisons. She found many ways to kill with poison and was amazed at the number of types that could be used. Fentanyl is a synthetic opiate painkiller that is at least 50 times more powerful than morphine. A related synthetic opioid, Carfentanyl, is 100 times as potent as Fentanyl, 10,000 more potent than morphine. These would be perfect, she thought, but where could she obtain fentanyl or carfentanyl? She read they could be purchased as a street drug. She didn't know anything about buying drugs on the street, and even if she did, the police could perhaps trace the sale back to her. She didn't like taking chances. Other poisons were even more interesting. Apparently, the Russians used a variety of more exotic poisons, Gelsemium, the Heartbreak Grass, Polonium210, Thallium, TCDD, commonly referred to as Dioxin and Ricin. This is ridiculous, she thought. She couldn't procure Fentanyl; how could she find these Russian killers?

She came across an article about common homicidal poisons. This sounded like an Agatha Christie novel to her. Perhaps these poisons were the answer. She continued reading about antifreeze, arsenic, botulinus toxin, cyanide, and strychnine. Maybe one of these poisons could be found? Perhaps sodium fluoroacetamide, also known as Compound 1080, used in pesticides, rodent, or predator poison. She learned it was sold only to licensed pest-control operators and remembered she'd seen rodent poison in the basement of one of her buildings a year or so ago. It looked really old, and she thought at the time she should throw it out and would have if she could have done it safely. Now she was glad she hadn't. This poison was odorless -- that was good -- she thought. It's water-soluble -- also good. Then she read the very best part, "as little as 1mg of 1080 is sufficient to cause severe poisoning. This poison is one of most toxic substances known, and there is no specific antidote." She'd finished her research. Now she'd go back to the basement of her building and find the rodent poison and read its ingredients.

On the way home, she'd planned how she would poison Nicky. She'd worked with Nicky and Lukas during the LPGA event before. Nicky always had a rum and coke in a plastic cup. She could simply add the poison to her drink. That's easy.

The bigger problem is avoiding being caught. Any police investigation would find that she had the motive, the opportunity, and arguably the means to kill Nicky. She needed to create reasonable doubt that someone else killed her. Lukas, she thought. Lukas could want revenge too. He could be blamed. It would be critical that the day she poisoned Nicky, Lukas would be there too, and then she'd point the murder towards him. She initially didn't know how to do that and would need to think more before deciding. She knew that Lukas was the person that could cause reasonable doubt.

Once back in Bay City, she was relieved to find the rodent poison in the basement, read the ingredients, and compared them to the notes she'd taken at the library. It was clear she was holding enough poison to kill Nicky many times over.

Two days later, she came up with the idea of how to direct the search for Nicky's murderer towards Lukas. She recalled that Lukas had invited

Adam and her to a barbeque in his backyard last summer. That day Lukas called Nicky and said he was running late and didn't want everyone waiting around. He told her that he hid his house key inside a light fixture by the backdoor. He asked her to make cocktails for everyone, and he'd be there as soon as he could. Until now, Natalie hadn't thought anymore about the hidden key. Was it still there? Later that day, she drove by Lukas' office and saw his car in the parking lot. She went to his house and checked the hiding place. The key was there. She smiled.

The police knew that Lukas was smart, she thought, and wouldn't leave evidence of murder in his home or office. She'd need to be subtle. Perhaps a trace of 1080 on the shirt he wore at the golf event would do the trick. I can make that happen, she thought.

Two days before the event started, Natalie called the golf event coordinator and confirmed that she'd be working with Lukas and Nicky on the last two days of the tournament in the suite between the 16th green and the 17th tee box. This was a good place, she thought; there'd be plenty of action with the crowd shifting its attention from the green on one side of the suite to the tee box on the other side, giving her plenty of opportunities to slip the poison in Nicky's drink.

After confirming that the key to Lukas's home was there, she started preparing the poison. She put on surgical gloves and a cover over her clothes and placed the poison solution in a vile. She securely closed the top and placed it carefully into a plastic bag when finished. She would watch the event on the first day and decide the best way to plant the poison the following day. According to her readings, the poison would begin affecting Nicky in about 8 to 12 hours. By then, the day's event would have ended, and she'd be safely home. Later that afternoon, she used a butane torch to burn the remainder of her rodent poison, gloves, and other evidence that could be traced to her and buried it in secluded woods.

The first day they worked the event, Natalie saw the volunteers were wearing red golf shirts with the tournament logo. Good, she thought; she'd be able to plant evidence on Lukas' shirt when she found it in his house. She did have one concern; Nicky was having so many rum and cokes that maybe she wouldn't feel like drinking on the following day.

During the first day they worked together, Natalie wanted to avoid any suspicion and was pleasant with Lukas and Nicky but not overly friendly.

On the morning of the second day, she parked her car a few blocks from Lukas' home and waited in a vacant wooded lot until he left for work before slipping on a pair of surgical gloves, finding his spare key, and letting herself into his house. She looked in his bedroom for the redshirt he had worn the day before. It wasn't there. She worried. Did he already wash it? The event had issued two shirts for each volunteer; surely, he didn't go home and wash the first shirt. She was relieved when she found it in his laundry room. She carefully took out the spray bottle with the poison and lightly applied a trace of poison to his shirt. Placing the bottle in the plastic bag, she returned his key to its hiding, removed her gloves, put them in the bag, and walked to her car.

When reaching the tournament, Natalie saw that Nicky had put her name on another plastic cup. She felt no regret as Nicky took her first sip, and Natalie said to herself, "Today, you'll be having your last rum and coke, you bitch." Natalie grinned, thinking about adding poison to Nicky's drink. The opportunity came when one of the most popular golfers made a birdie on the 16th hole. The crowd was cheering for her as she walked by the suite to the 17th tee. Natalie slipped the poison into Nicky's cup as everyone shifted their attention. The crowd cheered a booming drive by their favorite, and Natalie had a satisfied smile as Nicky drank from her marked cup. She had no idea she was ingesting tasteless rat poison. Natalie glowed with the warm feeling of revenge.

After the day's event, she asked Lukas and Nicky to have a drink. They declined, and Nicky said they needed to have drinks soon. Natalie laughed to herself while thinking, " Yes, I'll have a drink after your funeral."

On her way home, Natalie disposed of all the evidence just as she'd done before and then met a friend of hers at a favorite bar. Natalie was in an excellent mood, and her friend noticed. When she asked Natalie why she said, "I'm beginning to move forward in my life." After a glass of wine, she went home and waited for a phone call. It came, and she went to comfort Lukas at the hospital.

It was now days later, "Damn it," she said to herself, "why did I go to the hospital? Now I can't get Lukas out of my mind."

Chapter Forty-Seven

Manhattan, New York
September 2010

Beatrice Hirsch

Beatrice Hirsch's grandfather, Sergei Hirsch, entered the United States in 1919, right after World War I. He sought refuge from the social upheaval that continued in Russia, fleeing in fear for the lives of himself and his family. Sergei was a jeweler and established his business in New York City. He leveraged his contacts to become a successful diamond retailer.

He and his wife had one child, Pavel, raised in the jewelry and diamond sales business. Pavel used the family resources to start a construction company and was in the right place at the right time when the national trend began creating housing for the indigent. Federal funds became available for the demolition of neighborhoods and the construction of tenements in New York City. Pavel capitalized on the excessive payments made to contractors to carry out this progressive program.

Pavel and his wife, Sarah, had one child, Beatrice. Early in her life, it became clear that Beatrice was a particularly bright girl. She was gifted in art, music, and mathematics. After graduating from high school, Beatrice convinced her parents to let her attend New York University and study art history. Her father was unhappy about his daughter's choice and agreed only after she promised to study business too. After graduating with honors in Art History and Business Administration, she joined her father in the family construction business and quickly learned her trade. When the opportunity came to begin work in Russia and the Baltic and Eastern European countries, she immediately grasped the financial prospects. She was ready for a challenge as she had no husband, children, or real friends. Her life was work.

The construction business in these countries is built upon the black market and bribes. It was a ruthless world, and Beatrice was particularly well-suited to succeed. She had a gift for the dark side of running a company and thrived on the intrigue of finding ways to accomplish her goal of making as much money as possible in the shortest amount of time. For her, the ends always justified the means; in a ruthless world, Beatrice was unfeeling. She had no moral or ethical quarrels with paying bribes to construct buildings that failed to meet building specifications knowing that each was unsafe. If anyone stood in her way, she developed the contacts to eliminate the person.

Beatrice was a complex woman: ruthless but a loving heart for the arts. She often told herself, "Whatever steps I take to make money are justified because the money will be used to buy art. Not just art, but great art." Beatrice was a large woman with a large appetite for food and drink. Her most enormous appetite she saved for hoarding art that, like her appearance, swelled as she grew older.

Beatrice had little interest in the mainstream art world of impressionism, post-impressionism, or modern works, and although she owned some of these works, she didn't fully appreciate their paintings. She felt their spontaneously painted canvases were inferior to the great work of the Realist painters. She spent many hours in her youth trying to master the drawing and painting techniques of the painters she adored, Waterhouse, Sargent, and especially William Adolphe Bouguereau. She dreamed of having her own museum-quality paintings from these grandmasters. With the wealth generated from the family business, she began purchasing exceptional paintings. Beatrice, however, wasn't one to pay full prices at Christie's or Sotheby's; with her contacts in the black markets of Europe, she began finding paintings that had been illegally procured and were now available at discounted prices. Because these paintings were part of the art-theft world, they couldn't be shown to others and needed to remain hidden away. This didn't trouble Beatrice because she purchased these paintings for only herself. She could care less if anyone else ever saw them.

One of the contacts she made in Europe was another American in the demolition business, Deacon Black. She always thought his name so interesting: Deacon, a holy name for a man, almost as ruthless as she was. Black, however, fit his personality perfectly. It was also interesting that Deacon Black also loved art, although the works he had a taste for were of little interest to Beatrice. After one project in Latvia they worked on together, Black asked her if she wanted to purchase original museum-quality art. She said she would, depending on the painting, the cost, and the risk of buying the painting. He explained that a broker he used in New York had a friend who was an art conservationist and painter. He was working at smaller museums and willing to forge copies of the paintings he was cleaning. He then would sell the originals and return the forgeries to the museum.

Hirsch was interested as long as she had no direct contact with the forger or Black's broker. He told her the price would be 60% of the appraised price, paid in cash. Hirsch balked at this price. She was used to paying a much lower percentage. Black told Hirsch that his broker said that the conservationist wouldn't paint a forgery unless he received this amount.

"What are the paintings?" She asked

"A Camille Corot and a William Bouguereau,"

"Do you have pictures?"

"I'll send them over to you," he replied.

After studying the photographs, Hirsch called him back, "You can have Corot."

"Good, I want the Corot," Black said.

"I want the Bouguereau," she said.

"At his price?"

"If you can get it for less, if not, I'll take it for $600,000, no more," she replied.

Deacon Black reached out to Paul Rothstein, who talked to Adam in the following days.

"It's all agreed," Paul told Adam. "for the sale of the Corot and Bouguereau. They'll pay $600,000 for the Bouguereau alone."

Adam was taken aback. He didn't see himself as an art forger. Nevertheless, the money would answer all his financial concerns. As promised, he focused on the Corot and finished it in time to meet Deacon Black's deadline. He then turned his attention to Adolphe William Bouguereau's work of art. He was excited to start and enjoyed every moment of cleaning and then painting the copy.

Adam took his time and was very satisfied when he finished his work. The conservation went well, and the forgery was amazing. He called Paul and then delivered the original Bouguereau painting to Paul, who turned it over to Black and then to Hirsch.

She immediately had her expert study the work, and only after he declared it an original did she transfer the agreed-upon price to a specified account. She now owned her first William Adolphe Bouguereau. She was as excited, like a small child at Christmas.

Chapter Forty-Eight

New York City
July 12, 2019

Beatrice Hirsch

Over the years, Hirsch continued buying paintings from Adam in this fashion. She liked all of them, but a Bouguereau wasn't offered again until recently. One day, Black called her and said two Bouguereau paintings were available and sent her pictures. She thought both were wonderful. The second painting, two girls playing with a ball with an admiring mother, she knew was exceptional.

She called him right back.

"I want both paintings, the second one particularly. The one with two girls."

"He wants $5 million for that painting."

"I need to do some research and get back to you," she said.

The next day Hirsch called Deacon and told him that her experts put the value of the second Bouguereau at $8 to $10 million. She'd pay the heavy price of $5 million.

When the first Bouguereau arrived, she continued with her typical procedure of authenticating the painting before transferring the funds. She then impatiently waited for the second Bouguereau. After many months it arrived. When she unpacked it, she was taken back by its beauty. The little girls looked alive. She felt she could almost talk to the mother about her darlings playing with the ball. She hurried to have one of her workers place the painting in the most prominent place in her drawing-room. She sat for hours studying it. She couldn't have been happier and transferred $5 million to the designated account. Days later, when she was lying in bed, she remembered that she hadn't had her expert confirm the painting as an original before transferring the funds. She wasn't concerned; all the other purchases were originals. But to be safe, she asked her expert to come over the following day. He removed the painting and took it to his studio. Within days, after a thorough examination, he called and told her, "I believe it is one of the finest copies I have ever seen. How much did you pay for it?" He asked.

"$5 million."

"My god, you thought you were buying an original!" he stammered.

"I did. Are you sure it's a fake?" She asked.

"Yes, I'm positive. You may recall that many years ago, I was asked by the J. Paul Getty Museum to verify a 6th-century sculpture they'd purchased. I told them I thought it was a fake. I couldn't specifically tell them what was wrong. It just didn't feel right to me. They bought the sculpture, and later it was proved to be a fake. I had the same feeling about your Bouguereau when I saw it. It just didn't feel right. There's no question this is a forgery. The spectroscope tells me it was painted with all the right materials used in the 1880s. However, the aging of the paint is not right."

"I was told he had to do some conservation work on it. Could that be what happened?" She asked.

"I considered that, but no. The entire surface is consistent. Conservation repair wouldn't be so pervasive. I'm sorry, Ms. Hirsch. You've paid $5 million for a fake."

Hirsch thanked him for his services.

Chapter Forty-Nine

New York City
July 14, 2019

Beatrice Hirsch

Hirsch was furious. She'd been cheated. No one cheats Beatrice Hirsch, she thought. Her retribution would be severe. She called a person who worked for her many times, particularly in Eastern Europe.

"Konstantin?"

"Yes, Ms. Hirsch, what can I do for you?"

"Where are you? In Latvia?"

"No, I'm in New York. Why?"

"I need your services right away. How soon can you come to my home?"

"Later this morning, if it's urgent."

"It is. I'll see you at 11:00."

"Very well, 11:00."

Sergei Konstantin was Latvian because he was born in Latvia. His grandparents had moved there from Russia at the end of World War II. Many Russians took possession of most of the wealthy Latvians' finest homes at that time. No purchase price would be paid; they would come in the middle of the night and remove entire families. They would separate the fathers from their wives and children. Ultimately, children were separated from their mothers. Most parents and children were transferred to Siberia to work in the gulags. Many did not survive. This brutal and inhumane behavior with the Latvians was something Konstantin inherited. He was a cruel man that served him well as a hired assassin.

When he met with Hirsch, she explained that she had been cheated, that she'd been sold a forgery. He knew that this would not go well for those involved in the deception based on past dealings with her. She told him to visit her colleague, Deacon Black. She was sure he wasn't involved in the fraud because he had been buying paintings too.

"Tell him that all the other paintings she bought were originals. But the last one was a fake. You need to find out from Black the name of his broker in New York and identify everyone who was part of the fraud. Tell the broker I want my $5 million back immediately. Confirm with me that the money is in my account, and you have the forger's name, then find him. I want the original painting. Only this time, I won't be paying for it. Then make the forger suffer before you kill him."

Chapter Fifty

New York City
July 16, 2019

Sergei Konstantin

Konstantin met with Deacon Black at his home early that afternoon.

"Mr. Black, as I said on the phone, I work for Ms. Hirsch. She has great respect for you."

"You told me this has to do with the painting Beatrice recently purchased?" Black asked.

"Yes, that's right. Her art expert has determined that this one is a forgery, unlike all her other purchases. She does not hold you responsible in any way. I'm here to obtain the name of your contact whom you've been making these arrangements."

"His name is Paul Rothstein. He's one of my brokers. He's a partner at a small firm in Manhattan. Wait here while I get you his name, phone number, and address."

"Do you have his home address as well as his work address?" Konstantin asked.

"I do. Here you go."

"Thank you, Mr. Black."

"Please let me know how this turns out."

"I will not do that, Mr. Black. I think it best if you don't know. You're familiar with Ms. Hirsch's approach to people that try to take advantage of her."

After leaving his meeting with Black, Konstantin called Paul Rothstein.

"Hello, Mr. Rothstein; Mr. Deacon Black gave me your cell number. I have a wonderful opportunity for you. A potential client for you who is a friend of Mr. Black and also my client. Is it possible we can meet today? I'm only in the city for a short time," Konstantin asked.

"Yes, we can arrange that. What's your name?" Rothstein replied.

"Jonathon Cameron. I'm going to ask a favor. Is it possible we could meet around 8:00 tonight? It's the only time that will work in my schedule," Konstantin said.

"I suppose that could work. What did you say your client's name is? What do you think she would expect from me?" Rothstein asked.

"I prefer to withhold her name until we meet, for confidentiality purposes. This person is extremely wealthy and is unhappy with one of the people she's been involved. She's looking to move in a new direction. As I said, Mr. Black gave me your name and number."

"I understand. We can meet at 8:00, at my offices. Do you have my address?"

"Yes, Mr. Black gave that to me also."

"Very good. I'll wait for you in the lobby to let you in."

"Thank you very much, Mr. Rothstein. I'll see you at 8:00."

After the call, Konstantin reported back to Ms. Hirsch and informed her of his conversation with Deacon Black and his arranged appointment with Paul Rothstein. At exactly 8:00, Konstantin reached the lobby door of Paul Rothstein's office. Rothstein opened the door for a well-dressed man in his mid-forties.

"Hello, Mr. Cameron?"

"Thank you, Mr. Rothstein, for meeting with me so late. I'm sure you are going to find our meeting most interesting," Konstantin said.

Rothstein led the way to his office, and Konstantin took a seat across a large modern desk that included three computer screens and several open files that Rothstein placed in his desk drawers when Konstantin took a seat. He saw a large portrait of a younger Mr. Rothstein. He knew by the quality who painted it.

"Mr. Rothstein, you have never met my client, but you have been doing business with her for seven years. Do you recall the first paintings you arranged to sell to Mr. Black? Well, my client bought the Bouguereau. She has been the person buying almost all of your paintings since then. She realized she has been paying high dollars for these paintings compared to what she could pay on other black-market arrangements, but she's been happy because the transactions are clean. She always has a renowned art expert confirm the authenticity of each painting before wiring the sales monies to your account. She does this every time, except this last time. She was so excited and pleased with the latest Bouguereau that she transferred the money before she had it confirmed. That was unfortunate for her. The expert verified that she had purchased a fake."

"That's not possible. The person I work with would never be involved in such deception," Rothstein said.

"Oh, but he did. My client is very unhappy. She is not one to take these matters lightly. That is why I'm here. Let me be blunt. Do you have the painting?"

"No," Rothstein said.

"Do you know where the original can be found?"

"No."

"That's most unfortunate. So here is what is going to happen. You are going to transfer $5 million from your accounts to this account." Konstantin took a paper from his jacket pocket and handed it to Rothstein.

"You make this transfer right now, and I'll wait."

"I don't have access to that much money," Rothstein exclaimed.

Konstantin took a 9mm Glock 34 from his shoulder holster and casually placed it on the desk.

"I've done some research on you, Paul. I know, for instance, that you love your wife. Beth, isn't it? And your two children, Samuel and Frumeth? Now you want them to live, don't you? I know you do. So without further hesitation, you must find the funds to transfer to my client. I don't care whose accounts it comes from. Find it and transfer the money, now!"

Rothstein, clearly shaken, "If I do, you'll not harm my family?"

"Paul, that's the whole point of bringing their names to your attention. Now, start making the transfer," Konstantin sternly demanded.

Paul, with shaking hands, began transferring money, first from his accounts, then corporate funds. He then showed Konstantin that the transfers were complete.

"Excellent, Paul. Next, I need the name of the person who did the forgery and tried to take advantage of my client."

"His name is Adam Lindmark," Rothstein stammered.

"I need his address and mobile number. What does Mr. Lindmark do?"

"He works at the Great Lakes Bay Art Museum in Saginaw, Michigan. He does art conservation work. He's been conserving the paintings your client has purchased and replaced them at the museums with his forgeries."

"Are you sure he's still in Saginaw? You wouldn't want me to make the trip for nothing, would you?" Konstantin asked.

"Yes, he's there. I spoke to him yesterday. He is planning to leave Saginaw in the next few days."

"Where is he going?" Konstantin asked.

"I don't know; he wouldn't tell me. Somewhere in Europe, I believe."

"Now, Paul, don't play games with me. Remember Beth, Samuel, and Frumeth."

"I didn't forget. I'll tell you everything you ask. I don't know."

"Very well. I believe you."

Konstantin then called Ms. Hirsch.

"I'm setting with Mr. Rothstein. Can you confirm the money is now in your account? It is, good. I have the name and information of the art forger. He lives in Saginaw. Do you have further instructions for me? Yes, I understand."

"Paul, my client has a reputation to protect. If it got out to Mr. Black and others that she allowed this to happen without retribution, that wouldn't be good for her. The good news for you is I'm not going to kill your family unless I find the information you gave me is false. Now regarding you, my client says that I have the discretion to kill you tonight; however, I want you alive. Perhaps I'll need you to help me find your friend and the painting. If you have lied to me or knew of this fraud, I must reconsider. I don't' have to remind you to keep silent about our meeting, do I?"

Rothstein shook his head no.

"And don't talk to Mr. Lindmark or anyone else, or I will have no choice but kill your family and you. Understand?"

Rothstein nodded his head that he understood.

"No need to let me out, Paul; I'll find my way. I hope for your sake that I find that painting."

Konstantin picked up his gun, "And by the way, that's an excellent portrait of you. Did Mr. Lindmark paint it? Paul nodded his head yes. Konstantin stood up and left Paul's office and arranged for a private jet to take him to Saginaw early the following day.

Chapter Fifty-One

Saginaw, Michigan
July 17, 2019

Sergei Konstantin

Adam showered and packed the last of his things into a travel bag. He left the wine and the note for Natalie on the table. Just as he was about to leave, there was a knock on his door. When he opened it, a tall, well-dressed man in a dark gray suit and blue button-down shirt said, "Are you, Adam Lindmark?"

Adam nodded his head.

"Good, we need to talk. Your friend, Paul Rothstein, gave me your name. May I come in?"

"What did you say your name is?" Adam asked.

"Jonathon Cameron."

"What is it you want to talk about?"

"If I may come in, I'll explain in detail," Konstantin said.

Adam invited Konstantin into his living room and offered an oversized stuffed chair for him to sit. Both men sat down, and Konstantin looked around the house.

"Mr. Lindmark, it looks like you're ready to leave your home?"

"Mr. Cameron, to what do I owe the pleasure of meeting you?"

"I work for a person you've never met but whom you've been doing business with for many years. In fact, it's a person that Mr. Rothstein also had not met. Anyway, this person has been buying paintings from you for the past seven years. She's been pleased with the relationship and has been paying premium dollars for your work, they were all high quality, and she liked the cleanness of the transactions.

This person didn't know you or want to know you, but she is meticulous about these transactions. She employed some of the most knowledgeable art experts to measure the value of each painting. Once she received each of your paintings, she had a renowned conservationist authenticate it before transferring any funds to your account. This was her process until the last transaction. She was delighted with the painting of the little girls and their mother. Because you had a history of consistently delivering originals, she paid the purchase price before authentication. You can imagine her disappointment when she discovered it was a forgery."

Adam began to sweat and turn pale. His greatest fear was happening; he'd been discovered as an art forger. He always believed it would be an art museum to discover the truth. He was exposed the only time he passed a forgery to an individual. He wondered what was in store for him. The person he was looking at seemed a businessman and very professional. Perhaps he could give him the original, and everything would be set straight.

"Mr. Lindmark, my client wants the original. I can tell you that Mr. Rothstein couldn't provide me with the painting. He did, however, transfer the sale funds back to my client's account. She believes that she should receive the Bouguereau painting without further payment because of your indiscretion. I told Mr. Rothstein that I wouldn't kill him or his wife or two children if you turned over the painting. Where is the painting!" Konstantin demanded.

Adam felt like vomiting. He realized he wasn't going to be able to start his new life because the man across from him, with his unemotional and disturbing way of looking at him, made it clear that this wasn't ending well.

"OK. I have the original I can give it to you," Adam said in a shaky voice.

"Very good. Get it for me, now," Konstantin demanded.

"It's not here."

"Mr. Lindmark, I can tell you I'm not playing games with you. You will give me that painting."

"I know. I will give you the painting. I hid it in a mini-storage unit. I can take you to the painting right now."

"Very good. You're now being reasonable. We can go in my car."

At this point, Konstantin pulled out a gun from the back of his pants.

"I can not emphasize this enough—I am quite serious. If you do anything to prevent me from taking possession of this painting, things will not end well for you. Do you understand?" Konstantin said in a chilling voice.

"Yes. I fully understand. I promise I won't be playing any games. The storage unit is only a few minutes drive from here, and the original painting is in perfect condition."

Pointing the gun at Adam, Konstantin motioned him to head to his car.

"You drive."

Keeping the gun on Adam, both men got in the car.

"Tell me, Mr. Lindmark, whatever possessed you to sell my client a forgery. You were paid well for the painting. Why did you try to screw her?"

"I've been studying, working with, and painting great paintings most of my life. I never really wanted any of the paintings for myself. I've always admired the work of Bouguereau more than any other painter. When I saw this painting, I loved it so much that I decided to keep it. I became greedy. I wanted the money and the painting, a huge mistake on my part. I regret it very much, and I'm relieved to turn it over to your client," Adam whined.

They reached the storage units that Adam rented: one for his car the other for his belongings. Unlocking a door, he walked to the wooden box where he hid the painting. He opened it, to his horror, the painting was missing.

"Mr. Lindmark, is something wrong?"

"The Bouguereau is gone. Someone must have taken it!" Adam

exclaimed.

"Mr. Lindmark, I've warned you not to play games. I'm going to remind you of this warning before things become violent."

"I'm not playing games. I put the painting in this box. I planned to pick it up today when I left."

"Perhaps your mind is playing tricks on you. Maybe you left it somewhere else. Maybe even somewhere in this garage."

Adam began to panic. Perhaps he did. He started going through everything else in the garage. His mind was racing. Did he leave it at home? No, he specifically remembered bringing the painting here and putting it in the box. He recalled taking his time to make sure he locked the unit doors.

"Alright, Mr. Lindmark, time is up. I need to be more serious with you. Sit down on that kitchen chair."

Adam did as he was told.

"I told you I'm not playing games. I left the painting in the box. Someone stole it from me," Adam moaned.

"You shouldn't have been so careless," Konstantin said.

Konstantin turned on the lights in the unit, then closed the door, took plastic ties from his suit coat pockets, and zip-tied Adam's hands behind him and his legs to each side of the kitchen chair. He took out a scalpel from a small black zippered case he had in his suit pocket. Konstantin looked around the unit and found a toolbox that Adam had stored. How convenient, he thought as he took out a pair of pliers and walked behind Adam.

"Mr. Lindmark, maybe I can refresh your memory. Did anyone help you move your things to this garage?" Konstantin asked.

"No. I mean, no one that would steal from me."

"Well, someone knew because it's missing. Who are these people?"

"They are people that have no idea about my painting," Adam whimpered.

Konstantin moved close to Adam with a scalpel in his hand.

"Don't make me hurt you, Mr. Landmark, no more games. What are their names? I just need to talk to them. Their names, now."

"Lukas and Natalie," Adam stammered.

"Lukas and Natalie. Do they have last names?"

"Lukas Novak and Natalie Collins."

"They live here in Saginaw?" Konstantin asked.

"Lukas does, Natalie in Bay City."

Now Mr. Lindmark, before I visit your friends and make trouble for them, I'm going to give you one last chance to tell me: Where is the painting?"

"OK. I don't have it, and my friends don't have it either. I was trying to protect the original owner. I didn't want to tell you, but I have no other choice. I put the original back in the owner's house. I couldn't bear to take it from her," Adam lied.

"The original owner. It would help if you said that in the first place. Very well. It's too bad you've been lying to me. What's her name?"

"Janice Wendell,"

"Where does she live?"

"It would be easier if I showed you. We could go over there together, and I can make up a story and get the original back from Janice without any trouble. I could then paint her a forgery, and she'd never know," Adam offered.

"I think you're just buying time, Mr. Lindmark, and you no longer have any time left.

Konstantin then took out a handkerchief, placed it over Adam's mouth, and tied it tight.

"Mr. Lindmark, my client is an unusual woman. She has made a fortune in the construction industry in the Baltic and Eastern Europe. Frankly, everyone fears her. Personally? I think she is a psychopath. Most people who know her either believe that's true or have found out the hard way. Unfortunately for them, she has no conscience. What makes her interesting is her love of art, particularly portrait paintings. Her greatest love is, like you, Bouguereau. So, my instructions are to retrieve her money, bring her the painting, and teach the people who deceived her a terrible lesson. The lesson is important because she wants everyone who does business with her to understand the consequences of cheating on her.

Mr. Rothstein was kind enough to transfer the money to her account, and because I don't think he even knew that you were deceiving my client, he's still alive. But if I don't find that painting, it will be necessary for me to kill him and perhaps his wife and children. If I kill them, it will be with a single shot to the head. You're not going to be so fortunate and will suffer significantly. I know you are a gifted artist. So undoubtedly, you value your hands."

Konstantin placed a gag in Adam's mouth, then studied the tools in the box as Adam watched in horror. He finally selected pliers and held them up in front of Adam's face so he could study them and imagine what was going to happen to him.

Konstantin smiled, "Mr. Lindmark, I'm also a psychopath." He began crushing Adam's fingers. Adam screamed, but no one could hear him. Slowly Konstantin broke each finger on each hand. The pain was unbearable; Adam screamed and screamed into the handkerchief.

"You know Adam, you are such a pretty boy. It's a shame what I'm going to do your face."

Konstantin used his scalpel to remove layers of skin from Adam's face. His pain was unbearable.

"Mr. Lindmark, I told you I had to make an example of you. If Mrs. Wendell doesn't have the original, I will make an example of her. And then I will find your friends and make an example of them."

Konstantin then took out his Glock and screwed on his silencer. He shot Adam in each knee. Adam passed out. When he awoke, Konstantin looked at him.

"You should never have screwed my client, Mr. Lindmark."

He then shot Adam in the head.

"Goodbye, Mr. Lindmark. I hope things go better for your friends."

Days later, Carl Williams smelled a stench outside Adam's unit. He twice called Adam on his mobile phone, and there was no answer. He then called Liz and asked what he should do. She asked Lukas, and he drove over to the storage unit. He had a key, and when he opened the unit door, he was overwhelmed by the stench and the sight of Adam. Minutes later, the police arrived, and shortly after that, Detective Clark reached Adam's body and started the investigation.

Chapter Fifty-Two

Saginaw, Michigan
July 20, 2019

Sergei Konstantin

Konstantin called Hirsch, telling her what Lindmark said before he died. Should he go after Novak and Winters or Wendall's Bouguereau first? She told him to bring back the Wendall painting, and she'd have it analyzed to see if it was the original. If it was, then this episode was over. He could come back for the other two if it wasn't the original.

In the meantime, Sheila Reading, Executive Director at the Great Lakes Bay Art Museum, had a great idea of showing the two Bouguereau paintings as part of a big fundraiser. Janice was hesitant yet agreed to do it after Sheila told her that her painting's ownership would remain anonymous and help raise the museum's much-needed money.

Janice didn't want to give up possession of her painting but understood that it would be helpful to the museum, and she wanted other people to see her outstanding Bouguereau and admire its beauty.

Sheila didn't waste any time and began arranging the big event. She had Janice visit the museum and discuss arranging her painting and the other paintings to complement the showing. For Janice, understanding the museum's security system was most important. She didn't know much about alarm systems, and the museum's seemed adequate in her mind. Sheila assured her that they had other exhibits from major museums, and these museums had approved their security arrangements.

The following day the museum arranged to pick up the painting from Janice and place it in storage. They launched a marketing plan to showcase the artwork, and Reading contacted all the museum's major donors to ensure their support. Janice had a strange feeling that somehow this didn't feel right and longed to see her little girls and their mother.

Konstantin, too, longed to see the girls and their mother. After talking with Hirsch, he began planning to break into Wendall's home and take the painting. Locating her address and observing her home, he realized the woman never left. This wasn't a big problem for Konstantin; he could work around the issue.

Finally, Konstantin, dressed in a tailored suit, white shirt, and dark tie, knocked on Wendall's door. It took a bit for her to answer.

"Hello, are you Janice Wendall?"

"Who wants to know?" She suspiciously answered.

"My name is Jonathon Cameron. I'm an associate of Adam Lindmark. May I talk to you for a minute? It would be very beneficial to Mr. Lindmark."

"In what way would it be helpful to Adam?"

"A major museum in Madrid wants to show his works, and your name was listed as someone that could contribute," Konstantin lied.

Janice eyed him wearily through the keyhole and then agreed to allow him to come into her home.

"Come and sit down, Mr. Cameron," Janice said.

"Thank you. I understand Mr. Lindmark worked for you conserving one of your paintings."

"He did? I'm surprised he talked to you about me. What more did he say?"

"He told me he had worked on a William Bouguereau painting that you own," Konstantin said.

"I'm sorry he wasted your time Mr. Cameron. I know Adam and think very highly of him; however, I don't own a painting by the person you described."

"I'm quite sure I'm not mistaken, Mrs. Wendall. He was certain that you own this painting. I know he wouldn't have misled me."

"Mr. Cameron, I don't own such a painting, and I think you should leave," Janice curtly said.

"Of course, I will leave but not without that painting," Konstantin said, now without any reservations about his intentions.

At that point, Konstantin removed his pistol and pointed it at Wendall.

"No more game playing, Mrs. Wendall. Where's the painting?"

Konstantin started looking around Wendall's living room and could see a large open space on the far wall.

"I assume this is where you normally hang the painting. Now, where do you have it hidden?" Konstantin demanded.

"I don't have it. I sold it. That's why I told you I didn't own such a painting."

"Don't lie to me. Where is it?"

"I told you I sold it," Janice again sharply stated.

Konstantin pointed the gun at Wendall's head.

"Who did you sell it to, Mrs. Wendall?"

Janice remained utterly composed.

"I sold it to a museum. The Metropolitan Art Museum in New York," she said.

"That's too bad for you, Mrs. Wendall. I was willing to take the painting and leave peacefully. Now you give me no choice other than hurting you."

Again, he pointed his gun at Janice.

"Mrs. Wendall? Do you want to live or die?"

"Ok. I didn't sell it. It's at the Great Lakes Bay Art Museum. It's going to be part of a big exhibition fundraiser."

"Is this another of your lies?"

"No. It's the truth. They picked it up yesterday," Janice stoically stated.

"Let's make sure. Let's have you call the museum to confirm that it's safely stored, or maybe it's already hung for the exhibit," Konstantin said.

Wendall was still using a landline and called Sheila Reading. She confirmed that the painting was safe in the storage vaults downstairs.

"Ok. The Great Lakes Bay Art Museum. That will be my next visit. I appreciate your help, Mrs. Wendall."

Konstantin, knowing that he would remain in Saginaw for the time being, felt he had no choice and killed Janice with a shot to her head. It was unfortunate, he thought; she was a brave and defiant woman.

Making sure he left no trace that he had been in her home, he made his way to the museum to look it over. He paid a $5.00 visitor fee and walked around all the galleries. He could see they were preparing for an exhibition. More importantly, he determined that there were no cameras or motion detectors. He knew that meant he only had to circumvent the alarm system when he entered the building. He also took note of the stairs leading to the lower level. That must be where they store their art. He wondered if the vault was locked. He wouldn't be able to know until he entered that night. He'd be prepared to deal with any circumstances that presented themselves. When he talked to the person at the front desk, he was told that there'd be a showing of two Bouguereau paintings: one was owned by the museum and the other by an anonymous collector.

Later that evening, Konstantin disarmed the straightforward alarm system and quietly entered the museum. He found the stairs that he had seen earlier that day and made his way to an impressive vault storage system that was locked. It didn't take long for him to pick the lock and find the Wendall Bouguereau. He removed the canvas from the outer and inner framing. He looked at the second Bouguereau and decided this would make an excellent gift for Mrs. Hirsch.

Upon leaving the museum, he drove to O'Hare Airport in Chicago purchased a ticket for the first flight to JFK that left at 5:00 that morning. He was already in New York meeting with Ms. Hirsch before the Great Lakes Bay Art Museum discovered their two prized paintings were stolen.

Some days after the murder and before discovering that the paintings were missing, Sheila Reading decided she would meet with Janice and discuss the fundraising plans. When she arrived at her home, she rang the doorbell several times with no response. She knew Mrs. Wendall rarely left her home, so she looked through her living room window. Janice was slumped in a sofa chair. Reading called 911, the police entered her home and found her murdered body. Shortly after that, Detective Clark arrived to find that a single shot to Janice's head killed her. He talked to Reading, and she told him about the planned exhibition that would include a valuable painting owned by Janice.

Sheila and Clark drove to the museum to check if the painting was safe and found both Bougureau paintings missing. Clark found it interesting that whoever took the paintings relocked the vault and rearmed the alarm system when they left. Clark thought that it must be a professional to hide their theft long enough so they could leave Saginaw and be safely away before being discovered. Reading now recalled that Janice called her earlier to confirm her painting was safely stored.

Crying, Reading said, "The murderer must have been with her during the call to make sure they knew her painting was at the museum. I unknowingly helped the killer. Now Janice is dead and both paintings gone."

"It's not in any way your fault, Mrs. Reading," Clark said.

Clark deeply sighed when realizing the disturbing truth that Adam Lindmark was tortured and murdered, Janice Wendall murdered, and the Great Lakes Bay Art Museum robbed of two valuable paintings. My God, he thought, nothing in his long experience as a detective prepared him for this. Clark was convinced that the murders were by a professional killer. Meaning he'd most likely wrongfully believed that Lukas Novak was the killer. Someone else wanted these paintings, and they murdered anyone preventing them from taking the artwork. Who was that killer? He didn't have a clue. Perhaps it was time to talk to Novak again. Maybe he had some ideas.

Chapter Fifty-Three

New York City
July 22, 2019

Sergei Konstantin

Konstantin met a second time with Hirsch. He delivered the Wendall painting and the other Bouguereau painting he found at the Great Lakes Bay Art Museum. Hirsch laughed when he gave her the second Bouguereau painting.

"Konstantin, thank you for the gift; I already own the original painting. You took the forgery."

She was delighted to take possession of the other Bouguereau painting. She truly treasured this piece and couldn't believe that she would ever own a more beautiful painting.

Days later, when Konstantin walked into Hirsch's office, he could tell something was wrong. She was angry.

Konstantin asked, "Is something wrong, Ms. Hirsch?"

"Is there something wrong?" Pointing to the second Bouguereau painting, she said, do you know what this is?"

"Yes, Ms. Hirsch. It's the Bouguereau painting you so desire."

"Do you think I wouldn't find out that this painting is a fake? Just like the one I already own,"

Konstantin was a very hardened man, but that didn't mean he didn't fear Hirsch. She was known as a ruthless woman capable of unspeakable crimes against people who stood in her way. He knew that if she thought he had intentionally deceived her, she would eventually have him killed.

"Ms. Hirsch, I assure you that I didn't know it was a fake. Please remember, before I took it from the museum, I asked you should I take the painting or go after Novak. You said take the painting first; if it's not the original, you can go after Novak. So, I took the Bouguereau from the art museum after Wendall had told me it would be used for a fundraiser. I had no reason to believe it was a fake. I thought I was bringing you the original and nothing else. Nothing," Konstantin said in his most serious voice.

"Well, Konstantin, it's not an original. Where is the original, god damn it!"

Konstantin didn't answer and only looked at Hirsch.

"Who has that original painting? I want an answer."

"Ms. Hirsch, I don't know who has the painting; I assure you that I will find the painting and deliver it to you."

Hirsch staring angrily, asked, "What's your first step?"

"At the beginning of my interrogation of Lindmark, he said that he hid the original in a storage unit and said someone must have taken it. At the time, I didn't believe him, and he eventually told me about the Wendall painting. So, I didn't give more thought to what he first told me. He also said two people helped move his belonging to the storage, his girlfriend and his best friend. I will start there. They must know something and may have possession of the painting. If they don't, they'll tell me what I need to know. I will get that painting for you. I give you my word," Konstantin said.

"Konstantin, You don't want to disappoint me again. I want my beautiful painting."

After leaving his meeting with Hirsch, Konstantin returned to his hotel room and contemplated his next move. The more he thought about his time with Lindmark; he seemed certain that the painting had been stolen from storage. Would his girlfriend or best friend do that to him? Maybe they worked together? When you're talking about a painting worth millions, perhaps it's easier to steal from someone you know, even if you care for them. Like they always say, "money talks." He further thought that even if they didn't take the painting, he didn't have any other leads. So maybe they could help him find the person or people who took the painting. He knew, no matter what, he would find the painting. He wasn't going to disappoint Ms. Hirsch again.

Chapter Fifty-Four

Saginaw, Michigan
July 27, 2019

Lukas Novak

After being released from jail, I knew I would force myself to work today when I entered my office. I needed to move forward, and I knew Liz would be around, and she'd believe I had nothing to do with Nicky's murder, no matter how desperate things looked.

As I came into the kitchen, Liz was making coffee. She turned around and gave me a heartfelt hug.

"How are you, Lukas?" she asked.

"Never worse. Damn it, what the hell is going on in my life? Adam's dead. Nicky's dead. I'm arrested for Nicky's murder. I have no idea what the hell is going on, but I've made up my mind I will find Adam's and Nicky's killer, I promise you and myself."

Liz looked at me, and I could see a determination on her face too.

"Let's think about it and take one killing at a time. You didn't kill Adam, so who did? Do you think Natalie could have?" She asked.

"No. Adam told me she has a bad temper, so if he had been killed by a single gunshot or a hit to the head with a blunt object, then I'd think that maybe Natalie lost control and killed him. That's not what's happened; he was methodically tortured and killed," I said.

"So who else? Did you know anyone that hated him that much to torture him? How about a jealous husband?"

"I've thought about that a lot. I don't think Adam was involved with anyone from our area. I know he was seeing a woman from the Detroit Institute of Arts. Maybe she had someone in her life that could have been revengeful. That's a lead I need to give to my attorney and Clark."

"That's a good idea, Lukas," she said, "maybe that's a possibility."

"Also, do you remember me talking about Adam after he was back from Istanbul? He said he had an affair with a woman from Saudi Arabia. She was apparently from a very wealthy family. She and Adam evaded her security detail and went to his hotel. Afterward, she said her family would be very upset, and it would be best for him to hide. He took the threat seriously enough that he cut his stay short in Istanbul and took a train to Ankara, and then flew home from there. Perhaps they tracked him down and made an example of him. The torture would fit a killing of this type," I said.

"So we don't know who killed Adam. How about Nicky? Who would have killed her?" Liz asked.

I shook my head. "It wasn't me; that's all I know."

"Lukas, for Adam's and Nicky's murders, you're not going to prove you didn't do it. You don't have the facts on your side for that approach. You'll need to show other possibilities giving a jury reasonable doubt," Liz said.

"So we've listed some others who may have killed Adam. How about Nicky? I mean, thinking in terms of establishing reasonable doubt, who could have killed her? Maybe the killings aren't related. If a Saudi family killed Adam, why would they kill Nicky? I don't see any connection. Or if a jealous husband or boyfriend killed him, there wouldn't be any motivation to kill Nicky. So who else would want to see Nicky dead? Was she having trouble with anyone else that you knew about?" Liz asked.

"I don't think so. Only Natalie."

"Ok, what I'm saying is it making any sense? she continued. "Your game plan is to create reasonable doubt that someone other than you killed Nicky because you have others who may have murdered Adam."

"Liz, you're talking about creating reasonable doubt. I'm talking about finding the killer or killers of Adam and Nicky."

Chapter Fifty-Five

Saginaw, Michigan
July 23, 2019

Lukas Novak

When Clark called me and said he wanted to meet, I hotly said, "Not without my attorney."

Clark added that it was about the murder of Janice Wendall, and I wasn't a person of interest.

"What the hell? Janice is dead? How'd she die?"

"Murdered," Clark answered.

"I'll be right over." Clark was waiting for me and took me into his private office, making it clear this wasn't an interrogation.

"Mr. Novak, we found Janice Wendall in her home this morning with a single shot to her head. I'll be blunt, Mr. Novak, I think we're dealing with a professional killer. I'm sure you remember that Adam Lindmark was shot with a single bullet to the head, in addition to being tortured. We're running ballistics, and we'll find out if both shots came from the same gun."

"So, you don't think I'm the murderer?"

"What I think, Mr. Novak is that I need your help. After Mrs. Wendell's murder, two paintings were stolen from the Great Lakes Bay Art Museum. I talked with the museum's director, Sheila Reading, and she told me that both paintings were extremely valuable. Both were worth millions of dollars. The painting owned by Mrs. Wendall may be worth

$10 million. Both paintings were at the museum because of a planned fundraiser. Today, Mrs. Reading drove to Mrs. Wendall's home to discuss the fundraiser and discovered her dead in her living room. We believe she may have been killed soon after the time Lindmark was murdered. My question for you, who did Mr. Lindmark know who would know about his involvement with these paintings?"

I stared at Clark in disbelief.

"What to hell is going on, detective? My God, now Janice is dead."

Putting my head in my hands, I considered Clark's question.

"It was common knowledge that the museum owned a Bouguereau painting. It was on their website. The other painting was a different story. Janice knew the painting was very valuable. I'm not sure if she thought it was worth $10 million, but she loved that painting. It was a vivid reminder of the best times in her life with her husband. To keep the painting safe, she was very secretive about its existence. As far as I know, the only people that knew about her painting were Sheila, myself, and of course, Adam."

Clark thought about this a moment.

"I'll talk to Mrs. Reading to find out if she knew of anyone else who knew about the painting. Are you sure no one else knew?"

I shook my head, "No one."

Clark said, "Who do you know that Mr. Lindmark may have told about the painting?"

"The only person I know that Adam stayed in touch with was Paul Rothstein. They have known each other since their days at NYU. I know he went to New York to see Paul from time to time. I have no idea what they talked about."

Clark nodded, "I remember Paul Rothstein. I followed up with him after Lindmark's death. Three of the last calls on Lindmark's phone were to or from Rothstein. It's time I talked with him again."

Before I left, I told Clark about a woman Adam saw working at the Detroit Institute of Arts.

"Perhaps her jealous lover killed Adam and also wanted the painting?" I guessed.

"I'll look into the possibility," Clark said.

In the meantime, if anything else comes to mind about the painting or Janice's death, I'll be in touch," I said.

Clark nodded.

"Does this mean you don't think I murdered Nicky either?"

"I don't know what to think. Novak, how did that poison end up on your shirt? Think about that. If you didn't kill Winters, then who could have set you up? Answer that question, and maybe you'll prove you're not the murderer."

Chapter Fifty-Six

Saginaw, Michigan
July 25, 2019

Detective Tobias Clark

Clark arranged a meeting with Reading later that afternoon. She was in an awful state of mind. Having discovered her friend and supporter was murdered, coupled with the theft of two valuable art pieces, left Sheila mentally reeling. She knew she needed to help Clark all she could when she felt like hiding in her dark bedroom under her covers.

They met in Sheila's office at the art museum. Clark realized that she was having a hard time focusing.

"Sheila," Clark started, trying to pull her out of a distant stare, "I know this is very hard for you, and I'm sorry to ask you questions, but I need to find Mrs. Wendall's murderer. It seems clear that the theft of the paintings from the museum and her death are tied together. Mr. Novak told me that Mrs. Wendall tried to keep the ownership of her painting a secret and told very few people. He said that as far as he knew, only Adam Lindmark, you, and he were the people that knew. However, you said that you picked the painting up. I know it was a large framed canvas, and you couldn't have done that by yourself. So how many other people knew about Mrs. Wendall's painting?"

Sheila tried to focus, "I took my assistant with me to pick up the painting. He knew the ownership of the painting needed to be kept a secret. I don't think he talked to anyone about it. He's here today, and you can talk to him yourself. I don't know anyone else that Janice told about her painting. It was very valuable, and she was always concerned it would be stolen."

Clark followed up by asking, "I think her murder and the death of Mr. Lindmark are connected to the theft of the paintings. Does that make sense to you?"

"I don't know, detective. I'm not sure how to connect the dots. Why murder Adam? If they wanted to steal the paintings, they could just as easily have done that without killing him."

Clark suggested, "Maybe they needed information from him to find the paintings, and that's why they tortured him before killing him? Mrs. Reading, can you think of anyone else that may know something about this whole situation?"

"I'm sorry, detective, I don't. If I think of anything, I'll be sure to call you. In the meantime, I'll continue to work with the other police officers about the stolen art. I need to contact our insurance carrier, and I'm sure the insurance won't be close to covering our losses."

After leaving Sheila Reading, Clark called Paul Rothstein's office and asked to talk with him. He was told that Mr. Rothstein didn't work there anymore. After telling the receptionist that he was a police detective, she finally said that Mr. Rothstein was fired a few days earlier. Clark immediately called the NYPD and asked for homicide. He spoke with the homicide detective about the deaths of Adam Lindmark and Janice Wendall. He wanted help interviewing Paul Rothstein as he seemed to be involved in both murders. Clark explained that Lindmark and Wendall were all murdered in the same fashion, with a single shot to the head. He said they were looking to confirm it was from the same gun.

Clark also shared that he believed that the murders were somehow related to the theft of two valuable paintings. He said he'd send him the pictures of the paintings and further information about the artist, William Bouguereau. The NYPD detective said one of his colleagues was involved in art theft, and perhaps he could be some assistance. Maybe the Feds would also want to be involved. Clark told him the paintings were worth as much as $10 million, and he would appreciate all the help he could get because he didn't have anything firm to go on. The NYPD detective said he'd find Paul Rothstein and interview him about the murders and try to determine if they were tied to his dismissal from his brokerage firm.

Chapter Fifty-Seven

Saginaw, Bay City, and Midland
Michigan
September 28, 2019

Lukas Novak

It was well past 6:00, and Liz and I were still working in the office. We had concerns about how clients would react to my being charged with the murder of my girlfriend. Well, I was on a roll as I laughed to myself. The death of Adam may be overlooked, now the murder of Nicky and Janice was too much. Many of our clients had already called to say they were looking for another architect. A few stayed with us, primarily because of their loyalty to Liz. Laughing to myself again, could it get worse? Adam, Nicky, my arrest, Janice, and now losing my practice. If it weren't so ridiculous that my life could fall apart so dramatically in just a few days, I'd simply give up. Giving up wasn't my nature; my dad taught me as a boxer that you must never have that defeatist frame of mind. Always, always, think positive. That approach allowed me to overcome some tough opponents when I was boxing. Now, I needed to heed my dad's advice more than ever. It may save my life.

"We are going to survive all of this," Liz said. "The people that truly know you are behind you."

"No, Liz, the clients who stayed are with us because they believe in you. It's up to me to prove my innocence. And I will."

"You will. I know you will," she smiled with the warmth that made me realize once again what a loyal friend Liz continued to be.

"So, are we finished working for the night?" she asked. "Want to go for a drink?"

"Liz, I'd love to, and I know this seems a little odd; Natalie asked me to have dinner with her tonight."

"Really? Have you talked to her since Nicky's death?"

"No. However, she told me that she needed to talk to someone and thought I'd be the best person because I was suffering too."

"Well," Liz smiled, "that should make for a very intriguing dinner. At her condo?"

"No, Liz, we're meeting at a restaurant in Bay City. Hey, just to be clear, there's absolutely nothing romantic going on with her; after all, Nicky was just murdered."

"That was insensitive of me. Seriously, I know you're grieving. Besides, she's not your type. As usual, you're trying to be kind to someone that needs your help. I hope you have a good dinner and talking ends up being good for both of you," she said.

I arrived early at That's Michigan, which serves only Michigan-produced food and beverages. I thought perhaps I was dressed a bit too formally as I was still wearing the dark suit, button-down white shirt, and dark tie that I'd worn earlier that morning for an important first meeting with a client. Unfortunately, the new client didn't show up. So, I overdressed for no reason.

I should have gone home to change and didn't, so I took off my tie and unbuttoned my collar, and ordered a bourbon on the rocks. The bourbon was made in Northern Lower Michigan, and I wondered how it would taste and was pleasantly surprised. While sipping my drink, I worried about how difficult a meaningful conversation with Natalie might be. I knew we were both suffering from the loss of someone we loved. Maybe that would make the evening just maudlin, and I didn't need an outpouring of our grief.

Natalie's arrival reminded me of her incredible beauty. She was dressed in a dark blue skirt and light blue blouse that brought out the best in her tan skin—a gold necklace set off her sophisticated look. I got up to greet her, and though I wasn't sure that I should, I gave her a light hug.

"Lukas, thanks for having dinner with me."

I smiled and noticed a sadness in her eyes that added to her worn-down look.

"I'm sorry for not being a gentleman and waiting to order a drink until you joined me, but I was early and ..."

"No need to apologize. Whatever you're drinking looks good, and I think I'll have the same thing. Is it bourbon?" She asked.

"Yes, one of those Michigan bourbons made around Traverse City. It's pretty good."

The waitress came over and took Natalie's order and left us menus. The conversation was awkward, and Natalie started crying.

"I'm sorry, Lukas, I shouldn't have asked you to dinner. It's just that I'm horribly lonely and sad. I didn't know who else to talk to that could understand."

"Natalie, don't apologize; I'm going through the same feelings. I'm blessed because even though I've been charged with murdering Nicky, I have my work and some loyal friends. Whatever I do, I just keep thinking of Nicky's and Adam's murders."

"I want you to know that I don't believe for a moment that you had anything to do with Nicky's death. You're incapable of harming anyone, and if there's anything I can do to help, you can count on me to be there for you," she said.

When the waitress arrived with her drink, Natalie still had tears streaming down her cheeks. She took a tissue from her purse and dried her eyes.

"Have you eaten here before? I think everything is very good," she said, trying her best to lighten the mood.

Taking her lead, I started talking about the good times with Nicky and Adam. Natalie laughed about some of the silly things we did and asked me if I remembered when we went to New York. Adam knew all the great places to go.

"One night, we ended up in some Irish pub and drank shots of some special Irish whiskey, and Adam insisted it was so pure we wouldn't have a hangover the next morning," she said.

"Oh, I do, and was he ever wrong. I could barely get out of bed the next day," I painfully recalled.

Natalie giggled, "And Nicky couldn't or wouldn't get up, and so the three of us went out for breakfast and brought her back a bagel and coffee. She could barely drink the coffee and took a couple of nibbles from her bagel," she laughed.

Natalie continued to reminisce. "The following day, we were right back at it, and Nicky was leading the charge," she giggled again.

"Right, and we were all enjoying the Frick Museum, except Nicky, because she wanted to go to the Yankees baseball game. The one thing we agreed on was no Irish whiskey," I said.

We talked and laughed about the good times over dinner and eventually wondered who killed Adam.

"I think whoever killed Adam killed Nicky," she said.

"I don't know. Natalie?" I questioned. "If this was a revenge thing, why kill Nicky. You were Adam's girlfriend. Do you suppose that it was someone out to get me? Killing my best friend and my girlfriend? Then they set me up for the murder of Nicky."

"Who'd want to do that to you? Can you think of anybody?" she asked.

"I've thought and thought about it. I can't think of anyone that would have that type of grudge and hatred for me."

We continued talking about various explanations, and nothing seemed to make sense. Finally, being completely talked out, we agreed to call it a night. We enjoyed the evening enough and decided to have dinner on Saturday in Midland.

On my drive back to Saginaw, I was surprised by how much I enjoyed the evening and was taken aback by Natalie's caring side. I admitted that I looked forward to Saturday.

Chapter Fifty-Eight

Saginaw, Bay City, and Midland
Michigan
September 28, 2019

Natalie Collins

On the way home, Natalie thought about Lukas' sadness. Any remorse she felt was now gone. Lukas seemed to have recovered from that bitch's death just fine. She was also sure that he'd never be convicted; the reasonable doubt thing would save him. She was so proud of herself, the tears, the empathetic ear, and the willingness to help Lukas. Beautiful. He'd never guess that she was the one who killed her.

Natalie drove home and felt happy, happier than since the day Nicky died. The bottom line was that no matter how much it hurt Lukas, Nicky deserved to die.

Interestingly, she did enjoy talking and laughing with Lukas and found him more and more attractive as the evening went on. She began wondering what it would be like to go to bed with him. She smiled to herself, and she knew if she wanted that to happen, it would, just like it did with every other man she wanted.

Chapter Fifty-Nine

Saginaw, Bay City, and Midland
Michigan
September 28, 2019

Lukas Novak

The next morning I arrived early at the office and was enjoying my second cup of coffee when Liz arrived.

"Well, you're in early, Mr. Novak."

"So are you, Ms. Bowers. Can I get you a cup of coffee?"

"That's a rhetorical question, right? Of course, you can. And how was your dinner with Ms. Collins?"

"Liz, I was surprised that we truly enjoyed each other's company. It was a good evening. I've never seen Natalie in that light; she was thoughtful and a good listener. Caring is the word that comes to my mind. We talked about the past and laughed. It was the first time I've laughed since Nicky...."

"Lukas, I'm happy for you. You deserve it," Liz interrupted.

"Thank you, Liz. We've made plans to go out Saturday for dinner."

Liz paused and gave me a severe look. "Are you sure that's a good idea?"

"Why, because Nicky just died?" I asked.

"Yes, that and other reasons. People may view the two of you together as a reason for you to have killed Nicky."

"But Liz, it wasn't like I was married to Nicky. She wasn't my wife. I wouldn't need to kill her if I wanted to be with Natalie. Besides, yes, I loved Nicky very much, and I'm terribly sad she's no longer in my life, but Natalie and I are in similar circumstances. She lost Adam, and I lost Nicky. We're being supportive of each other. Don't you think this is good for both of us? Just to be clear, Liz, this isn't about romance."

"Lukas, whether it's about romance or not, I still think you should take a low profile for a while. Besides, did you ever think that maybe, just maybe, that Natalie is the killer?"

"What?"

"Yes, she could be. Adam had an affair with Nicky, and Natalie has a violent temper. Adam told you that many times. He was trying to get away from her, remember? He wasn't even going to tell her he was leaving town. If she is revengeful, then maybe, just maybe, she poisoned Nicky. Think about it. She could have known where you kept your hidden house key and slipped in and poisoned your shirt. Lukas, come on. Who else would want to kill Nicky?"

"Jesus, Liz, I can't believe you're saying this. If I didn't know better, I'd say you're jealous."

"I care for you, Lukas. I don't want any more bad things to happen to you. I know you're mourning and lonely. Just be careful with this woman. I think she could hurt you in more ways than one. I know you don't want to consider the possibility that she could have killed Adam and Nicky. Perhaps it was revenge, or maybe she wanted to be with you. I don't know. Somehow it doesn't seem right to me."

"Liz, I don't want to talk about this anymore," I said in a disappointed voice.

"Ok, ok. We've got plenty of work to do, so I won't mention it again," she said.

We worked in virtual silence the rest of the morning, only talking when necessary to go over a file. I said I was going out at lunch and asked if I could get anything for her. She said she was working through lunch and leaving early. After I got back, Liz came into my office.

"Hey boss, I'm sorry I didn't mean to offend you."

"It's ok, Liz. Why are you leaving early?"

"Carl said a deal that he'd been working on came through, and he wants to celebrate. He's planning for us to go to Detroit this weekend. Nice restaurant and hotel."

"Good for you, Liz. Have a great time and say hello to Carl."

Liz stopped outside of my door, "I'm sorry. You know I'd never do anything to hurt you. Please be careful."

I smiled at Liz, and she turned and left for the weekend.

As she got in her car, I worried that celebrating with Carl wouldn't be as much fun as it should be because she'd be concerned about me. She sensed that behind Natalie's beautiful face was an evil woman. I just couldn't believe that about Natalie.

Saturday late afternoon, I thought about dinner with Natalie and pondered what I should wear. It occurred to me this was something that I rarely gave much thought to doing. I selected light gray pants, a black dress tee shirt, and a dark gray sports jacket. Arriving at the Great Lakes Bay Country Club well ahead of Natalie, I ordered an Angel Envy Manhattan. The Club has an impressive entrance and waiting area with beautiful tapestries and a fireplace. Finding a cozy chair, I started enjoying my cocktail and looking forward to seeing Natalie. Liz's warning to be careful overtook my thoughts. By nature, I'm careful and wasn't going to be carried away by this woman, regardless of her beauty. When she walked through the elegant entrance doors, she was stunning. The club host asked if she was my guest. I nodded.

"Very well-done, Mr. Novak. Very well done," the host said approvingly.

Natalie was wearing a white skirt that showed off her long legs and a tight black knit top complimenting her slender shoulders. A colorful scarf set off her Parisian look. I greeted her, and unlike our last meeting, I didn't hesitate to give her a warm embrace that she returned.

As we were seated for dinner, she commented, "I see again you were gracious in waiting to order your first drink with me," she teased.

"Guilty, no gentleman here, unfortunately. I was here so early that I wanted to enjoy the peacefulness of the moment. What are you going to have?"

"A Kettle One martini," she told the server, "dirty, straight up, with blue cheese stuffed olives."

Once her drink arrived, we toasted, although I'm unsure what we had in mind with our toast.

She said to me, "I'm so glad we have each other. Truly, I think I was beginning to go mad. Thank you for helping me."

I smiled and told her that she was helping me as much as I was helping her. Our conversation was easy and interesting to both of us, and soon we found we'd had finished dinner and ordered a Port for dessert. Maybe it was the wine, but I found myself enjoying my time with Natalie. Liz's words came back to me when Natalie asked me if I wanted to return to her condo. Thinking of her warning, I told her it was terrible timing. She looked disappointingly at me.

"Is the evening ending already?" she asked in a pouty way.

"Natalie, I don't want it to end. Tomorrow morning my mother is visiting, and I need to go grocery shopping before she gets there. So it's bad timing. Let's get together next week."

She smiled at me and said, "You are a perfect son. I admire you for that. Yes, next week."

We agreed upon a day and time, and she said she was cooking for me. I walked her to her car, and we hugged. Natalie looked up at me, expecting a kiss. Two things occurred to me: I didn't want to kiss her; and how much I missed Nicky. Besides, maybe Liz's warning was something I should heed.

Later at home, I began thinking that maybe dinner at her condo next week could be a mistake. If Natalie wanted a deeper relationship with me, I knew that wouldn't happen and wondered about her legendary temper. Would I see it? I guess I'd find out.

I was wrong about Liz. Once she and Carl hit the casinos, she wasn't thinking much about anything else. She was having too much fun. She and Carl loved to gamble, maybe for the first time; he was paying for everything, making it many times more fun for Liz. After playing the slots, spending hours at the tables, and losing Carl's money, they had a lovely fine dining experience. As they started their second bottle of wine, Liz asked Carl about the source of their splurge.

He smiled. "It was something that just came up."

"Well, I'm happy it did," she said.

"Somebody's abandoned a storage unit, including some antique furniture that I was able to sell for $10 grand. Of course, I did it on the side, so there are no taxes," he boasted."

"Carl, never look a gift horse in the mouth," she said as she had another sip of her wine.

Chapter Sixty

Saginaw, Michigan
July 30, 2019

Sergei Konstantin

While landing at Midland-Bay City-Saginaw airport, Konstantin thought how interesting; only a short time ago, he'd never heard of Saginaw, Michigan, and now he was returning. But his job took him many places in the world, and this assignment was much less dangerous than his numerous experiences in Eastern Europe. After renting a car, he drove to the Black Cat Café. While visiting the café during his last trip to Saginaw, he discovered the smallness of Saginaw. By talking to just a few people, he found all about Adam Lindmark, including that he slept with his best friend's girlfriend, Nicky Winters, the night before he killed him.

Now he needed more information and found a seat next to women chatting away. As he sipped his black coffee, they looked at him, and he smiled back to the one facing him. Konstantin had been told that he was handsome, and he found that he could use his appearance to help him from time to time. He continued to exchange glances with the woman, and finally, he rose and approached their table.

"Excuse me, ladies, I'm not from here, and I was hoping to locate an old friend of mine that I understand is living in Saginaw. His name is Adam Lindmark. Would you happen to know him?"

The previously smiling woman's face turned blank. "Please sit down.

I'm sorry to tell you that your friend was murdered."

Konstantin expressed shock. "Murdered. My God, what happened?"

"Adam was a friend, and he spent time here having coffee with us. It was a complete shock."

Another woman at the table joined in. "We loved Adam."

The other women either murmured it was true or nodded their heads in sadness.

The woman continued, "He was not only murdered; but tortured first."

Two of the woman began to cry. "None of us can stand the thought of Adam being harmed that way."

Konstantin asked, "When did it happen?"

"Only a couple of weeks ago. I'm sorry you won't be able to see your friend. We had a wake for him, and he had so many friends."

"It turned out to be a celebration of Adam's life," another woman added.

The woman who initially smiled at Konstantin said, "It's been a terrible time for our community. A very dear woman, Mrs. Wendall, was also murdered in her home."

All the women were now staring at Konstantin, and he expressed shock and sadness.

"That's not all," exclaimed another woman. "There was another murder. A friend of Adam's."

"Yes, it was Adam's best friend's girlfriend, Nicky Winters. She used to work here."

"Poisoned," said two women at once.

"And Lukas Novak, her boyfriend, has been charged with murder."

In unison, all the women said, "We don't believe Lukas did it."

"He's a wonderful man and loved Nicky so much it couldn't have been him," said another.

Konstantin studied the women. "You mean to tell me in the last few weeks you've had three murders?" The women nodded. "And one of them was Adam's good friend Lukas?"

"No, no. Lukas's girlfriend was murdered. Lukas is charged with murder."

Now Konstantin was concerned. If in jail, it would be much harder to interrogate Novak. "Is he in jail?" he asked.

"No, he's out on bail and still working at his architectural office. We heard he had dinner the other night with Adam's girlfriend."

One of the women quickly added, "They're only friends. I'm sure nothing is going on between them. Lukas loved Nicky, and Natalie was crazy for Adam."

"Yes, almost sure nothing is going on," added another woman with a knowing smile on her face.

Konstantin responded, "So Adam had a close relationship with a woman here in Saginaw?"

"No, she wasn't from Saginaw. She lives in Bay City. Natalie Collins."

One woman commented, "You'll know it if you see her; she's beautiful and dresses like she's living in New York."

One woman laughed, "I'm sure it makes it easier to have dinner with her even though he cared for Nicky."

Other women frowned at her. One said, "That's a mean thing to say about Lukas."

"Well, ladies, I guess I've traveled a long way to see my friend only to hear bad news. It's probably best I leave Saginaw on the next flight before another murder happens. I don't want it to be me."

At that, Konstantin got up and left the café. The women were all watching him go when a barista joined them.

"Do any of you recognize that man?" The barista asked. The women at the table said they didn't.

"Well, I do. He came in here before Adam's death, and I was working, asking about him. He seemed very interested in finding out everything he could about Adam. Soon after that, Adam was dead."

All the women stared at the barista. "Do you think he had anything to do with Adam's murder?"

"I don't know, but I'm calling Detective Clark right now and telling him I've seen this man again. I don't think Lukas killed Adam. Someone else did. Now this man wants to know about Lukas and Natalie. Maybe he's back for them."

Within minutes Clark was at the Black Cat Café. He talked to the barista and all the women who spoke to Konstantin. He then asked everyone to go to the police station to describe the man to a police artist to create a likeness. They all said they would. One woman also told him that he spoke with a slight accent and flew into Saginaw. Clark began checking with the airport to see if he could determine who this man was and where he was from. Then he called Novak and told him they needed to meet and would come to his office right then.

As soon as Clark entered Lukas' office, Liz greeted him and led him into a conference room.

"Would you like a cup of coffee or water, detective?"

"No, thank you, Ms. Bowers. I need to have a quick meeting with Mr. Novak."

As I entered the room, Liz was leaving. I asked Clark what was so urgent.

"Mr. Novak, this is a matter that may also involve Ms. Bowers. Would you object to having her be part of our discussion?"

"Absolutely not. I'll get her."

After Liz and I sat down, Clark began to explain.

"I received a call an hour ago from a barista at the Black Cat Café. I met with her and four other women who were at the café. The barista told me that a man came in today that she recognized. She said she'd seen him once before. It was the day before Mr. Lindmark was murdered. She said that he had been asking about him and had mentioned it to me when I did my first investigation. It was a dead end. Anyway, today she saw him again. He was very interested in hearing about you, Mr. Novak and Ms. Collins. He talked with four women and, being chatty; they told him quite a bit about the two of you. Here's my point, the person who killed Mr. Lindmark and Mrs. Wendall is a professional. I'm not sure of the connection, but I am concerned he's now after Ms. Collins and you."

I stared at Clark, struggling to take in what he said.

"You think a professional killer is after Natalie and me?"

"I wouldn't be here right now if I didn't think your life is endangered.

I've called and left a message for Ms. Collins telling her what I've just told you. I don't think she's interested in talking to me. I want you to call her if you would please. Maybe she'll take your call. Tell her what I've told you. My advice to you and her is to take a vacation and leave town until I have a chance to find out more about this man. The women at the café are at the police station, having our artist do a composite sketch of the man. I should have it shortly; once I do, I'll send it to you and Ms. Bowers so you can be looking out for this person. Again, I strongly urge you to leave town for a while."

"Thank you, detective. I see how serious you're taking this man. Liz, cancel all our appointments for the next week. We're closing the office, and you're taking a paid vacation to go somewhere. You've been talking about going to Boyne City. I think now may be a good time to make that happen," I said.

Liz, with a look of surprise on her face, asked, "And where are you going?"

"Nowhere. Our chance of getting this guy is better if I'm around. I'm the bait."

Clark shook his head. "Mr. Novak, that's not a good idea. You need to go too."

"Detective, I can handle myself."

"Be realistic. If this man is after you, he's a professional killer. You won't stand a chance."

"That may be true, but if we are going to catch the man that killed Adam and Nicky, I'm willing to put my life at risk. Of course, detective, I'm counting on you to apprehend him first," I smiled.

With a resolute look, Clark said, "I see I'm not going to change your mind. I'll have officers watch your home and office."

As Clark left the office, he noticed a car he'd seen earlier parked a block and a half away was still there. He thought there was no one in the car but saw a man duck down at a second glance. This was not good.

Chapter Sixty-One

Saginaw, Michigan
July 30, 2019

Detective Tobias Clark

Detective Clark decided to take a closer look at the man in the black car, so when he left Lukas' office, he circled on a side street so that he could read the license plate number. He immediately called in for identification and was told shortly afterward that it was a rental car from the airport. His office also sent him a composite sketch of the person seen at the Black Cat Café.

Clark decided to talk to the people at the airport and called Lukas.

"Mr. Novak, as I was leaving your office, I noticed a car park down the street from you. It was there when I arrived, and it seemed suspicious to me. I called in the license plate number and found out it was a rental from the airport. I'm on my way there to find out the driver's name. In the meantime, I think you need to go somewhere safe. You may want to check and see if the car is still there. It's a black Honda Accord. Make sure the driver doesn't see you, and Ms. Bowers is out of your office before you go. I'm sending a police car over right now."

"Hold on, detective, I'll look. Detective, there's no black car on the street."

"Mr. Novak, I believe this could be the killer. He'll be back. Please go somewhere safe. Again, I'll have officers watching your home and office. Did you get a hold of Ms. Collins?"

"I was reaching out to her when your call came in. I'll call her again right now," I said.

"Tell her that her life may be endangered and get out of town and go somewhere safe. I'm also going to email you the composite sketch. Let me know if you recognize the man. I'm sending the sketch to Ms. Collins too. Please be careful," Clark stressed.

Clark arrived at MBS Airport and met with the rental car people and airline officials. By looking at the sketch, surveillance tapes, and rental car company's and the airlines' records, they determined that the car was rented by a Mr. Peter Snyder of New York City, and payments were made by a credit card owned by a limited liability company. Clark had his people trace the credit card ownership, again a dead end.

Clark called Lukas back and brought him up to speed on what he'd discovered and called the New York detective he'd been working with and filled him in on what was going on in Saginaw, sending him the sketch. The detective said he would do some searching and get back to Clark.

Clark called Natalie Collins again, left a message, and began worrying; did the killer already track her down? Was she already dead? He drove to Bay City to find her. On the way, he called Lukas again.

Chapter Sixty-Two

Bay City, Michigan
July 30, 2019

Sergei Konstantin

Konstantin watched Clark go into Novak's office and leave. Perhaps Clark was studying his car, and when he drove by the cross street behind him, he knew that Clark was in law enforcement. Concerned, Konstantin went to the local mall parking lot and was able to steal a white Chevy Impala. He then changed license plates with another car on the other side of the mall. This would buy him some time if the police were involved, he thought.

Konstantin's priority was finding and talking to Novak and Collins. He called Ms. Hirsch and gave her an update. She was impatient and reminded him that she wanted the Bouguereau painting sooner than later. He told her he understood and headed to Bay City to talk with Natalie Collins.

Chapter Sixty-Three

Bay City, Michigan
July 30, 2019

Lukas Novak

Perhaps an assassin was stalking Natalie and me, and I was taking the threat seriously. If anyone could get to me, it could be by threatening my mother's life, causing me to shiver, so I called her.

"Mom, how are you today? That's good. I have something serious to talk about with you. Yes, I'm ok. No, I wasn't in an accident. Mom, listen! There's a man that may be trying to hurt me. The police are watching over me, so I'm not worried. I'm worried about you. I am probably overacting, but I'm not taking any chances. You've been talking about visiting Aunt Sally. I want you to buy an airline ticket and leave today for that visit. No, I'm not being silly or crazy. I want you to call Aunt Sally as soon as I hang up. Then call and get a ticket to get out of town. As soon as you book the flight, call me. I'll drive to Royal Oak and take you to the airport. Mom, you need to do exactly as I've just told you. No arguments. Mom, I know you trust me. Make the calls right away. Ok, Mom. I love you too. I'll be waiting for your call."

An hour later, I received a call from my mother. She had a flight for 8:00 that night. I left for Mom's to ensure she'd get safely on the flight to her sister's.

On the way to Mom's, I received a call from Natalie.

"Lukas, Detective Clark was here. I'm scared, Lukas. If this man killed Adam and Mrs. Wendall and is now after you and me, I don't know what to do."

"Natalie, you need to get out of town, someplace that he wouldn't think of looking. I'm taking my mother to the airport right now. I want to make sure she's out of town, so she's not part of this mess."

"Your mother? Why?" Natalie asked.

"If this guy is trying to get to me and has done his homework, he'll find out the person I care about most is my mother. He could use my mother to leverage me. More importantly, he could harm my mother," I explained

"My God, I never thought of something like that. Maybe I'm glad I don't have anyone for the first time in my life. We've never talked about this; I'm an only child, I have no family. Lukas, I'm all alone. I don't know where to go. Can I stay with you? "

"I don't think that's a good idea. If the assassin is after both of us and we're together, that makes his job that much easier. Go on a vacation. Someplace you have been thinking of going. And don't wait. Pack up your things and go right now," I stressed

"Please, Lukas, let me stay with you," Natalie pleaded, "I'm scared."

"You can't, Natalie. It's just a bad idea. Now don't waste time. Pack and go."

"Ok, Lukas. I'll start packing now."

Chapter Sixty-Four

Bay City, Michigan
July 30, 2019

Detective Tobias Clark

Clark finally arrived at Natalie's apartment. He knocked, no answer. He knocked again, no response. Clark drove his shoulder into the door until it broke casing and flew open. He was in her apartment. It was quiet, and clothes were spread everywhere. He was too late.

Clark called Natalie and left a message in his most serious voice, "Ms. Collins, this is Detective Clark. I'm at the door of your condo. Where are you?"

Natalie immediately called him back.

"Hello detective, I just left my apartment, and I'm in my car to go away and hide."

"That's very wise of you. Get out of town and don't come back until you hear from me."

"Ok, detective."

Clark put Natalie's door back together as best he could, so it looked like it was locked, and decided to go back to talk to Novak.

No sooner had he left when Natalie realized she had forgotten her makeup bag in her bathroom. She turned around and parked in the lower-level parking lot. Feeling safer knowing that Clark had been at her apartment, she got to her door, finding it broken.

She slowly opened the door, "Detective Clark," she quietly called out. "Detective Clark," she said again as she entered. Looking around, she realized no one was there. Clark must have broken my door down, she thought. She found her bag. Maybe I should have a glass of wine to calm my nerves? She went into the kitchen, opened a white wine bottle, poured herself a glass, and gulped it down. Feeling more relaxed, she began thinking; she had no choice and decided where to hide.

Chapter Sixty-Five

Bay City, Michigan
July 30, 2019

Sergei Konstantin

Konstantin watched Clark leave his car, convinced that the tall African American was the police. He must have talked to the women in the café and surmised he was after Novak and Collins. Clark has warned them about me. That's going to make my job harder, but nothing I can't handle, he thought. Novak or Collins must have the painting, and he was going to find out who and take that damn painting to Ms. Hirsch before she sends someone after him.

When Clark came out of Natalie's building, Konstantin watched him. Clark sat in his car and was talking on his phone. Finally, he drove off, and Konstantin got out of his car and started towards Natalie's apartment. 302 was the number on the building entrance. He didn't think Collins would be there but hoped to learn more about her. He could also look for the painting. If she were there, he'd definitely find out all she knew.

Collins finished her glass of wine and thought about a second. No, she needed to keep her mind sharp and remembered to take her makeup bag and started for her door.

Chapter Sixty-Six

Bay City, Michigan
July 30, 2019

Sergei Konstantin

As Natalie went down the rear stairs of her building to the lower-level parking lot, Konstantin stepped out of the elevator on the third floor. The door to 302 was slightly ajar, and he pushed it open and slowly looked around, checking every room. He realized he'd missed Collins. It was clear she'd been packing her clothes. On the kitchen counter was an open bottle of wine and a glass that had been recently used. "Damn it," he said. "She's already running." It was time he focused on finding Mr. Novak.

Leaving Collins' apartment, Konstantin drove north and checked in to a rundown motel in Pinconning, a little town outside Saginaw. He decided to wait for darkness and then go back to Novak's house and study the situation. Just before midnight, he drove to Saginaw and parked three blocks from Novak's, and wearing all black, moved between houses until he had a clear view of Novak's. He spotted the unmarked police car watching the house. There didn't seem to be any sign of Novak. Maybe he'd already gone to bed. Perhaps he decided to leave town. He eventually worked his way up to Novak's garage and looked through the side door window. No car. Novak wasn't home. "Damn, he's made a run for it too." Konstantin decided there was no reason to wait around and walked back to his car and drove to his motel.

He needed to devise a new plan. The police were aware of his presence. It looked like Novak and Collins were hiding. He decided he'd drive back to New York and explain to Hirsch that things needed to cool down before finding the two targets and her painting. Reaching the motel, he gathered his clothes and drove to New York. Hirsch was not going to be happy. He was confident that he could convince her that he would find the painting, and she needed to be patient. He laughed at himself. Hirsch being patient, it would be a first. He realized he'd need to explain it to her another way. On the drive back, he'd have plenty of time to think things through.

Chapter Sixty-Seven

Bay City, Michigan
July 30, 2019

Detective Tobias Clark

When the police arrived to fix Collins' door, it was clear someone had gone through every room looking for something. The officer reported this to Clark, who called Collins and informed her that someone had searched her apartment.

"That's impossible, detective, and I just left the parking structure."

He just missed you. You're incredibly fortunate, Ms. Collins."

Natalie was more frightened than ever. She realized that having a glass of wine might have caused her death and thought about how Adam was tortured and murdered. All of this was going through her mind when she told Clark she would hide out. What she didn't tell him was that she'd gone back to her apartment and was lucky she wasn't there when the killer arrived. She shivered, thinking if she'd had that second glass of wine. She couldn't stop shaking. In her mind, she heard Clark urging her to get out of town, now!

Clark called Novak.

"Mr. Novak, I wanted you to know that someone was in Ms. Collins' apartment and searched for something. She's safe. I just talked to her. She told me she's going somewhere to hide for the time being until we catch this guy."

"Thanks for the update, detective. I'm on my way to my mother's home. I've convinced her to leave town to visit one of her sisters. I'll be taking her directly to the airport to make sure she's safe."

"Now listen, Novak, I know you think you're a tough guy, and you can handle yourself. Normally I'd agree with you. This is different. The man after you is an accomplished killer. I don't want you to go to your house. Find someplace, anyplace else to go. I'm going to get this guy, and when I do, you can come back," Clark sternly stated.

"Sorry, detective. This guy's not scaring me off."

"Damn you, Novak, you're being a complete fool and probably soon a dead fool."

"Thanks, detective. I love you too. Got to go. I'm almost at my mother's house."

Chapter Sixty-Eight

Bay City, Michigan
July 30, 2019

Lukas Novak

I got home at 2:00 in the morning after taking my mother to the Detroit airport. I saw the police car and waved to the officer watching my home. Everything seemed peaceful. I knew this wasn't going to last and was careful entering my home. Perhaps the killer was waiting for me. Carefully going from room to room with my Glock that I purchased when living in downtown Detroit. There was no intruder. No sooner was I in bed than my cell phone buzzed.

"Lukas, it's me, Natalie."

"Natalie, I'm glad you're safe. You're smart to get out of Dodge," I said.

"Lukas, I have nowhere to go, and I'm terrified. If this killer finds me, I know I'm dead. Maybe he has a way of tracking me or something. I'm only a few blocks from your house. Can I stay with you until I can meet with Detective Clark tomorrow and make sure I'm doing all I can?"

"Natalie, you're trouble. OK, come over, but it's just for tonight. Right? You understand?"

"I understand. Thank you, Lukas. I'll be there in a few minutes. Wait for me at the front door."

While waiting, I thought when Liz and Clark find out Natalie's with me, they will question my sanity. I questioned my sanity, but what else could I do? Natalie drove up to the front of my garage. I walked out to meet her and walked over to the police officer. I explained what was going on. Natalie took her things to my front porch. She looked terrible. Well, as awful as Natalie could look. I helped move her bags inside, and she gave me a big hug and repeatedly thanked me.

"You're welcome, Natalie. You can stay in the spare bedroom. It's already made up. The guest bathroom is just around the corner. I'm going to sleep. I'm exhausted. We can talk in the morning."

I went to my bedroom, closed my door, and lay in bed wondering what tomorrow would bring for Natalie and me.

Natalie lay in bed and wondered again how close she came to facing the man who tortured and killed Adam. Would she be so lucky next time? A dark feeling came over her that she hoped would disappear by morning.

Chapter Sixty-Nine

August 1, 2019
Saginaw, Michigan

Detective Tony Petrocelli

After receiving the artist sketch, Clark called his contact at the New York Police Department and forwarded it. Within an hour, he called back.

"Detective Clark, we've studied your composite sketch. We know this man. His name is Sergei Konstantin. He is a known hitman. He works closely with several underworld people and is closely affiliated with those who deal in the art and antiquities black market. From what you've told me of your case, it involves an art conservator who may have been stealing and forging original pieces of art. We have a person in our Manhattan Department specializing in this type of theft. His name is Tony Petrocelli. I know he'll be very interested in this case. He's had several run-ins with Mr. Konstantin and would like nothing better than to bring him to justice.

Later that morning, Petrocelli called and wanted to hear all Clark knew about Konstantin and the killings in specific detail. Clark also explained the sightings of Konstantin and his efforts to go after Novak and Collins. Clark promised to send him the entire file. As the call ended, Petrocelli said he would study the information and call Clark back as soon as he finished. In the meantime, he warned Clark to be very careful, that Konstantin was very clever and ruthless in his dealings. He added that torturing and killing victims gave him pleasure, and to take particular care to protect Novak and Collins.

Petrocelli was an anomaly in the NYPD. He was working in the art and antiques theft division, which was essentially him and one other detective. When his cases involved other matters such as underworld dealing, drugs, and murder, other departments would be involved. Petrocelli was the only son of a New York insurance agent. In high school, he was a gifted baseball player and received athletic and academic scholarships providing him with a full ride to Columbia University. There he studied philosophy and art history. It never occurred to him or his family to become an investigative detective. In his senior year in college, one of his friends joined the FBI, and the FBI hearing of Petrocelli recruited him. For five years, he worked for them, but when he heard about an art investigation involving the NYPD, he reached out to them, and after a series of interviews, he left the FBI and joined the New York police to work on several crimes involving art and the underworld.

Petrocelli had followed art theft cases for years and was well acquainted with the notion that organized crime used artwork as currency for illegal dealings. Hundreds of millions of dollars of artwork have been stolen worldwide and never recovered.

In 1992 the Art Loss Register was started. Tracking these thefts substantiated the belief that a large number of high-value artwork is recovered in parts of the world apart from the country that it was taken. Even though incredible amounts of money and value are involved, art theft is a low priority in almost all countries except Italy. The general public doesn't recognize the serious nature of this crime, and as a result, elected politicians are unwilling to devote tax dollars to address the problem meaningfully. Being one of the art world capitals, New York City has its share of art theft and has worked with the FBI to investigate and solve a few of these many crimes. New York commonly assigned one detective to specialize in art theft, and each of these specialists earned international acclaim for the art they recovered. The NYPD decided to employ an additional detective to focus on art recovery to enhance its public relations image. That's when Petrocelli was brought in due to his connections with the FBI and his art background.

The case in Saginaw was of particular interest to him because of his efforts to arrest Sergei Konstantin and one of his known employers, Beatrice Hirsch. Hirsch's reputation for corruption in Eastern Europe, her passion for buying stolen art, and New York being her permanent home made her a suspect in art thefts worldwide, particularly paintings taken from museums and individuals in New York. Each time Petrocelli attempted to arrest Hirsch, his key witnesses were murdered. Petrocelli was positive that Sergei Konstantin was the murderer in each case. The problem was that Konstantin covered up the murders each time, and there was insufficient evidence to arrest him.

The case in Saginaw sounded different. It appeared that Konstantin was not as careful as he usual. Perhaps being in the small town, he'd become careless. He had already been identified by several people and traced to the rental of a car and airline tickets from New York to Saginaw. Petrocelli thought that Konstantin would never make those errors in New York. Maybe this chance happening would be the opportunity to nail Konstantin and lead to Beatrice Hirsch's arrest.

From Petrocelli's study of Hirsch, he knew that she particularly cared for portraits by painters from the late 1880s, such as Waterhouse and Sargent. Apparently, the paintings involved in Saginaw were by William Bouguereau, one of the finest portrait painters from this period. He studied the pictures of the paintings in question and immediately recognized that one of the paintings, of two girls playing with a ball watched by their mother, was one of Bouguereau's finest works. He estimated the painting could be worth up to $10 million. He believed in Hirsch's mind this would justify any means necessary to acquire this unique piece of art, including torture and murder.

Petrocelli followed up his case study by calling Clark and filling him in on his past efforts to arrest Hirsch and the murders of key witnesses that Petrocelli was confident were done by Konstantin. They agreed that Petrocelli would fly to Saginaw to meet with Clark and talk with Novak and Collins. He stressed to Clark how dangerous Konstantin was and he should do everything he could to protect those two key persons.

After that conversation, Clark ordered two more officers to watch over Novak and Collins, although he wasn't sure where Collins was hiding. He called Novak to give him an update. Clark was surprised when Collins answered the phone.

"Natalie Collins, is that you?"

"I recognize your voice, Detective Clark. I planned on calling you later today," Natalie said.

"I'm sorry, Ms. Collins, I thought I was calling Mr. Novak's phone?"

"You are. He's in the shower, and I recognized your name on his cell phone when the call came in. Can I give him a message?"

"Yes, tell him I want to meet with you and him. I have new information on the man who is following you. I want you to stay where you are. I'm assigning an additional officer to watch over you at Novak's home. Don't leave the house. I'm coming over to talk with you."

"Ok, detective, we'll be waiting for you."

When I finished dressing, Natalie told me about her conversation with Clark. As we waited, we knew the assignment of another officer to watch over us wasn't good news.

When Clark arrived, I offered him a cup of coffee. To my surprise, he accepted, and the three of us sat down in the living room.

Clark started the conversation, "Natalie, I'm relieved you're safe."

"Thank you, Detective Clark. Really, I had nowhere to go. I called Lukas late last night and begged him to let me stay until I could talk to you. I need your help to protect me. I feel that if I hide away at some resort or hotel, he could find me. If he found me..." Natalie stopped short on her sentence and struggled not to cry. "If he found me, he'd probably do to me what he did to Adam, maybe even worse because I'm a woman."

Clark looked directly at Natalie. "We're not going to let that happen. You're safe, and we are going to keep it that way. Lukas and Natalie, what are your plans?"

I realized that Clark was referring to us by our first names for the first time. It was somehow reassuring.

I looked at Natalie. "I'm not sure *we* have a plan. We wanted to talk to you first. If you and Natalie believe she should stay here, I'm ok with that. It will start people talking, of course. Nothing stays a secret in this town."

Clark smiled. "I've already heard that the two of you have been seeing each other. So, you're right. Nothing is a secret. There being no secrets is why we can identify the person after you. The barista at the café identified him for us. I sent both of you the composite sketch. I also sent it to a detective in New York who've I've been working with on this matter. He recognized the man. The NYPD then assigned a detective that specializes in art theft. He also recognized the man as Sergei Konstantin. He is a known hitman for organized crime. At times he's been hired by a woman named Beatrice Hirsch. She's part of organized crime in Eastern Europe, lives in New York, and is a big-time art collector. The new detective we'll be working with is Tony Petrocelli. He's had many dealing with both Hirsch and Konstantin. I know I'm not going to relieve your stress level by telling you this, but you need to know; Petrocelli has been close to arresting Hirsch several times. His key witness was murdered each time, and he believes Konstantin killed them. He was never able to prove it because Konstantin left no evidence of his involvement."

Natalie and I stared blankly at Clark.

Finally, Natalie said, "Well, this confirms what we already believed. We're dealing with a professional killer. He's probably a psychopath based on what he did to Adam."

Clark nodded his head in agreement. "Detective Petrocelli is flying in from New York tomorrow. I want us to meet with him and develop a plan to protect you and capture Konstantin. If Hirsch is involved, arrest her."

I asked, "It seems to me if we knew what Konstantin was after, we'd have a better chance of being successful."

"I agree, Lukas, that's why I want us to meet with Petrocelli. He knows the world of art theft. I'm confident he'll have some thoughts on what's going on with us. I suggest that both of you stay here until we meet with Petrocelli and start developing a plan based on our best guess as to what he wants. Are both of you good with that? Natalie? Lukas?"

We nodded in agreement and said yes at the same time.

"Good, once Petrocelli is in town, I'll call you and set up a meeting. In the meantime, if you need anything, food, or Natalie, your things from your apartment, call me, and I'll have one of the officers come to your door and take the list of what you need. Does that make sense?" Clark asked.

In an attempt at a bit of humor, I looked at the very slender Natalie, "Yes, I've seen how much she eats. We better stock on a lot of food."

She frowned at me, and Clark just laughed and said he'd call us tomorrow. After he left, Natalie looked at me, "Thanks for letting me stay here, Lukas. I'm feeling better, and hopefully, Petrocelli can piece this all together so we can go back to our normal life."

"Your normal life, Natalie. I have a trial coming up for a murder I didn't commit of a woman I loved."

Natalie stared at me and said nothing.

Chapter Seventy

August 2, 2019
Saginaw, Michigan

Detective Tony Petrocelli

When Petrocelli arrived in Saginaw, his priority was meeting Novak and Collins. Clark set up a time for them to meet at Novak's office. When they were all together, and before introductions, Novak asked that his assistant, Liz Bowers, join them. Once Liz was in the conference room, introductions were made, Petrocelli began telling about his history with Konstantin, the person they believed killed Lindmark and Wendall, and maybe Winters.

"Hello everyone, as you've heard, I'm a detective with the NYPD in the art theft department. I'm here in Saginaw for two reasons. First, I believe you're involved in some form of art forgery. And second, I think the persons behind the murders are Sergei Konstantin and Beatrice Hirsch. I'll start with Hirsch. Her family controls several companies. The primary company constructs commercial buildings in Eastern Europe and the Baltic region. She's made a fortune by understanding the black-market underworld and has a ruthless approach to people that get in her way. She relies on a known assassin, Mr. Konstantin, when she has a problem. I know Ms. Hirsch through her purchase of high-end art that's been stolen. I believe she has a tremendous collection that features many genres of art; however, her passion is for romantic realistic portraits from the late

1880s to the early 1900s. She is particularly interested in a painter from that period, Adolphe William Bouguereau. After talking with Detective Clark, I understand that Mr. Lindmark was involved with two Bouguereau paintings, one owned by the art museum and the other by Mrs. Wendall.

I've researched Mr. Lindmark since I talked to you, Detective Clark. Before coming to Saginaw, he worked at several museums throughout the country. Each museum is about the same size as the Great Lakes Bay Art Museum. I have a theory that Mr. Lindmark, while claiming to conserve painting for each museum, actually painted a forgery that he returned to each museum and sold the original to people like Hirsch. I've talked to the CEOs at the six museums he worked at before coming to Saginaw. Each CEO said that it was impossible. Adam Lindmark was respected and admired, and it was inconceivable that he would take advantage of them. I convinced them to confirm their paintings' authenticity. Three of the museums agreed to do that immediately. The others said they would consult with their board of directors. Once examined, I'm sure they'll find their paintings are forgeries.

I believe Mr. Lindmark was working with a long-time friend of his, Paul Rothstein, a stockbroker in Manhattan. Mr. Rothstein has connections to people who would buy the originals from Lindmark. Here's what happened: Lindmark sold Hirsch the forgeries of either the museum painting and or the Wendall painting. It's most probable Lindmark sold her a forgery of Wendall's painting because that painting is worth between $8 to $10 million. He probably either sold the original to another buyer or kept the painting for himself. When Hirsch found out that she bought a fake, she hired Konstantin to locate and bring her the original. He started by visiting Mr. Rothstein. Rothstein transferred $5 million of his and his company's funds to an untraceable account. He's since been fired. I've tried to talk to him, but he refuses. I'm not surprised because I'm sure Konstantin has threatened him and his family.

Rothstein must have told Konstantin about Lindmark, and he came to Saginaw and met with him. I'm guessing he tortured Lindmark to satisfy Hirsch's need for revenge, and then Lindmark told him that Wendall had the original. When Konstantin paid her a visit, she told him the museum had the painting for an exhibit. He then killed Wendall, broke into the museum, stole the two Bouguereau paintings, and took them to Hirsch. But now, Konstantin is back in Saginaw and after you, Mr. Novak, and Ms. Collins. Why? I believe that Konstantin is still looking for the original Wendall painting, and he believes either you have it or you know where it's located.

I'll be blunt. If you have the paintings, turn them over to me now. If you don't, we need to figure out where this painting is before something else happens. What I mean by that is something bad happening to you. I know how Hirsch operates. Even if we apprehend Konstantin, I believe she'll hire someone else to find the painting."

Petrocelli stared at both Lukas and Natalie, "Well, do you have the painting? "No," they answered emphatically.

"Do you know where the painting might be?" Again they answered, "No."

"Well, good," Petrocelli sarcastically said, "that's really helpful. I suggest you focus all your energies on thinking about where we might start looking. In the meantime, you are in grave danger. Konstantin is cunning, clever, and brutal. We'll need to use our finest efforts to protect you."

Clark then added, "We have two officers watching Novak's home at all times. Both Novak and Collins are staying there and have agreed not to leave."

Clark, Collins, and Novak then explained the other security measures we're taking to Petrocelli. Everyone agreed that the police, including Clark and Petrocelli, would be immediately available anytime we sensed that something wasn't right at my home.

Being forthright, Petrocelli told Clark privately that he wasn't sure they could do anything to protect these two if Konstantin wanted them.

Chapter Seventy-One

August 6, 2019
New York City

Sergei Konstantin

Once back in New York, Konstantin talked to Hirsch and explained it would take more time and planning to track down the painting. He assured her that he was giving it his utmost attention. Hirsch was furious. She asked, "Do I need to bring someone else in to do your work for you, Sergei?"

"No, you don't," he replied. "I've got everything under control."

After leaving Hirsch, he followed through on a plan he devised on his way back from Saginaw. He called two people he had worked with many times, Allan and Doris Dean. The Deans were unique because there was nothing special about them. They were in their late 40s of average height and weight, and their facial features could be described as plain. They melted into the background by doing nothing—people no one ever noticed. Konstantin explained the situation and directed them to go to Saginaw and watch over Novak and Collins.

That day the Deans flew to Saginaw and immediately rented a house two and a half blocks from Novak's.

If asked why they were in Saginaw, they had their stories well-rehearsed. She was originally from Michigan and wanted to move back. He was looking for a new job. They thought that Saginaw's low cost of living would be a good place for them to search for a new home.

They took possession of the house, and each morning and evening, they made their slow walk through the neighborhood, eventually walking by Novak's. They noted that Novak's home was on a corner lot, and the police had officers stationed in cars on both streets. It was a 24-hour watch in eight-hour shifts. Deans' study was reported to Konstantin, explaining that Novak had installed a security system on his windows and doors and motion detectors throughout his property. And that Collins was living in Novak's house. From what they could determine, Novak and Collins slept in separate rooms. Both rooms were at the back of the house. Collins' room was closest to the back door. Novak's room was a few steps down the hall. They also told him that one officer on the side street fell asleep every night around 1:30 or 2:00.

Konstantin took all of this into account while building his plan. He would drive to Saginaw from New York, giving more time for the police, Novak, and Collins to become more complacent.

With the detailed information he received from the Deans, he wouldn't have any trouble avoiding the motion sensors and alarm systems. Once in the house, he'd abduct Collins and find out where the painting was or use her as leverage to get the information from Novak.

Konstantin was correct in his analysis. Novak and Collins were becoming very impatient. They talked to Clark and found out that Petrocelli had returned to New York. Despite Novak and Collins' best efforts, Clark insisted they remain under watch and stay in Novak's home. He did make a few concessions.

Chapter Seventy-Two

August 6, 2019
Saginaw, Michigan

Lukas Novak

Liz started meeting me at my home every day to continue working, making life bearable because I enjoyed working with Liz, and it felt good to accomplish something. Liz arranged meetings with clients at my office, and Clark agreed I could go to my office provided I used a police escort. The office allowed me to talk in private with Liz, and she was curious how the arrangement with Natalie was going. I think it may have surprised her when I explained we were sleeping in separate rooms and that I found Natalie to be thoughtful, intelligent, and kind. Liz, being an excellent listener, took this all in.

"I hear what you're saying. Please be careful and guarded around Natalie. Maybe I've got Natalie all wrong, and hopefully, we'll live through this ordeal, and I'll be happy to admit I was wrong about her."

Natalie continued working too. Explaining how her commercial properties struggled, we rewrote a business plan to get her out of trouble. She laid off everyone and still maintained her properties. "Maybe there was a silver lining in this nightmare drama," she said.

"I like working with you, Lukas; you're understanding and smart about finding solutions to my problems. You're what I need to go forward. Thank you," she said genuinely.

On the first or second day of staying with Lukas, Natalie heard a pounding coming from the basement. She ventured down to find that Lukas was in shorts and a sleeveless tee-shirt. He was drenched in sweat, pounding away on a body punching bag. He didn't notice her come down the stairs, so she secretly watched him. He hit the bag with such ferocity; it amazed her. The body bag was part of his entire gym, including a speed bag and a complete set of free weights, bench press, power rack, and training machines. She realized the power hiding under his white dress or baggy golf shirts. His utterly ripped and sweaty body took her in. He was beautiful, she thought, walking closer until he noticed her.

"I'm sorry if I'm bothering you," he said. "I need to work out, or I'll lose my mind."

"That's an amazing workout, and it's obviously working. You're very, very fit."

"Thanks, Natalie. I do work at it."

"Why the punching bag?"

"I enjoy it. I was once an amateur boxer."

"When?"

"A long time ago. My father loved to box and taught me at a very young age. I was a golden glove champ early on."

"You stopped even though you like it?" she asked.

"I did. I had a boxing match against an outstanding boxer. I hit with a full right hand to the face in the third round. He went down and stopped moving. They took him to the hospital. He was in a coma for days. Fortunately, he recovered. I vowed never again to box and risk hurting someone. These days, I compete against myself. I like to see how hard I can go against this bag or fast I can move against the speed bag."

"Show me," she said.

"All right, this is always the last thing I do."

He went to the speed bag and put on a remarkable demonstration of speed and power. He always worked out hard, but he put on a particular display with Natalie watching. When he stopped, the sweat dripped from his face and entire body.

"My God, remind me never to give you a hard time. You're amazing. Really amazing."

"Thanks, it does feel good to work out. Knowing I can handle myself in almost all situations also feels good. I never feel threatened."

"I feel better knowing you're around protecting me. Why don't you take a shower, and I'll make us dinner and open a bottle of wine," she said.

"Ok. I'll try not to drip all over the place," as he wiped himself down with a white bath towel. Red wine, please," he suggested.

Natalie went upstairs and opened a bottle of Pinot Noir to let it breathe, prepared a simple garden salad, and began baking chicken and slicing strawberries. While preparing the food, she became more aware that this understated man she was living with was exceptional. The loss of Nicky Winters may have more than one benefit to her. Lukas came out of his bedroom wearing shorts and a tight tee-shirt with a Wayne State University logo on the front.

"Can I help you with dinner?"

"Yep, you can slice the rest of these strawberries for dessert, and before you start, please pour us both a glass of wine," she said.

"Yes, my lady. I shall do as you wish because it's also in my best interest."

They laughed and, after pouring the wine, made a toast, "Here's to survival."

"So," she said, let's make the most of our time.".

She looked directly into my eyes, making her desire clear.

"Let me finish with the strawberries, and I'll set the table," I said.

She smiled with disappointment and returned to preparing the chicken and thought she wouldn't give up easily

After wine and dinner, we tried to figure out what was happening. If Konstantin took Janice's painting, why was he back after us?

"Perhaps Adam gave Janice a copy too and was planning on keeping the original for himself," Natalie said.

"That could make sense. So, Konstantin is still looking to find the original Bouguereau painting," I speculated.

"That does make sense."

That means the painting is still missing," I added.

We considered all the places that Adam might have hid the painting. We eventually agreed this idea didn't make any sense because he would surely have told Konstantin where it was hidden under torture.

"Because he didn't know where it was, he probably told him that Janice Wendall had the painting, not realizing Konstantin would kill him and Janice," she said.

"Considering what he did to Adam, I'm sure he'd tell him anything to have him stop," I said.

"That means that Adam didn't sell the painting to someone because he would have said so," she said.

"So if Adam didn't know where it was, then someone must have stolen it from him," I ventured.

"That could be. If so, then where was the painting so someone could steal it?" She asked.

"I'm guessing that everything he had was in the storage unit. Maybe he hid it there, and someone found it? Now, who was able to find a painting in the storage unit? I had a key, and Adam said I was the only person other than himself who had one. He was asking me to wrap up his affairs when he left, so that makes sense."

"Who else could get in?" She asked and then answered her own question, "The owner. The owner may have a key. If he knew Adam was leaving Saginaw, he might have taken the chance of going through his possessions in storage thinking that anything he took wouldn't be noticed."

"That makes sense, except storage unit owners don't have keys. I replied, but maybe he had another way of getting in. I wouldn't put anything past this guy."

"Lukas, who is it?"

"Carl Williams. Liz's boyfriend. He's a lazy slacker, and I can see him doing something like stealing. He'd steal even though he wouldn't know what he was stealing."

"What should we do?" She asked.

"I'll see Liz tomorrow at our office. We're meeting with clients. I'll talk to her then."

"Do you think she knows anything about Carl taking the painting?"

"I'm sure she doesn't," I answered. "Frankly, I don't know what Liz sees in him. I guess opposites do attract." I smiled weakly. "I suggest we head to our rooms and get some sleep and talk again in the morning."

In the morning, I was up before Natalie and called Liz and asked if she could bring over the work we needed before today's meetings. She said that would be fine, and we agreed to meet in an hour.

As I poured a second cup of coffee and got ready to jump in the shower, Natalie came into the kitchen. Wearing a very short tee shirt that exposed almost all her long slender legs, she smiled and said, "Sleep well?"

"Good morning. Want a cup of coffee?" I asked.

"Yes, that would be great."

"I'm glad you're up. I just talked to Liz, and she'll be here in an hour. I want to go over some files and talk to her about Carl and the painting," I said.

Natalie stepped back. "If she thinks her boyfriend knows anything about the painting, what will she do? What should we do?"

"Whether or not she thinks Carl knows about the painting, I'll have a private conversation with him. If he knows anything, I'm sure I can convince him to tell me."

As I was leaving to take my shower, I looked back at Natalie, who was reaching into the refrigerator for milk. Her short tee shirt raised almost to the top of her butt. I smiled. No underwear.

When Liz arrived, I invited her to meet on the patio in the backyard and asked if she wanted a cup of coffee.

She opened the sliding glass door that led to the patio. "I love your yard, Lukas. It's so private, and the flowers are gorgeous," she said.

Built in the 1920s, my home is red brick and has a steep roof. It includes an unattached garage, meaning I must go outside to my car in the cold Michigan winters. It sits on a corner lot, and years ago, someone planted evergreen trees along both sides and the back of the property. Now they're twenty feet tall and provide a natural privacy fence around the entire yard. I added my touches, planting flower beds along the front of the evergreens, including daylilies, coneflowers, daisies, and black-eyed-

Susans.

Liz was staring at the bees buzzing around the coneflowers. "I was just thinking," she said, "about all the good times we've had sitting around your firepit. Adam, Natalie, Nicky, and other friends sipping port wine. I can hear Adam talking about some interesting person or place and all of us laughing over some witty thing he'd said."

"Yeah, many good times," I agreed.

"And you and Adam talking baseball. You, the Detroit Tigers fan, and Adam loving his "Damn Yankees." I can't believe how much has changed since I was last here, Lukas." I nodded in agreement.

"Adam dead. Nicky dead. Mrs. Wendall dead. An assassin trying to kill Natalie and me. I feel like I've been sucked into a vortex and can't make out what's happening," I commented. I didn't say it out loud, but thought how badly this nightmare could end.

Liz stared at me, then smiled, "Hey, we have files to review and clients to meet today."

When finished, she asked, "So how's it working out with Natalie?"

"Surprising well. We made dinner together and tried to figure out who's trying to kill us and why."

"What are your best guesses?" She asked.

"Well, we believe that Konstantin is after Janice's Bouguereau painting. That's the only reason for him to be in Saginaw. If Adam knew where the painting was, he would have told Konstantin. After all, who could possibly withstand the torture inflicted on him? He told him about Janet Wendall's painting in desperation, probably hoping it would distract the killer, although he already knew she had a forgery. Obviously, that didn't make a difference to Konstantin because he killed Adam and Janet when he found out that her painting was at the museum.

"He then stole what he thought was the original painting from the museum and took it to his client. By the way, we now believe that the client is Beatrice Hirsch. After analyzing the painting from the museum, she found it too was a forgery. Konstantin returns to Saginaw for the painting. Who are the two closest people to Adam who might know the whereabouts of the painting? Natalie and me, except we have no idea where to find the paintings.

Leading us to believe that someone must have stolen the painting from Adam, but who? It seems logical that Adam hid the painting in his storage unit. Who had access to the unit? Adam and I had the only keys. I don't have the painting, so who else had access to the unit?

At this point, Liz interrupted me. "The owner of the storage units, Carl?"

"Normally, an owner doesn't have a key," I said.

"Maybe Carl had another way of getting in," Liz responded.

"How?"

"One time after he'd been drinking, Carl was bragging about his skill as a locksmith. He said the renters of his units had no idea that he could go into them anytime he wanted and search through their stuff. Lukas, he could have taken the painting," she offered.

"Maybe," I said.

"Ok, I'll talk to Carl tonight and find out what he knows or doesn't know," she said.

"Thanks, Liz. That may lead us to the end of this whole mess. And then, if I can find out who murdered Nicky and find her killer, I can grieve her death and move forward."

The following day, I walked outside and approached the police car parked at the front of my home. The officer rolled down his window when he saw me in the driveway.

"Need a ride to your office Mr. Novak?"

"Thank you, officer. I'd appreciate that very much." The officer walked me to the front door and waited while I punched in the code to the alarm system. We searched every room before his leaving. He said he'd be waiting in his car to take me back. I thanked the officer, sat down at my desk, and waited for Liz to arrive. In minutes she came, and after she poured herself a coffee, sat down in the chair across the desk from me.

"Liz, did you talk to Carl about the painting?" I asked.

"I did."

"What did he say?"

"He said he didn't know anything about a painting and was sure that neither he nor anyone that works for him was in Adam's unit."

"Do you believe him?"

"I want to believe him," she answered.

"But you don't. Do you?"

"I think he knows something, Lukas. It wasn't just how he answered, but there's something else. Do you remember when Carl took me to Detroit for the weekend? We stayed in the honeymoon suite in the most expensive hotel. We gambled away a lot of money, and I asked him where this newfound money came from. He told me that he had just sold some antiques someone had abandoned. Maybe that's true, but I also remember that it was soon after Adam's death. Maybe he stole the painting when Adam was alive then sold the painting after Adam's death when he became anxious about holding on to it."

"I need to talk to him, Liz, I said.

"Lukas, let me talk to him one more time. I don't think I'm getting through how serious this whole painting thing is."

"Ok, talk to him again. If he doesn't give you answers that you believe are straightforward, I'll talk to him too," I said.

"Lukas, you won't hurt him, will you?" She asked.

"I don't intend to, but we need answers."

Liz nodded that she understood.

"Liz, we have to find that painting. I have a feeling time is running out for Natalie and me."

Chapter Seventy-Three

August 8, 2019
Saginaw, Michigan

Sergei Konstantin

After talking to the Deans, Konstantin decided to return to Saginaw. His plan was simple. He'd break into Novak's house kidnap Collins. He'd force her to tell him where he could find the painting. If she didn't know, he'd use her to force Novak to tell him where the painting was hidden.

It took him only one day to drive to Saginaw, and he arrived late in the evening, parking his car in the garage that the Deans had rented. That night and early the next morning, he went over all the Deans' information. He paid particular attention to Novak's motion sensors and alarm system. He believed both were easily circumvented. The Deans then drew out a map of Novak's house and showed Konstantin where the rooms in the house were located, particularly the rooms where Novak and Collins would be sleeping. He also considered that the one police officer was usually sleeping by 2:00 am. That's when he'd break into Novak's house.

At 2:00, dressed all in black, he left Deans' house, working his way down the backyards of the nearby homes until he could see the police officer's car parked on the side street. He could see the police officer was already slumped down and sleeping in his car with his binoculars. Konstantin moved across Novak's backyard, avoiding the motion detectors. He made it to the backdoor and unarmed the security alarm system. Using a pick, Konstantin unlocked the door and quietly eased himself into the house. He made his way to Collins' bedroom and found her soundly sleeping. He moved next to her and placed his hand over her mouth. She tried to cry out, but Konstantin's grip was so firm she had no chance. He bent over her and whispered in her ear.

"Make no sound, or I'll slice your throat with this."

He showed her a knife he was holding in his left hand.

"Do you understand? Do you?"

Natalie nodded yes.

He told her to get out of bed slowly. When she did, he stepped behind her, still holding his knife in front of her so she could see that this was no idle threat. Slowly they made their way across the bedroom.

When they reached the hallway, Konstantin felt a terrific blow to the side of his head. It threw him against the door casing, causing him to drop his knife and release Natalie.

"Go, Natalie! Get help from the police officer," I yelled.

Natalie bolted through the backdoor.

I stepped next to Konstantin and delivered a right-hand punch to his midsection. He groaned and bent over. He surprised me with a karate chop to my throat when he came up. It stunned me, giving Konstantin time to draw his Glock out of his holster from the waist behind his back. Before he could point the gun at me, I drove my shoulder into his stomach, driving him against the wall with such force it knocked the lamp and other things off the table next to the bed. Konstantin held his gun and tried to fire it as we fell to the floor. I hit him with a vicious head butt that broke his nose, and he was bleeding from his mouth. That didn't stop him; he fired a shot that grazed my ribs. I didn't think I'd be that lucky again and hit him in the face with my best right hand. It dazed him and gave me the chance to knock the gun out of hand, and while he struggled to his feet, I groped along the floor, searching for his weapon, giving Konstantin a moment's chance to slip out of the bedroom, go down the hall and retreat out my backdoor before the police arrived.

Konstantin had planned the route he'd take back to the Deans' assuming he'd be forcing Natalie to go with him. Nevertheless, this exit path would work, and he made sure no one was following him when he made it to the side door of Deans' house facing away from Novak's house. He labored to go inside.

Both Allan and Doris were waiting for him with the lights off.

"Where's Collins?" Doris asked.

"I didn't get her," Konstantin said.

"What the hell happened?" Allan said.

"Novak. He surprised me as I was taking Collins. He hit me with a punch to the head that almost knocked me out. We struggled. I was lucky to get out of there before the police arrived.

"Wait, you mean to tell me that the architect got the best of you?" Asked Doris.

"He's no ordinary architect. He's strong as a bull, and he caught me off guard. I did fire a shot, and I think it hit him because I heard him moan. It didn't stop him, and he drove me into a wall so hard I could barely get up."

Allan asked, "Do you think it's safe to stay here?"

Konstantin replied, "We have no choice. The police will be swarming the area. I'm sure they will go house to house looking for me. You'll have to convince them that you've not seen me."

Doris said, "We can do that. No one lies better than Allan and I. In the meantime, I better help clean you up. It looks like you have a broken nose. I can fix that too."

"He loosened some of my teeth, too," he mumbled.

While Doris was cleaning Konstantin up, Clark arrived at Novak's house. He found a police officer and Natalie looking at Lukas's ribcage wound.

"Lukas, what happened?" Clark said.

"Konstantin broke in through the backdoor and was trying to kidnap Natalie. Something I heard woke me up, and when he came out of Natalie's room, I hit with a right hand to the side of the head. He went down, and we struggled. He got a shot off; it only scratched me. I screwed up. I let him get away, and he disappeared outside. I'm not sure what direction he went."

Natalie joined in, "Lukas hit him so hard that he let go of me and dropped his knife. He yelled for me to go outside and get a police officer. When I got to the car, I had to wake the officer up. By the time we got in the house, the fight was over, and he was gone."

"The gun wound doesn't look too bad. Are you hurt otherwise?" Clark asked Lukas.

"No, I'm fine."

"Natalie, how are you?" Asked Clark.

"Other than being scared to death, I'm ok. He threatened to kill me if I made any sound. I think he would have. If it wasn't for Lukas, God only knows what he'd be doing to me now. I keep thinking about what he did to Adam. Lukas, you saved my life."

Clark looked at one of the police officers as both were listening to what Lukas and Natalie were saying. Staring at one officer, he said, "Were you asleep?"

"Yes, sir."

"I want you to head to the station and wait in my office. When I finish here, I want to talk to you," Clark said.

The other officer took Lukas and Natalie to the hospital to look at Lukas' wound.

As they left, Clark told them, "We better enhance the security on your doors and windows, and I need to do a better job of having competent officers protecting you. When you get back from the hospital, call me. I want to go over everything again, and I'll call Petrocelli and tell him what's happened."

While we were at the hospital, Natalie called a security specialist that worked for her rental company. She explained that they needed a highly secure system for Lukas' house. She then called the company providing Lukas' system and demanded they immediately do what was necessary and work with her guy to make sure she and Lukas were protected and no one could get in again. She yelled at them, "I could have been killed, damn it."

After leaving the hospital, Natalie and I met with Clark at my house. We went over the details. Clark told us he'd found the gun Konstantin was using, and he'd ordered police officers to go house to house in the area looking for Konstantin or at least for clues as to where he went after he left my home.

After Clark left, it was already early evening, and I made double dirty vodka martinis for Natalie and me. We were exhausted by the day's confrontation, and my mind drifted off as Natalie was talking. I realized I hadn't had a dirty martini since having one with Nicky. I missed her and wished she were with me now.

"Don't you think that's true?" Natalie asked me.

"I'm sorry I drifted off. What did you say?"

"I said I'm damned lucky you're in my life, and I'll never be able to thank you enough for what you did tonight."

"You don't need to thank me. I did what I needed to do. I'm sure this isn't the end of all of this. That killer isn't going to just walk away after what happened tonight. I'm guessing he believes in revenge."

As we worked on our drinks, my phone rang. It was Liz. She told me that she had heard what happened from Clark. I assured her that Natalie and I were alright and had taken security measures since the break-in to make sure someone couldn't break into the house again. "At least I hope they can't because I'm tired," I said.

"I hope you're protecting yourself," Liz said. "I'll let you go and get some rest. We can talk tomorrow. I can't tell you how relieved I am that you're ok. I'm not sure what I'd do without Lukas Novak in my life."

"I feel the same way about you, Liz. By the way, did you get a chance to talk with Carl?"

"I did, and he wasn't much help. We can talk about it tomorrow and tell Natalie I'm relieved that she's safe too. Good night, Lukas."

"Good night. Liz."

"Is she in love with you?" Natalie asked.

"No. We just make a really good team, and we're important in each other."

"I'm glad she doesn't love you, Lukas."

Although I smiled at Natalie, I thought about Liz's warning about her. I finished my drink and told Natalie that I was going to bed. She looked disappointed.

"All right. Thank you again for saving my life. Lukas, I need you. I want to be with you and show you how appreciative I am."

"Natalie, let's just try to get through all of this."

I went to my room, and before falling asleep, I thought about Nicky and wished she was beside me, giving me the strength to go forward. I had the feeling that luck was running out for us.

Chapter Seventy-Four

Manhattan, New York
August 9, 2019

Tony Petrocelli

After hearing from Clark what happened at Novak's house, Petrocelli decided it was time to visit Beatrice Hirsch. She agreed to meet him only after making threats, and she was very displeased when he met her in the library of her city mansion.

"Detective Petrocelli, to what do I owe the pleasure?" She said sarcastically.

Petrocelli smiled and thought to himself that she'd grown even fatter than the last time he saw her, and she was huge then.

"I wanted to let you know that your colleague, Sergei Konstantin, broke into a person's home last night in Saginaw. He was attempting to abduct a young woman. Fortunately for the woman and unfortunately for him, a man was waiting for him and beat him up quite badly. The Saginaw police are looking for him now. It's a small town, and I'm sure they'll find him. If they do, I hope they don't connect him to you. Two William Bouguereau paintings are missing, and I know how much you appreciate Bouguereau. Ms. Hirsch, I hope this is just a coincidence," Petrocelli said.

"You came all the way here to tell me about a man I don't know. In a city I've never heard of. About paintings, I know nothing about. Detective Petrocelli, you again prove to me that you know nothing about your work. Please leave," she calmly responded.

"I'm leaving Ms. Hirsch, but I know this is all about you and those paintings. This time I believe your appetite for stolen artwork will be your undoing. Goodbye, Ms. Hirsch."

As Petrocelli turned to leave, he added, "I don't think this will be the last time we talk about this matter," he smiled again as he left her library.

After he left, she called Konstantin.

"Konstantin, I just had a visit from Detective Petrocelli. He tells me you had some trouble in Saginaw. He said you were beat up while attempting a kidnapping. Tell me this isn't true."

"It not true. It's all a lie to make you nervous," Konstantin said.

"I don't believe you. I think you're the liar. I'm bringing this matter to an end. I have one Bouguereau painting, I have my $5 million back, and the other Bouguereau will probably show up on the black market sooner or later. I want you to come back to New York and call an end to your botched efforts in Saginaw. Do I make myself clear, Konstantin?"

"Yes. I understand. I will return to New York," he said.

He hung up and turned to Allan and Doris.

"That was Ms. Hirsch. She heard about what happened last night and has ordered me back to New York."

"Well, that's probably good," Allan said.

"Things haven't gone so well here, and the police are looking for you. Besides, even if you can get a hold of Novak and Collins, there's no guarantee they know where the painting is," Doris added.

Konstantin defiantly responded, "We are not leaving. We are going to teach Mr. Novak and Ms. Collins a painful lesson, and we will find that painting."

"How?" Doris asked.

"We've learned that Novak is a very caring person. In particular, there are two people he cares about. We know someone recently killed his girlfriend, so he'll be even more protective of the others. There's his mother. You found out that she has left her home and we don't know where she's gone. Then there's his colleague, Liz Bowers. We are going to kidnap Bowers, and we'll make sure that Mr. Novak comes to us, and when he does, he is going to suffer."

Konstantin then reached up and touched his broken nose and loosened front teeth.

Chapter Seventy-Five

Saginaw, Michigan
August 10, 2019

Sergei Konstantin

"Here's what I want you to do," Konstantin said "when you're sure that Bowers is at their office alone, I want you to go there and pretend to be new clients. When she lets you in, force her to get into your car at gunpoint. Bring her here, and we will have a nice chat with her and Novak."

That afternoon Allan and Doris approached Novak's office. It was a building with double glass front doors and a small entryway leading into a lobby area with carefully arranged stuffed chairs and coffee tables with current magazines. There was a reception desk and, to the right, a large conference room. A hallway led to Liz's office, another smaller conference room, Lukas' office, and a small kitchen to the left. A second door off the kitchen led to a parking lot at the back of the office.

When threats to Lukas' life began, Liz decided to be proactive and took security measures. One morning when Lukas arrived, workers were installing an intercom so Liz could talk to the people that were ringing the front doorbell. She added an alarm button at the reception desk that notified the security company and police that there was an intruder. Liz also decided she'd be able to protect herself if needed. She bought a Magnum Research Micro Desert Eagle handgun that used .380 caliber bullets. She had Carl show her how to use the pistol, taking her to a gun club where she practiced using the gun on the firing range. She practiced shooting many times until she began to feel comfortable using the pistol and started wearing the weapon when she was at the office alone.

Late in the afternoon, when the Deans were sure Liz was alone, they rang the doorbell, and Liz came into the reception area to see who was at the front door. She saw a middle-aged couple who looked as if they had worked hard their whole lives and never indulged in any frills. Liz, through the intercom, asked them what they wanted.

"We want to make an appointment to see Mr. Novak," Allan said.

Liz was about the open the front doors when her intuition told her that was a mistake.

"The office is closed right now," Liz told them. "I don't have Mr. Novak's schedule. Could you call the office to make the appointment?"

"That would be fine," Allan said.

He then reached underneath his sports jacket, taking out his handgun. Liz saw Doris' face change from friendly to malicious. Liz stepped back into the reception area as Allan pointed the gun at her. She dove to the side of the room and heard Allan demanding she open the door. Without hesitation, Liz sprinted to the hallway that led to the kitchen. She was wearing her handgun in a holster.

"Damn it, Doris go to the backdoor and stop her," Allan said.

He fired two shots from his pistol with a silencer and kicked the front door open. Alarms went off, and he ran into the office. When Doris reached the back of the office, she saw Liz running for the trees at the end of the parking lot.

"Stop," Doris shouted, "or I'll shoot you in the back."

Liz dove to the ground just as Doris fired. Liz raised and placed two hands on her pistol and fired at Doris. A shot hit her in her side, and she slumped to the parking lot. Liz jumped up and ran to the trees across another parking lot between two buildings. She called 911 and told them what had just happened as she was running. Now completely out of breath, Liz pushed on until collapsing in some bushes. After laying on the ground for a few moments, she turned, looked back, and was relieved not to see anyone. She called Clark. To her surprise, he answered immediately.

She quickly explained what had happened. He said he was on his way with other police officers. She told him she would work her way over to the back of the McDonald's parking lot and wait for him.

Allan ran through the office and out the back door. He found Doris lying in blood. He looked at where she was shot and helped her to her feet.

"Come on," he said, "we've got to get out of here."

He helped her to their car, drove back to their house, and parked in the garage.

Allan helped Doris out of the car and into the house.

"What happened?" Demanded Konstantin.

"Doris is shot," Allan answered.

"By whom?"

"That Bowers woman."

Allan helped Doris into the bedroom and began examining her wound.

"Doris, the bullet went straight through and didn't appear to have hit any organs. You're going to be ok," Allan said.

The Deans always carried a medical bag for situations like this. It wasn't the first time they'd been shot. Knowing they couldn't go to a hospital, Allan cleaned and bandaged the wound.

"Konstantin, this over for us. Doris and I are heading home. Things have gone wrong on this painting business from the very beginning."

"To hell you are. You'll leave when I tell you to leave. I'm going to get Novak, and you're going to help me. Doris will be ok. I want you to go to Bowers' house and see what she does next."

"Are you crazy?" Allan said, "She's seen me."

"Then you need to disguise yourself, and you can take my car. She hasn't seen it. Now go, and I'll watch over Doris."

Allan knew that Konstantin was a violent killer. He was afraid of him, and to go against his demands would not end well for him or Doris. He went to Doris and explained what was happening. Doris knew that following Konstantin's orders was the only thing they could do.

"It's alright, Allan. I'll be alright. Go do what you need to do," Doris said.

He reached down and gave her a light kiss on the forehead.

"I'll be back as soon as I can," he whispered.

Allan already knew where Bowers lived based on his previous research. He put on a baseball cap and dark sunglasses, drove to her house in Konstantin's car, and waited for her to return from a safe distance away. In a few hours, she arrived home and soon came out carrying a large suitcase and then back in again, coming out with another bag. She loaded them in her car and headed out.

Allan followed her to Carl's home on the other side of Saginaw. He watched her as she carried her bags to the front door and let herself in. In fifteen minutes, a man arrived, parked on the driveway, and let himself in the house. Allan assumed this was Bower's boyfriend. He called Konstantin and reported what he had seen. Konstantin told him to continue to watch the house and call him when he saw any activity.

Chapter Seventy-Six

Saginaw, Michigan
August 10, 2019

Lukas Novak

On her way to his house, Liz called Carl and explained what had happened, and then called Lukas and told him how she had escaped.

"Thank God for the intercom and my pistol training," she said. "I'm on my way to Carl's."

"I'm so relieved you're not hurt and so sorry for bringing this mess into your life," I said.

"Lukas, I'm proud of myself. I didn't lose my cool. She threatened to shoot me in the back. I dove to the ground and rolled over to get a shot at her. I took my time and fired. I hit her in her side, when she fell to the ground, I ran," Liz explained.

"Who were these people? I asked.

"Some middle-aged man and woman I'd never seen. When they came to the office door, I got a funny feeling they were involved with Konstantin. I wouldn't let them in. That's when the husband threatened to shoot me through the door. I dove to the side and ran out the kitchen door. That's when the woman tried to kill me. I called Clark and met him at the McDonald's parking lot."

"You're incredible, Ms. Bowers. I'm so very proud of you. Now you need to stay safe. You said you're at Carl's?"

"Yes, I'm just getting there now. Carl's on his way too."

"Good. I want to talk to you and Carl. I'll be over in a few minutes," I said.

I hung up and told Natalie what had happened and that I was going over to Carl's house to see Liz and talk to Carl.

"I'm going with you."

"No, you're not. You're staying here. It's too dangerous for you to be driving around," I said.

"Too dangerous?" she shouted. "The only time I'm safe is when I'm with you. I'm scared to death to stay in this house by myself. You know the police are less than competent. There is no arguing, Lukas. I'm going with you."

I knew Natalie was right. It was too dangerous for her to stay alone in my house. I also knew it was dangerous to be driving around with me.

"You can go, but you're staying in the car."

I went into my bedroom and came out with my gun. I don't believe in carrying guns, but this was an exception.

Do you know how to shoot a gun?" I asked Natalie.

"Hell no. Who do you think I am? Annie Oakley?"

"Ok. Come here. I stood behind her and told her to raise her arms. Holding the gun between her arms, I showed her how to use two hands, take the safety off, aim, and fire. I explained it twice more.

"Lukas, I'm not sure I can do this," she said.

"If your life depends upon it, just be calm and do what I showed you. You can do that. I know you can, Natalie. Right?"

"Right, I can if I need to," she said hesitantly.

Chapter Seventy-Seven

Saginaw, Michigan
August 10, 2019

Lukas Novak

We left and drove in my car to Carl's. I was surprised that the police car out front didn't follow us. I was glad they didn't. When we arrived, although Natalie said she'd stay in the car, she said she was too scared and wanted to go in the house too. I agreed that was a good idea, we knocked on Carl's door, and Liz let us in and took a seat on the couch next to Carl. Liz asked me if it was a good idea to have Natalie with me.

"I'm thinking it's too dangerous," Liz said.

"It is dangerous, but probably more dangerous for her to stay by herself. The police haven't been much help," I said.

Liz nodded in agreement. Then she told the story again about the two middle-aged people trying to adduct her and how she escaped.

"I'm so thankful you're ok," Carl said and reached over to hug her.

"Carl, you know this is all about a missing painting, don't you?" I said.

"I know. Liz told me."

"And you don't know anything about the missing painting?" I said while studying Carl's face.

Carl turned away from me and looked toward Liz. "I said I don't."

"I think you're lying, Carl. I think you know everything about the painting. Adam is dead. Mrs. Wendell is dead. They tried to kill me,

Natalie, and Liz over this missing painting. Now I want the truth. Did you steal the painting?" I demanded.

Carl looked down and said, "No."

I got up and walked over to Carl on the couch and stood over him. Reaching down, I grabbed him by his shirt and pulled him to his feet.

"I don't know," Carl whimpered.

"You're lying, Carl. Everyone's lives are threatened. You're going to tell us the truth, right now,"

Carl refused to answer. I hit him with a right to his stomach and knocked the wind out of him. He started gasping for air and begged Liz to make me stop.

"The truth, Carl," Liz demanded.

Carl said nothing. I pulled him to his feet, hit him, knocking him hard against the back of the couch. He groaned again. I reached down, pulled him up, and hit him even harder.

"Alright, alright," Carl stammered. "Stop. I know about the painting."

Pulling his face close to mine, "Tell me everything, Carl, or I swear I'm going to kick the shit out of you.."

"Ok, after Adam put all his stuff in the unit, I heard he was leaving town and going to sell everything. I decided to look around. I picked the lock to his unit. I saw some things I thought would be valuable and found this wooden box hidden under some carpets in the corner. I forced the lock open and found the painting. When I unrolled it, I saw a picture of these two kids playing with a red ball. It looked cool, and I thought I could sell it."

"Where is the painting, Carl?" I shouted.

"I don't have it. I sold it."

"Who did you sell it to?"

"A guy I know who's bought jewelry and antiques from me in the past."

"What's his name, and where does he live?" I yelled.

"His name is Sidney, and he lives in Detroit."

"Sidney what? And where in Detroit?"

"I don't know his last name, only Sidney."

"Can you get a hold of him?" I asked.

"Yes, I've got his cell number."

I pushed Carl back on the couch and looked at Liz.

"Carl, you put all our lives in danger by not telling us what you knew," Liz said. "This time, you better not be lying and do everything you can to make up for it."

I needed to decide what to do next. I told everyone to find a seat and let me think." After sitting quietly, I said, "I have a plan."

Chapter Seventy-Eight

Saginaw, Michigan
August 10, 2019

Lukas Novak

"Carl, you're going to call Sidney and tell him you have some diamond rings and bracelets to sell. Tell him you've already checked them out, and they're genuine. Let him know you want to show them to him and ask him what he'd pay? Casually ask him if he's sold the painting. Whether he has or not doesn't matter. We want to meet him, and I'll find out where he's keeping the painting or to whom he's sold it. The only important thing for you, Carl, is to set up the meeting. Can you do that?"

"Ok, I'll call, but this guy is no one to fuck around with. I think he's killed people in the past. Anyway, that's what I've heard."

I laughed. "He can't be any more deadly than Konstantin, a known assassin. Now make that call. Let's meet with him today."

Carl called, and he must be a good customer because Sidney picked up right away. He said he could meet today at 5:00 at the usual place, and no, he didn't sell the painting, and he told Carl not to ask for any more money because it's hard to sell stolen artwork. He'd meet him at 5:00.

"Well?" I asked.

"Today at 5:00 at his place in Detroit. We always meet in the parking lot behind his apartment building. It's called the Kane Building, and it's on Jefferson Avenue by Belle Isle. The parking lot has a dumpster and a bunch of old cars. From Sidney's window on the 8th floor, you can see the lot where we meet."

"I know the Kane Building, but I haven't been there in years. Is there any place for me to hide so I can surprise Sidney?" I asked.

"Lots of places there's the dumpster and cars even on the side of the building where Sidney can't see from his window," he answered.

"Ok, it's 2:00, and it will take us close to two hours to drive to Detroit, so we better leave now. Carl, you'll ride with me, Natalie you stay here with Liz."

"To hell I am," Natalie said. "I'm going with you, and I promise I'll say in the car this time."

"Natalie, you can stay with me if you want," Liz said. "I'm not going. I've had way too much excitement already today."

"Thanks, Liz, I appreciate the offer, but I'd feel better being with Lukas."

"It's settled. We're leaving now. Ok, Natalie, you're going with us. Liz, I want to confront Sidney alone and don't want any interference from Clark. So, around 4:00, give him a call and tell him what's going on. By the time he gets to Detroit, I'll have the painting in our hands," I said.

"Ok, Lukas, I'll call Clark. Be careful, and I know Carl is an idiot, but please bring him back safe," she asked me.

I drove with Carl in the passenger seat and Natalie in the back. I knew the Kane Building, one of my friends that I went to Wayne State University with had lived there. I'd been in his apartment several times. It was a magnificent 12-story building constructed in the 1930s. Looking down from above the building, you can see it's shaped like a cross. Each arm of the cross has a separate apartment with windows that look in three directions. When built, it was an exclusive building. Today, it's not as well cared for, but still beautiful. I remembered the parking lot because my friend's VW Bug was broken into several times, even though there was nothing to steal.

I knew that there'd many places for me to hide, and that's important. I'd need to get the jump on Sidney. If I could, I knew I could take him down, and I'd dominate him.

I calculated it would take less than two hours from Carl's, down I-75 to the Jefferson Avenue exit and the Kane Building, allowing me at least 30 minutes to park and find a hiding place to surprise Sidney.

I was worried about Natalie going with us but didn't have time to convince or argue with her to stay with Liz.

"Natalie, when we get to the Kane Building, you must promise me that you'll stay in the car. Don't get out no matter what happens," I said in a voice that was caring but demanding.

"I promise Lukas I'll stay in the car."

"Promise?" I asked again."

"Promise," she replied.

"Carl, we'll park behind the McDonald's that's on Jefferson a block away. Then I'll come in from the back streets and hide off to the side of the building. You come in from Jefferson. That way, we won't create any suspicion. Does that make sense," I asked?

"It does," Carl replied.

Fortunately, traffic was light, and I made good time getting to Detroit. When reaching the Jefferson Avenue exit, I realized we were too early to set things up at the Kane Building.

"We've got time. Let's go get a drink somewhere," Carl said.

"God damn it, Carl, get serious. We're not down here to drink. You need all your wits to make this happen," I said.

"I know. It's just that I'm so nervous my hands are shaking, and I think this might give me away. I'm never this nervous meeting Sidney,"

"Ok, we'll go over to Woodbridge Street. There's a tavern there."

We entered the tavern that was a bar dating back to the 1940s. I'd been there from time to time when I was going to school at Wayne State. It'd been years since I was there, and it didn't look like there'd been any changes. It had the dark, dank smell of a bar that had been around 80 years. We sat down at one of many empty tables.

"Sort of quiet in here," Natalie said.

"It doesn't get busy until folks get off work. Around 5:30 or 6:00," I said.

The waitress came over and took our drink orders. Carl had a double shot of tequila that caused me to shake my head. Natalie ordered a glass of Chardonnay, and I had a Coke. When the waitress brought over our drinks, Carl shot his back and ordered another. I stopped him and ordered him a Bud lite.

"Let's go over how this is going to work. Carl, you told him you have some jewelry. I've got a bag in my trunk. I'll put some stuff in it to look like you're carrying jewelry. While you're making small talk, I'll come from his back and put my gun on him. We'll march him up to his apartment and take the painting," I said.

"If we take the painting, he's going to want his money back," Carl said.

"How much did he pay you?" I asked.

"Five thousand."

"Five thousand for a $10 million painting."

I just shook my head. I wasn't sure if I said it out loud, but I thought, what a fucking idiot.

"I didn't know what it was worth," Carl said.

So maybe I did say it out loud.

"If you want to pay him back, that's up to you. You can tell him I'm forcing you to do this to buy you some time," I said.

"And Natalie, what are you going to do?" I asked.

"I'm going to stay in the car-- no matter what," she said.

We finished our drinks; I paid our bill and wondered if I'd ever see this tavern or any tavern again.

Chapter Seventy-Nine

Saginaw, Michigan
August 10, 2019

Sergei Konstantin

While Lukas and Natalie were meeting with Liz and Carl, Allan watched. He called Konstantin with an update.

"Sergei, I'm watching Liz's boyfriend's house; she's here with him. You're not going to believe it. Novak and Collins just went inside."

"Text me the address. I'm on my way," Konstantin said.

Allan called Konstantin again in a few minutes, "Are you on your way? Hold off. Novak, Collins, and Bower's boyfriend are leaving in Novak's car."

"Ok, follow them, and as soon as you see the direction they're heading, call me, and I'll catch up."

"I'm following them right now, and they just got on I-75 going south," Allan said.

"Don't lose them, and I'll be right behind you. Let me know which exit they're getting off."

Chapter Eighty

Detroit, Michigan
August 10, 2019

Lukas Novak

As planned, I drove over to the McDonald's and parked on the side street a block away from the Kane Building.

"Carl, if you do what I've told you, you're going to be fine, so relax," I said in the most soothing voice that I could muster, "just remember you're doing this for Liz."

I'd already decided to take a back street to the other side of the building from where Carl would be arriving.

Once I reached the building, I found a place to hide behind two cars, no more than ten or fifteen steps from the dumpster where Carl would meet Sidney. I was relieved when Carl arrived and stood next to the dumpster as he agreed with Sidney. I thought there'd be a good chance he'd lose his nerve and not show up. I figured he was drawing all his strength from Liz and trying to redeem himself. I watched him make the call to Sidney, telling him to come down to meet.

I thought it strange that Sidney insisted on meeting outside rather than in his apartment. Perhaps he didn't want Carl or anyone else to see what he kept there or thought letting people inside wasn't safe. Nevertheless, I was happy Sidney was meeting in the parking lot because it would be much easier to take him by surprise.

When Sidney came out the back door of the apartment building, he stood by the door until he saw Carl. He motioned for Carl to come over to him, and Carl motioned back for Sidney to join him. Sidney shook his head and again waved Carl over. Carl didn't move. He froze and couldn't decide what to do next. Sidney seemed to realize that something wasn't right and began to go back inside.

I couldn't wait. I knew that this was our best chance to find the painting. I jumped up from my hiding place and, ducking behind the cars, moved toward Sidney. Once I hit the open space in the parking lot, I darted toward him. He caught sight of something to his left and then saw me racing towards him from his right. Startled, he pulled out a gun from the back of the waist of his pants and turned and fired three shots. I dove to the ground and returned fire as he tried to go back inside the building. One shot hit him in the back of the arm, and he screamed out. I jumped up, reached him, and slammed him to the ground next to where his gun had fallen. I helped him to his feet.

"Now, Sidney, it doesn't look like you're hurt too badly. Let's head up to your apartment, and we'll put something on your wound. By the way, the painting you bought from Carl wasn't his, and I want it back. Now let's get going," I said

Sidney looked stunned. He held his hand over the wound on this arm and marched into the apartment building as I pushed him along. We were inside when Carl ran up and said, "Sorry, Sidney. He made me set you up. It wasn't my idea."

"Shut up, Carl, for Christ's sake, I said. Sidney is going to be busy showing me his apartment where he's going to give me the stolen painting that you sold him."

"What's this is all about? Do you want the painting that Mr. Stupid sold to me?" Sidney asked, pointing at Carl. "I thought you were going to kill me," he said.

"Why would you think that, Sidney?" I asked

"What would you think with three people running at you?"

"Three people?" Asked Carl.

"Yeah. You, your friend with the gun and the woman along the side of the building."

"Ok, whatever," I said, "let's focus on you taking us to your apartment. When we get there, we can take the painting and stop your bleeding."

When we reached apartment 8 North, it was clear why Sidney didn't want anyone up here. It was a warehouse of stolen goods, including furniture, televisions, video equipment, and jewelry. Obviously, he was selling drugs, and he quickly tried to hide some sitting out.

"We don't want your drugs, Sidney," I said, "just the painting."

Sidney went into a bedroom, and from the back of his closet, he came out with the painting. He handed it to me. I unrolled it, and staring at me were two beautiful young girls playing with a red ball. "To think that two, maybe three people have died over this painting," I said.

"What the hell," said Sidney. "Is it that valuable?"

"It is, and more of us may die before this is all over. Thank God we finally have it. Now let's clean that wound and get you bandaged up," I said.

Chapter Eighty-One

Detroit, Michigan
August 10, 2019

Sergei Konstantin

Arriving at the Kane Building, Allan did what he was told. Staying out of sight so Novak wouldn't be scared off, he waited until Konstantin arrived. Allan was relieved when he showed up and told Konstantin that Novak and Bowers' boyfriend confronted someone who came out of the building.

"The guy from the building fired three shots, and I think one of them might have hit a woman. I'm not positive because I didn't have a clear view from my car."

"Ok, Allan, you did well. Now go home and take care of Doris. I'll handle everything from here," Konstantin said.

As he moved carefully toward the back entrance of the building, he saw a woman lying by the wall of a neighboring building. He looked her over and smiled when he realized it was Collins. Based on her wound and the amount of blood on the pavement, Konstantin guessed she needed an ambulance immediately.

"Good, you caused me a lot of trouble, woman," he said to himself.

Walking to the apartment building door, he saw blood on the ground. The door had automatically closed, so he fired two shots from his pistol into the lock and pulled the door open. He had no idea which apartment they were going to, but he would follow the drops of blood, like Hansel and Gretel and their breadcrumbs. The blood told him that they had entered the elevator, so he stopped at every floor looking for more. Finally, on the 8th floor, drops were leading down the hallway to apartment 8N. The door was closed, and he assumed locked. He didn't want to bust in because it would give Novak time to put a fight. Waiting by the door, after about ten minutes, it started to open, and Konstantin slammed it wide open against Sidney's face. He pushed his way in and shot Sidney in the head. Carl hid behind a loveseat covered with boxes, so he was out of sight.

"Novak," Konstantin said, "don't try reaching for your gun, or I'll kill you. You see, that's what I do," he paused, "kill people. Now slowly pull out your weapon and drop it on the floor."

I did what I was told.

"Now kick the gun over to me," he said.

I kicked the gun halfway between Konstantin and me. He laughed.

"I underestimated you once, Novak. I won't again. Now step back."

I stepped back, and Konstantin picked up my gun.

He walked up to me and suddenly slammed his pistol into my face. I could feel the blood running down from my nose.

"I'm glad I didn't have to shoot you, Novak. Do you know you broke my nose and loosened my front teeth? That's ok because you won't have any teeth or much of a face when I'm done with you. Remember what I did to your friend, Lindmark? Well, it's going to be much worse for you. When I'm finished, you'll never use your hands, ever again. You'll never walk again. I'm not going to kill you. That should give you some relief. But I will batter your head so much that you won't have much of a mind left. That's the way you're going to spend the rest of your life."

I stared back at Konstantin. I knew he was capable of everything he said. I also knew I'd never let him take me that way. I'd wait for my best opportunity to try to overtake him, and if he killed me, so be it. It was better than the torture he had in mind.

"Novak, I see you're holding a canvas. Gently toss it to me," he said.

I thought maybe this was my chance, but Konstantin stepped back so I would have no opportunity to reach him in time to do any damage. I tossed him the painting. He unrolled the canvas and saw the children with the red ball.

"So this is the painting that's caused all the trouble. I don't mind telling you; I relish the thought of giving this to Ms. Hirsch. You know she was quite unhappy when your friend sold her a forgery. It amazes even me how vindictive she can be. Choosing me to inflict the vengeance was a good choice on her part because I enjoyed it very much."

Chapter Eighty-Two

Detroit, Michigan
August 10, 2019

Liz Bowers

Liz Bowers knew that staying at Carl's house was the prudent thing but couldn't, and an hour after Carl, Lukas, and Natalie left, she decided to follow. She headed to the Kane Building using her car's GPS, not knowing if she could help, but she had to try. On the way, she did as Lukas suggested and called Clark, informed him of what was taking place, and gave him the directions to the Kane Building. Furious, Clark already knew from one of his officers that Lukas and Natalie had left.

Arriving at the Kane Building, Liz drove by slowly and saw a woman's body lying in the parking lot. "Oh no," she said out loud. The light blue dress the woman was wearing looked like Natalie's. She parked her car on the street and was about to run over to Natalie when she saw a man shooting the lock off the back door of the building. She knew it was Konstantin and guessed that Lukas and Carl were inside.

She called Lukas' number to warn him. No answer. Running to Natalie, Liz found that she'd been shot and had lost a lot of blood, but she was still alive. She called 911 and explained in detail that a woman needed immediate medical attention and where she could be found. Torn, Liz couldn't decide, should she stay with Natalie or try to warn Lukas?

"I'm sorry to leave you, Natalie. There's not much more that I can do but wait for the ambulance. I think Lukas and Carl need me," she said to Natalie, although she doubted she could hear her. Then Natalie nodded her head.

Chapter Eighty-Three

Detroit, Michigan
August 10, 2019

Liz Bowers

Liz made her way to the backdoor. It was open, and blood was on the ground. She hoped it wasn't Lukas' or Carl's. Entering the building, she found more blood leading to the elevator. Just as she was about to press the up button, the elevator's bell rang, indicating someone was coming down.

Stepping into a hallway, she hid behind a credenza with a vase of artificial flowers. Liz could see the elevator, heard the elevator doors open, and saw Lukas slowly walking towards the back door. Behind him was Konstantin pointing his weapon at Lukas. Liz pulled her gun from the waist of her slacks, didn't hesitate, aimed, and fired at Konstantin.

Konstantin saw Liz move and pivoted to fire at her. Before he could, I pushed him hoping his shot would miss. It didn't. I heard Liz scream and fall to the floor.

Her shot hit Konstantin in the upper part of his leg, causing him to fall. I tried to take his gun away, but he recovered quickly and pointed it at me.

"Step back, Novak," he shouted.

I had no choice and did and, at the same time, looked over towards Liz. She was lying on her back, and I couldn't see if she was alive or dead.

Konstantin got back on his feet and motioned for me to walk towards the door. I thought I'd probably missed my best chance to get away from him. It was too late for that, and I hoped I'd have another chance. If I did, I wouldn't let it slip away.

We walked to the parking lot with Konstantin pointing the way, reaching his car parked at the rear of the building.

"Get in and drive," he said.

Keeping his gun on me, he said, "Drive back to Jefferson Avenue. Head east away from the I-75. You and I will make a little stop before I head back to New York. I know I'm going to enjoy it. I think not so much for you, Novak."

Chapter Eighty-Four

Detroit, Michigan
August 10, 2019

Liz Bowers

Liz had never been shot before and felt the searing pain in her shoulder. But she didn't think she was dying and pulled herself up using the credenza as support, making her way to the apartment building door and hoping to get a shot at Konstantin. She saw him and Lukas heading between cars and noticed Detective Clark kneeling over Natalie and talking to the ambulance people. She yelled to him, "Detective, Konstantin has Lukas. They're heading towards the back street."

Clark ran over to Liz. "You've been shot."

"No kidding, detective. We need to get to your car and see if we can catch up with Lukas."

Clark helped Liz as they made their way to his car, roared onto the side street, and headed to where they hoped they could spot Konstantin and Lukas.

They saw a car turning and heading to Jefferson Avenue at the first side street intersection. Konstantin's car turned east on Jefferson Avenue, and Clark followed. He opened his window and placed his flasher light on top of his car.

"Do you think that's a good idea?" Liz asked. "Let's just follow them."

Clark nodded in agreement, decided not to turn the flasher on, and accelerated to close the distance between them and Konstantin, weaving around cars blocking their way.

Konstantin told me to keep driving to the east. We were entering a very run-down area of East Detroit. I was sure this was exactly what he had waiting for me. As I looked in the side mirror, I saw a dark sedan closing in behind us. I thought it might be Clark's car. I could only hope.

Just then, Konstantin told me to turn left down a side street with deserted houses on each side. There was nobody in sight. This is where it all comes to an end, I thought.

"Go until I tell you to stop," he said.

I slowed down, hoping that it was Clark following us and he'd be able to catch us.

"You're going too slow," Konstantin said.

I increased my speed and looked in the mirror and saw the car behind us was turning too. Damn, it's Clark, I thought. I must have looked too long in the mirror because Konstantin turned the rearview mirror so he could look behind us too.

Finally, he said, "I see what you're looking at, Novak. Someone is following us, and you think it's your friend. I don't think you can be that lucky. Speed up and run this next stop sign."

I did as I was told. Konstantin watched to see if the car behind us would stop at the sign. It didn't.

"Well, well, that is one of your friends, and I see he has a flasher on the top of his car. Regardless of what happens, Novak, it looks like you're not going to live after all."

As Konstantin said those words, I decided to take control of my fate, pushed down on the accelerator, jumped the curb, and now airborne, violently smashed into a large maple tree.

Chapter Eighty-Five

Detroit, Michigan
August 12, 2019

Lukas Novak

When I opened my eyes, I wasn't sure if I was alive. It took some time to realize I was in a hospital. I had all sorts of tubes running from my arms, and I wondered how badly I was hurt. I moved my arms, then turned my head. Ok, so far, I thought. I wiggled my toes on my left then right foot. They both worked.

When I began to sit up, a nurse came into the room. "He's conscious," I heard her tell someone in the hallway. "Call the doctor and tell him." The nurse came back into the room.

"Hello, Mr. Novak. I'm happy to see you're awake," she said.

I was a bit confused and took a moment to answer.

"Where am I?"

"You're in Hope Memorial. You've been in a coma."

"For how long?"

"Two days. We've let your doctor know you're awake. He'll be here shortly."

When she told me who my doctor was, I was relieved. He was a client of mine. I'd designed the addition to his vacation home in Northern Michigan.

The nurse came over to me and said she was happy to see me moving. As she checked my vital signs, my doctor came into the room.

"Well, Lukas," he laughed, "you've decided to join us once again."

"I think so, doctor," I said, "how long have I been here?"

"Oh, about two days."

"So, I'm lucky to be alive."

"Not lucky to be alive, so much, as fortunate to be knowing who you are and talking to me.

"You took a terrible hit to the head and have been unconscious. We've been monitoring you. Because you're young, we believed you'd come out of the coma in a relatively short time. However, with brain injuries, you never know. I'm happy to see you're so responsive."

It was then that a nurse came into the room and asked the doctor if it was okay for her to call my mother and Liz. He said it was fine and to tell them I was doing well. Let them know I need to do a series of tests, and we'll reach out to them when Lukas can see them. Tell them not to worry."

"How's your vacation house working out?" I asked.

He laughed. "I see you're already in full recovery. Yes, it's working out just as we planned, and my family loves it up there. I wish I could join them more often."

Over the next few hours, I was given several tests and told that it was somewhat unusual for a person to come out of a coma with little or no side effects. I considered myself very lucky. Later that evening, they said I could receive guests.

While one of the nurses talked to me, Liz and my mother arrived. My mother ran over to me, hugged me, and cried.

"My prayers are answered. You're awake."

When she finally let me go, I saw Liz standing behind her, crying too.

"Well, you sure have a dramatic side to you," she came over and hugged me as well.

After about five minutes, a doctor came in. It must have been one of my doctor's associates. He said that Liz and my Mom could stay for a little while more and then I should rest. He suggested they come back tomorrow.

It was late morning the next day. My window faced east, and the sun was shining through the window. I was feeling better and ready to leave the hospital. When Liz came into the room, she was carrying flowers. She said my mother was so emotional that she thought it best that she'd wait to see me later.

"Do you recognize these?"

They were geraniums and black-eyed Susans. Bright red and yellow.

"Are those some of my friends from my backyard?"

"Yes, they said they missed you," Liz said with a big smile.

"I can't tell you how much I missed them."

While putting the vase of flowers on the stand next to my bed, she said, "My God, you're so lucky after hitting that tree."

"What tree?"

"You don't remember hitting the tree?"

"Nope."

"What's the last thing you remember?"

"Let's see, I recall thinking that Clark might be following us," I said.

"That's right. I was in the car with him."

"Wait, I remember that I thought you were shot at the apartment building, and you might be dead, I said.

"Lucky for me and you, his shot hit me in the shoulder."

I could see that there were bandages under her sweater.

"If you hadn't pushed him while he was firing, I'm sure I'd be dead. Anyway, I was able to get up, and Clark was in the parking lot with Natalie. Natalie must have gotten out of the car and wandered over to the lot. The guy with the painting shot her. I found her when I arrived."

"Liz, I thought you were staying in Saginaw?" I asked. This was all confusing to me. I looked blankly at her.

"I was and then changed my mind. Anyway, Natalie was on the ground when I arrived, so I called her an ambulance. The ambulance was there when Clark arrived," Liz said.

"How's Natalie?" I asked.

"She's dead. Her wound was too severe."

"Oh no. I told her to stay in the car. You heard me."

"I know. I think she was too frightened to stay alone."

"Before the ambulance took her away, she talked to Clark. I think she knew she was dying. She told Clark that she poisoned Nicky."

"What?"

"Yes, she was the one," Liz said.

"You were right for me not to trust her," I mumbled.

"Well, I was sort of right. Natalie told Clark how different life would have been if you had loved her and not Nicky, and if she had known at the beginning what a great person you were, she would have loved you and not Adam."

I was more confused than ever, too much to take in for me, and what she was saying wasn't making any sense to me.

"Clark and I followed you out to Jefferson Avenue. As we got closer, you turned down a side street, and we turned too. You suddenly sped up and turned directly into a big tree. We're guessing you were going at least forty miles an hour."

"I don't remember that at all. I remember thinking that I wouldn't allow Konstantin to torture me. Maybe that's why I drove into the tree?"

"Maybe. Anyway, your car was destroyed. Clark and I pulled you out and then Konstantin."

"Is Konstantin alive?" I shouted.

"No, he died in the collision," Liz said, "we won't have to worry about him."

"The painting? What about the painting?"

"I found it in the back seat of Konstantin's car. It's now at the art museum."

"Good," I said. "I hope they've upgraded their security system."

"They did. Clark contacted Petrocelli, and he's trying to determine if there's any case against Beatrice Hirsch. He believes there is provided you survive and are willing to testify. He told Clark that maybe, finally, he'd have a witness that could help bring her down. In any case, he doubts that she'd be willing to risk trying to get the painting again."

"How about the couple that tried to kill you? What happened?"

"They've not been seen again," Liz said.

A thousand questions were running through my mind.

"How's our office doing?"

"It's been unbelievable. Almost all our clients have come back."

"When Clark found out you'd gone to Detroit without telling him, he was furious. He was blaming you for Natalie's death. After Carl explained how you insisted on her staying in the car, he calmed down. He also told Clark she was afraid to stay in Saginaw because the police couldn't protect her and insisted she go with you. I think Carter finally understood about Natalie and realized you might have to do something illegal to get the painting back. Later, I told him you didn't want to put him in a compromising position."

"I guess shooting a guy is sort of illegal," I mused.

"Exactly," Liz said.

"I assume he's dead. What was his name?"

"Sidney, yes, he's dead, but you didn't kill him."

"No, I shot him in the arm. Konstantin killed him. He gave him no chance when he pushed into Sidney's apartment. He shot him in the face from a few feet away."

"He's killed a lot of people," Liz added.

"Clark's not going to arrest me again, is he?"

"No, in fact, he used his influence to make sure the Detroit Police didn't charge you for shooting that Sidney guy," she explained.

"Well, I thank Clark for that."

"Lukas, all charges against you have been dropped, of course. Clark had a news conference and explained the deaths of Adam, Mrs. Wendall, and Nicky. He gave you credit for your courage, if not your common sense," she said.

"I appreciate that too. Apparently, that helped get our clients back."

Liz smiled at me. "Well, you're sort of a Rockstar in Saginaw right now. But don't let it go to your head."

"It's hard for it to go to my head when I can't even remember what happened."

Chapter Eighty-Six

Saginaw, Michigan
August 22, 2019

Lukas Novak

After leaving the hospital, Liz and I were sitting in Jack's 1866 Bistro. I realized we were at the same table where Nicky and I were sitting when we first talked about Adam's murder. So much had happened since then. It seemed like years ago, but it was just over a month. Liz sipped some fruity martini while I enjoyed an Angel's Envy Manhattan.

"I spoke to Petrocelli today," I said. "I told him I'm willing to testify that Konstantin said Hirsch hired him to kill Adam and Janice." He feels he has enough evidence to bring charges against Beatrice Hirsch for conspiracy to commit the murders."

"How does it feel to be on the other side of a murder charge?" Asked Liz.

"When people want to convict you of murder, it's stressful. There were times I thought I'd end up in prison. I'm thankful that Natalie told Clark the truth. At the same time, I still can't believe she killed Nicky. She was a very jealous woman, and Adam said she could be violent too. Still, that's different than planning a detailed murder," I said.

"And planting evidence against you. That's very cold," added Liz.

"For her to confess, she must have thought she was going to die, or maybe she did love me. You know I'm so irresistible," I said with a grin.

"It's good to see your weird humor returning," Liz laughed. "Talking about returning, well actually not returning, I let Carl fly."

"That must have been hard for you, Liz. I know you cared for him."

"I did and still do. The reality is he's a lazy slouch and never changing. I couldn't get past all the lying to you and me about the painting. He caused so many deaths and put many others' lives in danger. It was time for me to move on. He said it would kill him if I left. I don't think he is courageous enough to kill himself. If he does, he brought it on himself," Liz said in a very downhearted voice.

"I guess Carl and Natalie, like all people, have their strengths and weaknesses. Although I admit, Natalie's were extreme," I said.

"Those with extremes include Adam. He developed wonderful relationships with people across the country. They cared for and trusted him. Everyone was crying and talking about what a wonderful human being he was at his wake. As it turns out, he didn't really care and was just using them," she said.

"And boy, was he good at it. Everybody loved Adam," I added, "Nicky, Natalie, Janice, and me too."

We both sat quietly, sipping our drinks and thinking about all the terrible things that happened to so many friends and loved ones. All were dead, even Carl, in a manner of speaking.

Finally, I said, "I also talked to Clark. I think he's finally forgiving me for not taking him to Detroit. He thanked me for helping end Konstantin's killing spree. Petrocelli said the same thing."

"I guess everyone is happy that you killed Konstantin, except Beatrice Hirsch," Liz said, "I wonder how many people Konstantin has killed?"

"Petrocelli said it's hard to truly know because many of the murders occurred in the Baltic and Eastern Europe."

"You know if you testify against Hirsch, she may come at you with another killer. Did you think of that?"

"Yes, I've thought about it. I just have to do it. I couldn't face myself if I didn't. But let's not think about that now. Let's enjoy our time together and have another drink."

I changed the subject because I didn't want to think of facing another assassin.

"I've got another big surprise I haven't had the chance to tell you. An attorney representing Janice Wendall's estate called me. I didn't know this, but right before Adam's death, she amended her trust."

"Yes, and?" Liz asked.

"I'm named in it."

"No way!" she exclaimed.

"I am. Janice gave her Bouguereau painting to the Great Lakes Bay Art Museum. The Detroit Institute of Art has already agreed to display it with their Bouguereau's "Nut Gatherers." Of course, that's after Sheila uses it for her big fundraiser, then it's going to on display not only at the DIA but other places, including Paris, as part of a larger Bouguereau exhibition."

"I'm glad it's staying at our museum, and it's great those two Bouguereau's will be seen together by so many," Liz added.

"So the painting goes to the museum. How about the remainder of Janice's trust?" She asked.

"One-third to the museum's endowment with only income to be distributed. One-third to Sheila. And one-third to Adam. Because Adam didn't survive, his share goes to me," I said.

"That's crazy. How large is Janice's trust?" She asked.

"The attorney didn't know for sure. It doesn't matter. I'm so humbled that Janice thought that highly of me."

"Well, that part of her estate is going to the right person because Adam used her, and his greed caused her death," Liz snarled.

"I've been thinking so much about Adam. He had so many gifts, but his greed was his undoing. He not only stole from all those museums, in the end, from Hirsch too. Konstantin told me that Hirsch paid Adam $5 million for Janice's Bouguereau painting. Then Adam sold her a forgery so he could keep the original."

"It not only killed him and Janice but killed Natalie too," Liz said.

"And Natalie, with her jealousy and revenge, killed Nicky, I added.

"And Nicky wouldn't have died if she didn't have sex with Adam one last time before he left town."

All of this was overwhelming as I started thinking about everyone's faults, particularly Nicky.

Changing the subject, I asked, "Can you believe Janice's kindness? Her legacy is giving to others, particularly the painting she loved so much. Those little girls and their mother were like family to her."

"Now they'll be there for generations to admire and appreciate. And her gift to you, how kind. I hope it's not too large, so you give up architecture," Liz said jokingly.

"I'm not going to stop working. I am going to take some time off. I rented a condo in Charlevoix for two weeks next month, and I'm taking my mother away for us to relax. Mom has been so worried about me she's taking anxiety medication, and she's never believed in taking meds. She's the one that needs a vacation more than me. It will be good for both of us," I said.

"Why are you waiting until next month? Go now, Liz suggested.

"I can't. Someone has to watch the office. Liz, I want you to take a break for the next two weeks. I want you to take time off, and beginning now, for the next two weeks, you're on a paid vacation for any place you want to go. And I mean it! I'm paying for everything for you to recharge your batteries and have a good time."

"Really? I was just talking to one of my girlfriends, and we want to get out of town and have some fun. Thanks, Lukas, really the timing couldn't be better."

"Where are you going?" I asked.

"I don't know. Florida, New York, California, maybe Europe. I have to rethink our plans now that I have two weeks.'

I enjoyed watching Liz being happy. I couldn't imagine getting through the last month without her never-doubting support.

"Thank you, Lukas. You're very generous."

"You'll never know how much your support meant to me. I mean, you literally took a bullet for me, not to mention that you saved me from being tortured and murdered. I think you've earned your vacation!"

Again we sat quietly.

"I know this sounds ridiculous, but I'm going to vacation without

Carl for the first time in quite a while."

I was not surprised the conversation returned to Carl.

"By the way, he told me that he pleaded guilty to a misdemeanor for stealing the painting. I know you don't like him, but he's to me like Nicky was to you. You cared for her. She made you happy, and you forgave her weaknesses. That's the way it's with Carl and me, except I couldn't forgive him anymore."

"I won't have the chance to make that decision with Nicky. I understand all about people's strengths and weaknesses, including my own. With Carl, I know you're making the right decision. I think you can forgive him, but still move on."

Liz smiled and reached over and hugged me.

"Thank you. I needed that," Liz said.

The waitress stopped by and asked if we wanted another round. "Yes," we said at the same time.

"We're on vacation, well, at least I am," Liz said.

"We're celebrating," I added.

"What are you celebrating?" the waitress asked.

Liz and I started laughing.

"It's a long story," I said.

"They should make it into a movie," Liz sarcastically said.

"Well, if they do, I'd go see it," said the waitress.

"I know I wouldn't," Liz grimaced

"Nor would I. I hope never to live through that again."

Suddenly Liz stared at me as if something scared her. She reached over and put her arm around me.

"I hope so too."

Acknowledgments

Without the patient editing and continuous encouragement from my best friend, Paul Chaffee, I would have given up writing this book many times (perhaps readers will think that would have been best!). When it comes to editing, many thanks to my publisher and friend, Robin Moyer; again, she helped me push through all the times I needed to go back and rewrite portions of the book. Thanks also to my friends, Jim Perkins, for the portrait on the front book cover, Mike Kolleth for his enthusiasm and photo on the back cover, Thor Rasmussen for my photo, the Saginaw Art Museum for allowing me to use their beautiful facilities, Peter Shaheen for finding me a quiet place to write in splendid Costa Rica, Tom Lawler for his good advice, my daughter, Lija, for her enthusiasm at just the right time and lastly my long time (really long!) friend and colleague, Debra Briguglio.

Author's Biography

Larry L. Preston is a former business and estate planning attorney; co-founder and CEO of Tri-Star Trust, a private bank; and CEO of TempleArts, a public charity that operates a performing arts center and art museum. Mr. Preston is actively involved in his community and has served as chairperson of the Saginaw Community Foundation and Saginaw Chamber of Commerce. He's received several honors from Junior Achievement, Boys and Girls Club, Boy Scouts, Saginaw Chamber of Commerce, and Saginaw State University's Businessperson of the Year. He's also been a trustee of The Great Lakes Bay Alliance, Michigan Humanities, Heroes for Kids, FORCE, and Midland Center for the Arts. He and his wife, Maija, of over thirty years, have three successful children and live in Freeland, Michigan, and Marina Del Rey, California.